May the Author of Life
guide you always.

Annie Cole

Bell Forest

Annie M. Cole

INFIƆ∞ITY
PUBLISHING

Copyright © 2010 by Annie M. Cole

ISBN 0-7414-5848-9

Printed in the United States of America

This is a work of fiction. Names, characters, places, and incidents either are the product of the author's imagination or are used fictitiously. Any resemblance to actual events or locales or persons, living or dead, is entirely coincidental.

Published June 2010

INFINITY PUBLISHING
1094 New DeHaven Street, Suite 100
West Conshohocken, PA 19428-2713
Toll-free (877) BUY BOOK
Local Phone (610) 941-9999
Fax (610) 941-9959
Info@buybooksontheweb.com
www.buybooksontheweb.com

With love and admiration,
I dedicate this book to my daughter, Hannah.

Chapter 1

The place was haunted. Not just the house, but the entire town of Coldwater, Alabama.

In a thousand small ways, Telie McCain saw her past surrounding her, choking her with suppressed grief. She let out a shuddered sigh, mourning the loss of what once was.

Stepping through the empty shell of a house, she watched from the front window as the realtor slammed the post down into the ground with the word SOLD displayed in bright yellow. Lifting her gaze, her throat tightened. She stared at the magnolia tree in the front yard, and her thoughts inadvertently shifted to her father.

As a young girl, she would climb up into the branches of the stately magnolia, wrap her skinny legs around a thick branch and wait for her father to return home from work. As soon as his truck appeared in the distance, she would stand on the shaky limb, ready to scramble down as soon as he pulled into the dirt drive. She worshipped her father, Mack McCain.

Most people liked Mack. He was known to be a hard worker, a good neighbor, a regular church attendee and a devoted family man. Most evenings you could find him in

1

the garage, hammering a nail in a chair leg or replacing a neighbor's bicycle chain...something like that. He had a special gift with nature too: he could turn something overgrown and wild into a thing of beauty.

With dust flying behind her dirty tennis shoes, Telie would run and jump on the tailgate of his slow-moving truck, as it headed for the latest piece of scrubland he had purchased. He'd taught his daughter how to work with her hands, respecting the land and making it beautiful.

I can't believe it's been twelve years, she thought. *Twelve years since he left.* He'd fallen in love with someone else, simply saying he would not live without her. She sat in stunned silence as her father declared his love for this other woman. Shocked beyond belief, she could only stare at him. Devastated, confused...too much for her fourteen-year-old adolescent mind to grasp, she struggled to make sense of it all.

Time passed and distance divided. After her parents' divorce, Mack moved out west to Texas with his new wife and her three children. Her father slowly faded from her life. His presence was gone, but he had not abandoned her heart.

Telie's mom, Mila, moved out of the house when Telie turned eighteen. She was anxious to put the pain of her own rejection behind her and begin a new life. It had been painful to watch her mother suffer the same feelings of rejection she had suffered, but the joy was back in her mother's eyes and that was enough. Now, it was Telie's turn for a new beginning.

Telie's house sold quickly. Letting out a sigh, she walked out, closing the door behind her.

Convincing her mother that she needed to move away had been difficult, to say the least. But the need to escape came storming through her until it settled there, within her. She would leave, no matter what.

Telie's employer, Paul Grayson, helped her find a job in South Alabama, near Mobile Bay in the little town of Moss Bay.

Having dealt with "Christenberry's Landscaping Company" outside of Moss Bay for the past nine years, Paul Grayson knew he was sending Telie to a first-class outfit. He respected Michael Christenberry and his father before him. Nothing but the best would do for Telie. Although Paul would miss her greatly, he considered her a daughter and wanted only what was best for her.

"You think I'm doing the right thing, Mr. Grayson?" Telie asked, the day she was to leave. Staring down at the gravel, she slid her foot back and forth, scattering rocks, waiting for his answer. She felt more anxious about leaving him than leaving her mother. Paul Grayson had been an anchor to her when she'd felt like drifting. His approval mattered. She heard a long inhale before he answered.

"Yes, I do, Telie. You need a change worse than anybody I know. I'm certain Michael will be thrilled with you, especially when he sees how hard you work. I've told them all about you."

He hesitated in that awkward way people do when they're not sure what to say next. "I know it's difficult to leave, but trust me, you need a do-over." He placed a reassuring hand on her shoulder. "When I talked to Martha the other day, she was so excited about you coming down she wanted you to leave right away. Business is good down there, and they're thrilled to have someone with your experience come on board. I told her that as soon as your house sold, you'd be down. I had no idea it would sell so quickly. It's meant to be, and that's all there is to it." He took his hat off, wiped his brow and then put it back on again.

It was evident that Martha Ashton, not Michael Christenberry, made all the day-to-day business decisions at

Christenberry's. She was Michael's bookkeeper and second in command. You seldom, if ever, talked directly to Michael; he was always outside, or out on a job, hardly ever in the office. Martha called weekly for Mr. Grayson, and the girls in the office teased him relentlessly about it. "Your girlfriend is on the phone and needs you bad," they would say. Always mumbling something incoherent, he would snatch the phone, and in no time at all Martha would have him laughing.

Paul Grayson was a confirmed bachelor now that his wife had passed away. She had been "a piece of work" as a few of his close friends had described her. After his thirty-year sentence of marriage to Ethel, he'd stayed away from women, as a general rule.

Telie could always tell when Michael had been up though…the girls in the office had no shame when it came to good-looking men. "If I wasn't married," they would say… or worse. She always seemed to be somewhere else on those rare occasions; now she wished she had at least met the man, her future employer. All the information she could squeeze out of the girls concerning him had nothing to do with the character of the man.

Paul lifted a crate of pansies, turned and said, "We're sure gonna miss you around here, Telie girl, but I think this is a good opportunity for you. Those people are *good* people; they'll treat you right."

"Thanks, Mr. Grayson. I can't tell you how much I appreciate all you've done for me over the years. I'll miss you too."

Chapter 2

A rainstorm blew up suddenly, pelting the asphalt with large drops of water, as steam began to rise in the parking lot. Making a run for her truck, she lifted a hand over her head, trying to dodge the rain. She tossed her purse down in the seat beside her and cranked the truck.

The bed of the truck was loaded down with plants and a few boxes of her belongings. A bright green tarp covered all of it, fastened down tightly with cords. Mr. Grayson had asked if she would make a delivery for him. He loaded her down with the plants Michael asked for and gave her instructions concerning the pecan trees he had ordered.

She traveled light, only wanting things that brought her comfort: like her grandmother's embroidered pillowcases, her books and an oscillating fan she couldn't sleep without. She knew she was way overdue for a new wardrobe, but she packed what few clothes she wanted and gave the rest away along with all of her other possessions. She reveled in her new sense of freedom, enjoying the lightness of it all.

The rain and wind played havoc with the tarp. As she traveled south, it slapped and popped in a fierce struggle to break free. She felt like that tarp, anxious to be free of the past that bound her.

Seven hours later, flat land, sandy soil and Spanish moss on twisted trees greeted her at every glance. Squinting in the afternoon light, just as the sun broke through the clouds, she reached for her sunglasses. Driving down the muddy unfamiliar roads, past farmhouses in the distance with open fields of freshly turned soil, she rolled down the window to take it all in, inhaling the smell of wet fields after the rain. "I'm really gonna love it here. This place is unbelievable. Thank you, Lord," she whispered. She reached for the map and the directions she'd scribbled down before leaving.

Looking around for landmarks, all of which were few and far between, she noticed a white wooden sign with green faded letters that read "Christenberry's Landscaping." It was worn from time and salty air and stuck up out of the ground by two posts. A long and sandy, mud puddle-ridden dirt road stretched out in the distance. The straight narrow road led to a compound that sprawled out on both sides of the flat, almost tree barren land. It looked as if it sat out in the middle of an old cotton field. She turned onto the road, traveling slowly as she scanned the area. A grouping of structures in the center of the acreage looked low to the ground and shady with colorful pots of flowers scattered around. The metal roof was blinding as it reflected the hot afternoon sun. "Wow," she said, "what a massive spread!"

Michael Christenberry walked steadily as he carried a heavy bag of soil on his shoulder. Leaning over, he stacked it on a pile near the fence. Lifting his sunglasses to his head, he watched as a gray truck made its way down the road. *No dust today,* he thought, remembering the white trail of dust that usually rose in the air behind every vehicle that came up the road. He felt like he had already swallowed his fair share of dust for the year. He surveyed his progress. Tugging the worn-out work gloves off his hands, he turned as the gray truck caught his eye once more, pulling onto the gravel parking lot. As he watched, he saw a young woman hop out of the truck. She looked rather small with slender legs and graceful arms. Her honey-wheat wavy hair was pulled back and secured loosely at the back of her neck. Looking down, he realized she had landed in the middle of a mud hole, splattering mud and water all over her faded jeans. He pulled his lips over to one side to conceal his amusement but kept watching her. The young girl seemed not to notice. She stepped out of the puddle with her muddy boots, her full lips spread into a warm smile as she walked toward him. He waited as she approached.

"Mr. Christenberry?" she asked, already knowing this *had* to be Michael from the detailed description the "office girls" had given her. He had a strong look about him, a weathered look, tanned skin, a square jaw and sun-lightened brown hair. His bluish-green eyes wrinkled around the corners from too much squinting in the glaring South Alabama sun. His muscular build told her he was a man accustomed to physical labor.

"Yes, can I help you?" he said, clearly intrigued by this girl who didn't seem to mind being covered in splashes of mud and water, or care what he thought about it either.

Telie stuck out her hand to introduce herself. "I'm Telie McCain," she replied confidently. "Did Martha tell you I was coming?"

A smile flashed across his face. "Martha rarely troubles me with the important details of my business," he said teasingly, as he walked over to take her extended hand. "Michael Christenberry," he stated. Pulling his attention away from her to keep from staring, he eyed the truck bed and noticed a few branches sticking out from under the tarp. "Did Paul send down a load?" Looking back, he waited for her answer.

"Yes…Mr. Grayson asked me to bring these to you and let you know that you can send the pecan trees up anytime." She found it hard to pull away from his penetrating eyes.

"Oh sure, sure," he said, looking away from her and turning his attention to the plants. "Looks like you ran into a little rain on the way down," he said, seeing the puddles of water that had collected on top of the tarp. "Did you have a difficult drive?"

"Oh no, not at all. It was relaxing really." She turned around to the truck and began unfastening the cords; pulling the tarp back, she shook it gently allowing the water to roll off the sides.

"Here, let me help with that." He grabbed the fabric and tossed it back in one smooth movement. Michael leaned toward Telie. "Martha tells me you have *years* of experience," he said with a dazzling smile. His white teeth looked even whiter next to his sun-weathered skin. "I can hardly believe *that*," he said, looking skeptical. "You must have started work at about…what, eight?"

"Not quite eight," she corrected playfully. Stepping away to the back of the truck, she began unloading the pots of plants. "It only feels that way sometimes," she added, smiling.

"You must be tired from the long drive. Go on inside and meet Martha, she can show you around, I'll get this." He dismissed her with a wave of his hand and continued unloading the truck.

"If you're sure…oh, those boxes stay…they're mine," she indicated, pointing to the boxes in the back of the truck bed.

"Yeah okay, I got this. You go on in. It'll make Martha's day to see you here." He smiled at her as she headed off in the direction of the office. "My goodness," he said, "she'll certainly brighten up this old place."

Joe, "the water boy" as Michael liked to call him, stopped his watering and stared after Telie as she crossed in front of him. None of that escaped Michael's notice. *Great,* he thought. *That's all that boy needs is another distraction. He can barely concentrate on what he's doing as it is!* Shaking his head, he lifted another pot out of the truck and placed it near the fence.

Martha was not at all what Telie had expected. She was small with tiny features and somewhat plump…somewhere in her sixties. Her silver hair was short and neat. With tiny glasses perched on the end of her nose she looked pixie-like, almost. Her voice was so gruff and commanding over the phone; Telie fought to keep from laughing in the face of this little woman. She reminded her of what Tinkerbell might have looked like if she had ever grown old and out of shape. It would not have surprised her if at that very moment two iridescent wings flopped out right in front of her.

Telie extended her hand toward Martha with a smile, grateful for the chance to hide her laugh. "I'm Telie, Miss Martha."

"Good gracious, girl, come here and let me get a look at you," she said gruffly. She jumped up from behind her desk. "I bet you're just worn out from that long drive." Her shining blue eyes danced over the top of her glasses. "Here, sit down, let me go get you a Co-Cola."

Telie smiled. She hadn't heard anyone refer to a Coke that way.

"That sounds wonderful, Martha." She sat down, glancing around the room. Plants and pots and a hodgepodge of garden tools lined the walls. Martha's desk sat facing the front windows that looked directly out over the parking lot. A collection of brightly colored birdhouses and gourds hung on the wall behind her desk. To the left, a long hall disappeared toward the back. On the other side of the room, a door opened to a large office.

Coming back into the room, Martha said excitedly, "I believe I'll have one too. We'll celebrate your arrival with a toast! To happy gardens everywhere!" she said, tipping her bottle to Telie. Martha seemed as if she were looking for someone. "Did you bring a load down with you, sweetie? Is Paul with you?" she asked, looking excited at the possibility.

"Mr. Grayson sent all that you asked for…but he didn't come with me," she replied, looking over her shoulder to see what had captured Martha's attention.

"Is that rascal seeing anybody up there?" Martha cut her eyes at Telie over the rims of her glasses. "A man like that is sure to have women crawling all over him."

"Oh no, not Mr. Grayson, he says he is not interested in 'No John Brown Woman' – whatever that means."

Martha let out a laugh, slapping her hand on her thigh. "That sure sounds like him." Changing the subject rather abruptly, she remarked, "I always get the bottled drinks; they taste better. I've got Michael hooked on them too."

Telie turned up the cold drink, swallowing down an icy swig.

"Where you plan on stayin' tonight, sweetie? We'll be closing up in about an hour or so."

"A hotel, I guess. Something to get me by until I can find a place," Telie answered.

"Nonsense." She dismissed the comment with a wave of her hand. "You'll stay here until you find something. There's a bed and a shower in the bunkroom and a kitchen across the hall in the break room…all the comforts of home. I've got some leftover chicken salad in the refrigerator and plenty of drinks. Michael only uses the bunkroom when the temperature drops below freezing…and from the looks of it he won't be using that room for at least another ten months. It's just what you need…won't cost you a thing." Martha slapped the desk. "Now that's settled."

"Are you sure?" She looked at Martha skeptically. "What about Michael?"

"He won't care, if that's what you're asking. Now come on and let me show you around so you can try and get your bearings."

Michael observed Martha and Telie as they surveyed the place. He could only imagine what Martha was bending her ear about. "Heaven help her," he said out loud with a grin, shaking his head.

"Who's the new girl with Martha?" Joe asked, in his lazy southern drawl. Joe's voice could only be described as country with a little dab of Cajun mixed in just for fun.

"Telie McCain. She comes from Grayson's, highly recommended I might add." He eyed the boy, seeing his interest. "So I hope you'll show Miss Telie around, Joe. I'm sure she'd appreciate your help while she gets adjusted."

"Sure boss, you can count on me," Joe answered, stretching out the word "sure" into two syllables.

Joe Gregory was twenty years old with gangly legs and a laid-back disposition. Uneven poker-straight brown hair stuck out in all directions from beneath his camouflaged cap. His long and lanky build had the slightest stoop. He had never been accused of ever letting anything rush him. His steps were always slow and deliberate.

Michael liked the boy. His easygoing manner reminded him of a faithful, but lazy dog. Nice to have around, but you just couldn't expect too much out of him. On more than one

11

occasion he had caught Joe napping in one of the outbuildings. He'd always have some excuse about resting his eyes
from all the dust or how he suffered from heat exhaustion,
then he'd stumble back to work, grabbing up the hose as he
went along.

Michael wondered if Joe could keep from stumbling over
his own feet as he quickened his pace to catch up with the
girls. "I hope he doesn't trip and fall. He's liable to maul her
to death with his knees and elbows just trying to get up."

Chapter 3

The sun was sinking in the distance, melting behind the trees. Telie unloaded a small overnight bag from her truck and went back inside to lock up as Martha instructed.

I can't believe they trust me to do this, she thought to herself. Martha told her to make herself at home and to please eat up the rest of the chicken salad in the fridge. She'd handed her a huge set of keys and instructed her how to lock up everything, which keys went to the shop out back and which ones locked the tractor shed. She fumbled with the heavy key ring, trying to find the right match as a swarm of gnats followed her every step, not quite touching her. Crickets sang and everything seemed to let out a deep exaggerated breath. The day was done.

Michael left a little before closing. He handed over his orders for the next day to Martha before he left for the evening. Martha had teased him relentlessly about his "big fancy dinner plans" all afternoon. He seemed anxious to leave.

Locking herself inside the office, Telie walked down the hall to find the bunkroom. Placing her stuff on the bed, she pulled out her pajamas and headed for the shower. *This feels so good*, she thought, as the hot water ran down her back.

The soft fragrant soap helped relieve the stress as she worked it into a thick lather over her tense muscles.

Drying off, she quickly pulled her pink cotton top over her head and stepped into a pair of gray pajama bottoms. Taking out a brush and a book from her bag she sat cross-legged on the bed, brushing her hair. She opened her book and managed to read a page or two before her stomach growled. "Must be time to find Martha's chicken salad," she said to herself. Sliding across the bed she stepped into her slippers and shuffled over to the break room across the hall.

Yanking open the refrigerator door, she was surprised to see a variety of drinks filling the shelves. She spied the chicken salad in a plastic tub and grabbed it along with a drink. A sleeve of crackers sat on top of the microwave, so she helped herself to them and began spreading the salad on thickly. "Unbelievable," she said out loud, piling the mixture on a few more saltines as she hungrily devoured them.

Her mind whirled around all the things she needed to do in the next few days. *Oh well*, she thought, *I can't do anything about it tonight. You'll just have to lead the way as usual, Lord.* Curling up in the bed, she pulled the covers around her shoulders and snuggled in. The place was deathly quiet. All she could hear was the hum of the refrigerator across the hall. Loneliness crept over her, enveloping her with a sudden sense of sadness, or was it homesickness? She tried to push it back, reasoning with herself that she was just tired. Turning the pillow over to the cool side, she caught a whiff of aftershave on the pillowcase. Pulling it closer, she thought, *This bed belongs to Michael.* A warm, comforting feeling encompassed her as she sighed and drifted off to sleep.

With her eyes barely opened, she saw the faint gray light of morning filtering in between the slats of the window blinds. Untangling herself from the covers, she slid out of bed, dropping her feet to the cold linoleum floor. Her toes felt for her slippers under the bed. She slipped them on, crossing the hall to put on a pot of coffee. Just as she poured a mug full of the black brew, she turned around swiftly and plowed right into Michael!

"Oh!" she exclaimed. The hot coffee splashed back, sloshing down the front of her pajamas and burning the tender skin on the underside of her arm. She stood frozen, bending forward, trying not to let the hot liquid scald her skin. She looked up, staring with wide-open eyes at Michael.

"I'm so sorry!" His voice held both compassion and surprise. "I should have said something...I didn't know anyone was here!" Taking hold of her elbow he led her to the sink and turned on the tap. Grabbing a towel from the top shelf, he handed it to her to wipe away the coffee that had splashed on her face. Gently taking her arm, he turned it slowly; the red patch on her skin ran from her elbow to her wrist. He moved her arm under the faucet and let the cold water pour over her tender flesh.

"Ouch," he said. "I know that's gotta hurt." He squinted, looking away from the burn and into her eyes, inches from her face.

She returned his gaze, lost in the compassion she saw there. His bluish-green eyes deepened with intensity; she stopped breathing momentarily. "I'm okay...it's just a little burn." Feeling embarrassed, she turned from him to watch the water run over her skin.

"I had no idea you were here. You kinda scared me too, ya know," he said, trying to make light of the situation. "I caught a glimpse of something floating across the hall and for a minute I thought all those stories about the grounds being haunted just might be true after all." He was trying to distract her from her injury and wrestle a smile from her deeply blushing face.

"Most people run the other way when they think they've seen a ghost," she said, looking up at him. "I guess I wasn't scary enough for you. I'll have to work on that."

He carefully patted her arm dry, then reached around and pulled out a chair. "Sit down...let's put a little aloe on that burn. I've got a plant up front...hold on, I'll be right back."

As soon as he left the room, unexpected tears welled up in her eyes. *What's the matter with me? Why am I crying? I never cry! It doesn't hurt that bad,* she thought, aggravated at her sudden meltdown. The tears spilled over onto her reddened cheeks. Her throat tightened as she swallowed down the knot. Quickly wiping her face with the back of her hand, she fought to gain control over the escalating emotions that threatened to embarrass her. "I can't believe I'm acting like such a crybaby over this!" she whispered. *Why does he have to be so nice and caring? I wish he had just told me to get over it already. I'd be fine by now.*

When Michael returned, he noticed her flushed cheeks and damp eyes, but decided not to say anything. She looked as if she was trying hard to keep it together, whether from pain or embarrassment, he couldn't tell.

"I hope you don't think this is going to keep you from work today," he said jokingly. "I mean, just because I throw scalding hot coffee on you, that's no excuse for you to lay out on me."

Telie smiled. "I guess I'm just a little embarrassed by all of this. I mean...here I am sleeping in your bed, at your place of business, drinking your coffee...I even ate your crackers last night." She shook her head in disgust. "I should have asked your permission instead of assuming it would be all right. I thought Martha told you. It's not her fault; it was my responsibility to ask." She let her voice trail off. "You must feel like one of the three bears."

"As long as you're not calling me Goldilocks, I mean, I really don't think my manhood could take that kind of a blow!" He raised one eyebrow, studying her face for a long moment, hoping for another smile. "Like I said before, Martha rarely troubles me with day-to-day decisions, but..." he added, letting out a sigh, "now that I know you're here *and* can make coffee, I'll expect to have it waiting on me every morning from now on – you got that? And I'll try and forget the whole Goldilocks thing, okay?" he said with a wink.

"I think I can handle that for you, Mr. Christenberry. Hopefully I'll be out of here soon; that is if Joe's grandfather decides to rent his cabin to me. He's supposed to let me know something today."

"You mean that old hunting cabin...at French Camp?" Michael asked, looking confused.

"Yeah, that's the one," she answered excitedly. "I asked Joe if he knew of a place out from town that I could rent. That's when he told me about the cabin. He said it was small and secluded and would be perfect for just one person."

Her smile and excitement quickly removed his protest. He didn't have the heart to say anything about that old two-room cabin way out in the wilderness. How hunters used it mostly as a getaway to party and raise Cain away from their wives. Squeezing the aloe out of the succulent plant, he smoothly covered her skin with the sticky juice. His calloused fingers were surprisingly gentle. "There you go. You're all set," he said, wiping the aloe from his hands with a paper towel. "Take a few ibuprofen, the bottle's behind you, and you'll be good to go."

Later that day, Michael spied Joe walking across the property. "Hey Joe, hold up," Michael said, as he walked toward him.

17

"Yeah boss?" Joe put down the water hose and ambled over to Michael. Wiping the sweat from his forehead, he blew out a deep, exhausted breath.

Michael tried to conceal his aggravation. Tightening his jaw, he said, "Telie mentioned to me this morning that she wants to rent your grandfather's hunting cabin at the old French Camp – is that true?"

"Yeah, I asked him about it last night. He said she can have it until October…hunting season and all."

"Why in the world would you tell her about that old place? I mean it's out in the middle of nowhere! It's dangerous! Every hunter in the county knows about it. There's no telling who might walk up on her out there." He waited for him to explain his ridiculous idea.

Joe nodded slowly. "That's what I told her. I even tried to convince her to let me show her some apartments in town, but she wouldn't hear of it," he said, sensing the anger beneath Michael's words.

His eyes narrowed. "Why not?"

He could have laughed but decided against it, seeing the look on Michael's face. "She told me that she would rather live in a boxcar than in an apartment complex," Joe stated as a matter of fact. "Can you believe that?"

"What?" he snapped. Disbelief showing on his face, he waited for further explanation.

"I don't understand it either, man, but that's what she told me." Joe shrugged, raising his eyebrows. "I get the feeling she likes nature or something. Maybe she's one of those Greenpeace treehuggers or something, man, I don't know."

Michael looked up and saw Telie walking toward them. "All right Joe, we'll talk about this later," he said, dismissing him quietly.

"How's that arm of yours?" Michael's voice took on a sincere tone.

"Good as new...that aloe really works!" she said, smiling up at him warmly. "Thanks for doctoring me up. I really appreciate it...and I'm sorry for all the trouble I've caused you. I'm really not a 'high maintenance' type of girl."

He didn't reply, but fixed his eyes on her intently. "Let's see," he pondered, removing his work gloves, "I hear from Grayson that you know a lot about landscaping design. That true?"

"I know a little about it. That's mostly what I did for him. But I can do whatever you need me to do. I can adapt to whatever work needs to be done. I did a variety of things at Grayson's."

"Such as?" he asked, looking her over, still finding it hard to believe that this little wisp of a girl could work as hard as Paul Grayson said she could.

"Yard work, tree trimming, pond cleaning – I've done it all," she said proudly, tucking her hair behind her ear. "It doesn't matter to me. I'll do anything you need me to do."

"Anything?" he asked quizzically.

"Almost anything," she replied, stealing a glance at Joe. They exchanged a knowing smile, although hers had been forced.

An uncomfortable silence followed. Michael cocked his head to the side and asked, "Did I miss something?" He was not entirely sure he wanted to know.

"Telie doesn't like snakes," Joe answered, then turned and grinned mischievously at her.

"Since when do we have a problem with snakes?" Michael inquired, directing his attention to Joe.

"Since that idiot found out I don't like snakes!" Telie replied sharply, not giving Joe time to comment.

Both men seemed surprised at the sudden outburst from Telie. Laughing, Joe turned to explain to Michael. "You see, boss, I found a green snake in one of those plants over there. I was just going to show it to her...but she freaked! It dropped out of my hand and slithered over there," he said, pointing to a group of clay pots. "I've been pickin' on her a little, you know, asking her to move them around and stuff... sorry, boss."

Michael shook his head and then spoke sternly to Joe. "You find that snake and get rid of it. Off the property...do you understand me? Oh...one more thing. If I ever hear of you frightening Telie again, you'll have to answer to me. Clear enough?"

"Yeah boss. I'll get the snake." With that, Joe ambled off in search of the snake, biting his lips to keep from smiling. He glanced back at Telie, seeing her peek out from behind Michael, sticking her tongue out at him.

Michael turned around to face Telie, and she smiled sweetly up at him. "Do you have any objection to helping out with the nursery?" He looked around at all of the plants scattered around. "It's turned into more than I bargained for and fast becoming a real handful to keep up with. I let Martha talk me into adding all of this last summer." He took a skinny cigar out of his pocket and stuck it between his teeth, squinting as he appraised her.

"Not at all, I'm familiar with most of the plants. I do see a few that I'm not so sure about, but that won't be a problem,

I can look them up on-line and find out about them. I can usually educate myself pretty quickly. I'll do whatever you need me to do."

"Fair enough," he said. "I'll be out most of the time with my crew. We get an early start around here so I'll probably be gone by the time you get here in the morning. Martha will let you know what needs to be done each day. We get paid on Friday, and if you ever need off for anything, just let Martha know. We're like family around here, so whatever I can do to help you, just let me know. We're glad you're with us, Telie, and we hope you like it here."

"Thank you, Mr. Christenberry, I'm sure I will."

"One more thing, my name is Michael. Mr. Christenberry was my father," he said with a wink, and then turned to leave.

Telie looked around after Michael left, marveling at the size of the place. It spread out in both directions. The largest complex housed the office, break room and the small bunkroom and bath where she had spent the night. At the back of the property there were several outbuildings that held tractors and equipment, the kind of things you need for large landscaping projects. It was also the place she noticed Michael spent most of his time. Around the rest of the property, scattered here and there, was an assortment of flowers and blooming shrubs. Fountains and large slabs of stone mingled among the plants.

Spying a large potted tree in the middle of the path, she decided to move it to the side, out of the way. She bent down and wrestled it, both hands firmly around the base of the pot. Looking up, she noticed a shadow growing in front of her. Glancing over her shoulder, she saw Michael standing there with his arms folded, watching her.

"Do you think that's wise?" He gave her a stern look.

"I was just trying to move it from the path," she explained.

"If you want something moved, you should ask me to move it for you. That tree is too heavy for you. In the future, if I'm not here, ask Joe...he'll be glad to help you. I don't want you hurting yourself. Do I make myself clear?"

"Yes, sir," she replied, blinking in disbelief. *What's with this guy? He's really upset with me and all I'm trying to do is work,* she thought. No one had ever tried to stop her from doing *anything* before. Not her father, not Paul Grayson, no one. *Does he think I'm weak and helpless?* She wondered. She didn't quite know what to think of Michael Christenberry. He was certainly a different kind of man than what she was accustomed to.

Walking away, confused, she sensed his eyes on her. Looking around for something to do, she began pulling dead blooms off of a few plants and checking to see if they'd been properly watered. "They bloom more frequently when their spent flowers are removed," she spoke under her breath, to no one in particular, still a little miffed at being corrected.

At Grayson's she'd had the run of the place. No one had ever told her what to do. She could do anything she wanted to, no matter how difficult. Certainly no one had ever reprimanded her before.

Everything was scattered about, not in any particular order. Deciding to arrange a little, she found a wagon nearby and used it to load a few plants, moving them to other locations. She grouped several together in a colorful display. Stepping back from the flowers, she tilted her head to appraise her work. Pursing her lips, she said, "Much better. Now, what about another display up front with a gurgling fountain." She spied out the perfect spot. Loading her wagon with bright blooms, she made her way over to the spot she had selected. Eyeing the fountain she wanted, she looked around to see where Michael was before trying to move it. "On second thought," she mumbled to herself, "I better get Joe."

She found Joe behind the tractor shed cleaning his fingernails with his pocketknife. He was more than willing to help her after the little snake incident. They moved the fountain into place and filled it with distilled water. Finding an outlet, they plugged it in. "It's amazing how a little trickling water can transform a place, isn't it, Joe?" Happy with the outcome, she moved a large planter around to the front and clipped off the dead flowers to encourage new blooms.

"Joe, what kind of a plant is this?" she asked, running her fingers along a long spiky blade.

"That's a sago palm," he answered.

"I want it in the middle of this lantana. Can you pick it up for me? The large scale will work well in the front here. I'm going to put this creeping Jenny in so it will trail down and soften the container…to make it more relaxed."

"Oh, sure, we're all about having our containers relaxed around here. We wouldn't want any of them to stress out or anything." Laughing, Joe shook his head. "Next, you'll have me singing lullabies to them."

Ignoring his comment, she walked away from the display and looked back, impressed by the transformation. The splashing fountain and the colorful containers of flowers had made the entrance to the nursery come to life. *Before you even get out of your car, you're hit with the incredible beauty of the surroundings,* she thought. *The visual interest as well as the soothing sound of the fountain captures your attention.* "This will be a draw, you wait and see," she said to Joe, with a look of satisfaction. "I can't wait for Michael to see it. You think he'll like what we've done?"

"Yeah…I think he'll like whatever *you* do," he complained, rolling his eyes.

Disliking the implication, Telie could not resist a retort. "Well, in that case he wouldn't mind if I haul off and smack you upside the head, then would he?"

Telie sat down in the gravel and crossed her legs Indian style. Ignoring Joe, she started loosening the soil around a plant that looked like it needed life support. Hearing the crunch of gravel and squeaky brakes behind her, she looked back in time to see Michael. His elbow was propped on the window of the truck, a huge smile on his face. "Looks good!" he yelled to her.

"Thanks," she responded. "Like the fountain?"

"I do, I really do," he answered, pulling away slowly, his eyes surveying the area before settling back on her.

Telie drew in her breath and held it for a long moment.

Chapter 4

Rounding the corner with an armload of garden tools, Telie set out to load her truck and head over to June Meyers' house. June is a longtime friend of Martha's and a regular customer. Shortly after lunch, Martha mentioned that Joe usually goes to June's, but she wanted to send her this time to see what she was made of.

Martha followed her to the truck. "I'm giving you fair warning, Telie girl, she's something else. I love her dearly, but not many people can please that woman or put up with her for very long." Martha peered over the top of her glasses. "Plan on spending all day...she'll have you doing everything from fixing her rickety old screen door to taking down her Christmas lights from four months ago. Last year, Joe had to be rushed to the emergency room after she had him remove a wasp nest from under the eave of her house. Poor Joe, he hides every time she sets foot on the place. I think he's scared to death of her," she said with a laugh. "She pays well and that's the only reason I put up with her, friend or no friend. The lawn will be the easiest part; it's all those 'little' jobs that will do you in."

Telie called back over her shoulder, as she walked to the truck, "If I'm not back by sundown, come and get me!"

25

Making her way up the road, she soon came across large spacious lawns and old timeless homes. The houses were positioned away from the road and elevated slightly to take advantage of the view of the bay across the road. "This must be the house," she said, as she spotted one fitting the description Martha had given her.

It was white clapboard, fitted with grayish-green plantation shutters. The yard was full of mature trees and shrubs that looked as if they had been there for generations. *They've survived a hurricane or two*, she thought, as she gazed up into the gnarled limbs.

Pulling into the driveway, she noticed a tall slender woman standing on the porch. Her salt and pepper hair was pulled back severely from her face into a tight bun. She was wearing a loose pair of black pants and a crisp white blouse tucked in around her small waist. She had a regal look about her.

Taking a deep breath, Telie stepped out of her truck and walked toward her. "Miss June, I'm Telie, Martha sent me to help you out today."

"Don't they know about child labor laws over there at Christenberry's?" June said, sizing her up and down, a skeptical look on her stern face.

"I'm stronger than I look, Miss June. You just tell me what you want me to do, and I'll do it, just the way you want it, deal?" She stuck out her hand, clasping June's bony fingers, giving them a firm squeeze.

"Fair enough," she said, pulling her hand back with a smile. "Start with the lawn. After you finish, come inside and I'll tell you what else needs to be done."

Michael dropped into the chair beside Martha's desk, and let out a deep sigh, raking his hand through his hair. "Where's Telie?"

"I sent her over to June's after lunch. You know how June gets, she's been about to drive me crazy wanting someone over there yesterday."

"You what?" Michael's mouth fell open. "What are you tryin' to do – run her off?"

"Who Telie? Don't be ridiculous…or did you mean June?"

"Telie. We can't run June off, I've tried!" He shook his head. "What possessed you to do that to Telie? Sometimes I just don't understand you, Martha. If she survives this, it'll be a miracle."

"She can handle June, Michael. When are you going to stop thinking every woman in the world is helpless? I heard how you jumped Joe over the whole cabin thing. You should be ashamed of yourself. You're the one that told him to help her out, didn't you? If French Camp doesn't suit you, why don't you let her stay at your place?"

"My place?" he sounded shocked.

"Bell Forest…what the heck did you think I meant? At least she would have neighbors. It's close to work, too. All she wants is to be left alone, apparently; why else would she insist on living way out in the boonies? The monastery is nearby and those old monks won't bother her. Another thing while I'm speaking my mind, if you don't stop playing watchdog over that girl, you're gonna wear us all out! She doesn't need you watching over her every move. Telie is anything but helpless, Michael, and it's high time you realized it. Not every woman in the world is like your wife, Emily."

"Are you finished with your little tirade?" he asked, annoyed.

"Not quite, but that will do for now. I've got work to do," she said, as she opened her account book and started posting.

Michael couldn't get Martha's words out of his head. He hated it when she was right. Of course he was overprotective; he knew that. Maybe she could handle it out at the cabin. But there was no way he could stand the thought of that. *It would make more sense for Telie to live closer to work*, he told himself. *I can at least offer Bell Forest to her. Who knows, she just might like it, anything to keep her from moving out to the old French Camp.*

Michael missed Bell Forest. It had been years since he'd stayed out there. His wife had not cared for the place; it was too "woodsy" for her taste. She preferred their house in town, and because *she* loved it there, that's where he chose to stay even after her death. He couldn't bear to leave it anyway; it reminded him of her. It was exactly the way she'd left it three years earlier.

Bell Forest had been his mother's favorite place on earth, her sanctuary. It had been a gift to her from his dad. Michael didn't have the heart to ever sell it. He could still see his mother walking along the shore of the bay. She picked up anything that interested her: bits of driftwood, a shell, maybe even a smooth stone or a piece of glass. She placed her collections on the rail of the porch for all to admire. He missed that about her…he missed everything about her.

Maybe I could make a trade out of some sort, he thought. *I'll ask her later. On second thought, I better ask her now, just in case she decides to take Joe's granddad up on his offer.*

28

Pulling up into June's driveway, he noticed the two of them sitting on the front porch. Telie was seated in the swing, pushing slowly back and forth with her foot.

"Enjoying the afternoon, ladies?" He called to them with a smirk on his face, wondering what they'd been sipping to paste that silly grin across June's face. He couldn't recall ever seeing her smile before, and it startled him.

June's voice pealed across the yard, sounding young and vibrant. "Yes, we certainly are. Come on up, I'll get you something cold to drink." She went into the house as Michael climbed the steps to the porch and took a seat, opposite Telie.

"You've survived, I see, going in where angels fear to tread."

Telie flashed a grin baring white teeth that sparkled against her dusty, dirty face.

The front screen door banged as June stepped out onto the porch and handed Michael his drink. "Here you go... now let me tell you something, Michael, this girl here has worked! You better never send that boy around here no more, you hear?"

"Oh, I hear," he said, hiding his grin, as he gulped down his lemonade. After finishing his drink, he wiped the corner of his mouth with the back of his hand. A smile spread across his face as he thought how overjoyed Joe would be with the news that he'd been banned from the property.

"We were just discussing our plans to go 'rose rustling' this Sunday. Turns out, Telie and I have a lot in common." A mischievous look crossed her face before she winked at Telie.

"The less I know about the plans you two devise, the better off I'll be," he said, handing back his empty glass. "That hit the spot. Thank you."

"I plan to introduce Telie to every available bachelor in Moss Bay. It's not often you find an attractive girl that's not afraid to work!"

Michael appraised Telie, then smiled. "Or one that's not afraid to get dirty!"

A deep blush flamed Telie's cheeks. For once she was thankful for the dirt mask she wore. "A little dirt never hurt anybody," she declared. She stood up and said goodbye to June with the promise that she'd be back next week.

Michael stood, placed his hand in the small of Telie's back and led her down the porch steps and out onto the lawn.

The heat of the day was finally catching up with Telie. She felt heavy, drained and exhausted, as if her feet were made of lead. Her head wanted desperately to lean back on the broad chest behind her.

"Would you like to see another property before you make a decision on the cabin?" Michael asked, jingling his truck keys in his hand.

"Another place, you mean a place to live? Where is it?" she asked, sounding interested.

Michael nodded. "Oh, it's out from town. It's kind of secluded and run-down a little bit, but it has a great view of the bay," he explained.

"Whose place is it?" she asked, stopping as she lifted her weary eyes to search his face. The sound of cicadas hummed through the trees as she waited a moment for his answer.

"It's mine...I mean it belongs to me." He faced her directly, noticing how tired she looked with her golden-brown eyes half closed.

"You want to rent it?" She tried to make sense of what he was suggesting.

"Well," he hesitated a moment, then grinned, "I thought we could work out some sort of an arrangement."

Telie's face flushed hot pink. She bit her lip to gain control over her flaring temper. She spoke calmly. "I don't think I'm interested in making an 'arrangement' with you, Mr. Christenberry. Whatever you have in your mind, you have the wrong girl." She turned to leave, digging in her purse to retrieve her keys.

Seeing the look on her face, he suddenly realized how his words must have sounded. Quickly, he rushed up to her and said, "No, no, wait! What I meant to say is that the old place is in such bad shape, I'll be glad to trade out rent for labor. Just don't answer until you see it though; it's been neglected a long time." He felt suddenly helpless. "I'm sorry...that came out all wrong. I didn't mean to imply anything other than that." Watching her face soften, he breathed a sigh of relief.

"Oh," she said, relief and embarrassment playing across her face. "Sure...I mean, yes, I'd like to see it. When can we go?"

"How about now? You can follow me down there," he said, not giving her a chance to change her mind. "It's not far from work...but don't think you'll hurt my feelings if you don't care for the place. My wife, Emily, never liked it much."

They drove down the two-lane road, past flat farmland dotted with cattle and large stands of pecan trees. A few ancient live oaks dripping with moss leaned over the road and seemed to wave as they passed by, stirred by the wind.

"Welcome to Bell Forest," he announced, as they stepped out, slamming the truck doors behind them.

Telie's head turned slowly, taking in the wild beauty of the place. She was captivated immediately.

"I warned you," he said, looking around at all of the fallen branches and limbs that cluttered the ground. Vines and undergrowth grew over long forgotten azaleas and forsythia shrubs and tangled around everything in its path as it made its way up from the lush marshland. "That's Bayou Bell over there," he motioned past the cottage. "The bay is out front, beyond those trees. Come on, I'll show you the house."

Making their way carefully down the path, Michael reached back and took Telie's elbow, gently leading her over the fallen tree limbs. His nearness caused her heartbeat to quicken suddenly, giving her renewed energy. She wasn't used to being looked after, especially by a man. The men in her life treated her like a boy. The feeling of being protected was both strange and wonderful at the same time. She was certain that Mrs. Michael Christenberry was an incredibly blessed woman.

"This place is unreal." She spoke softly as if it might all disappear. Dappled sunlight filtered through the trees above their heads as a breeze gently stirred around them. A dove cooed a mournful sound from a nearby branch.

"On warm nights, it's pleasant out here…always a slight breeze." He cleared the porch steps of debris with his foot and helped her up.

The house complemented the surroundings and didn't compete with it. The front porch was ample, covered by a broad metal roof that hung low, perfect for shading and shedding rainwater. A large wooden door, painted dark gray, stood facing them with a well-worn, slightly warped screen door covering it. There were two oversized windows on each side of the door, fitted with small glass panes. The porch held two white, time-worn wicker rockers and a large willow chair with a small table tucked neatly against the wall.

Michael reached the door in two steps and unlocked it. Seeing her expression, he remarked, "Don't be so impressed; you haven't seen the inside yet." Opening the door he said, "Wait here, I'll go flip the breaker."

Trying to adjust her eyes, she peered around the tiny cottage and beamed. "Perfect," she whispered.

In the small living room there stood a stone fireplace that covered much of one wall. An arrangement of two chairs in a soft faded green fabric faced a small overstuffed cream-colored couch. A coffee table scattered with a collection of books, a jar of seashells and smooth stones sat next to them. The bedroom could be seen from the living room and was just large enough for the bed, dresser and nightstand. A small porcelain lamp was all that sat on the nightstand. Much of the furniture had a bleached look, aged and worn. A collection of lavender-blue and pale-green pillows tossed over a cream-colored bedspread gave the room a splash of color. The same colors carried over into the small bathroom.

Making a gesture toward the kitchen he said, "The kitchen is pretty much empty…I'll take you down the road and show you what passes for a grocery store around here. You can get everything from night crawlers to homemade bread. But don't make the mistake of telling the storeowner, Mrs. Davis, your business. She'll tell the whole town. Of course you can always go into town to buy groceries at the one and only real grocery store around."

Telie smiled at his comment, but her attention was on the kitchen. She liked it the best.

It was mostly white: white walls, white cabinets with bright blue glass jars placed neatly on the windowsill over the sink. The window faced the road out back. She could tell it was a place that captured the warm morning sun. The rear kitchen door led out to a narrow screened-in porch with three small steps down to the yard. The overgrown path led back around to the side of the house as it joined the main path to the dirt drive.

"It's not very fancy, but there's a bed with clean sheets in the closet and plenty of *soap* in the bathroom." He eyed her mud-streaked face and tousled hair with amusement.

"Yeah, I sure could use a bath," she mumbled under her breath. "June had me clean out her fireplace!" she exclaimed. "But at least I managed to stay out of the emergency room. I hear others haven't been so fortunate."

"That's quite an accomplishment. The name 'June Meyers' is legendary in this town. It was a memorable day when she decided to burn down an old building on her property a few years back. She doused it with gasoline. After it ignited, half the town got involved trying to put it out. They say the flames could be seen as far away as Mobile! Thankfully no one died…but it was close." He smiled broadly, exaggerating the story.

Focusing on the matter at hand, trying hard not to be distracted by his smile, or by the way his eyes lit up when telling the story. "When can I move in?" Suddenly self-conscious about her appearance, she tucked her hair behind her ears, waiting for his answer.

"You really want to live out here?" he asked in disbelief. "I mean…it's no boxcar or anything," he said, jokingly.

Raising her eyebrows, she thought, *Joe has been running his big mouth.* "It's perfect. I love it. It's absolutely perfect for me."

His heart beat a little faster at the sound of her enthusiasm, surprising him. "Do you have your stuff with you or did you leave it back in the bunkroom?"

"No, I've got my stuff with me. It's all in the truck," she said. "I don't have furniture, so this will really work well for me. I can't tell you how much I appreciate this, Michael. I'll start cleaning up the place right away. You won't recognize it when I'm finished." She sighed deeply, grateful for her chance to have a place of her own.

"Good...I'll stop by in the morning and check on you... take you to town if you like. Whatever else you might need just let me know. Sound good?"

"Sounds good to me. I'll need to do some banking if that's not too much trouble. I need to open an account. I'd also like to find that grocery store in town. I don't think I'm ready to meet Mrs. Davis yet," she said, grinning. "I'm kind of a private person."

"Oh, I gathered that." He smiled back. "We'll get an early start then. The bank stays open until noon on Saturdays." He walked to the door. "I'll see you in the morning." Hesitating, he closed the door softly behind him.

He walked back to the truck telling himself that she'd be okay; it was safe – safer than French Camp anyway. Backing out, his eyes scanned the place. *This is too much work for that young girl. Well, I'll see how things go,* he thought.

Chapter 5

The air was thick with the fragrance of honeysuckle. It clung to the morning air, rich and heady, as Michael walked down the path at Bell Forest. Today, he was to drive Telie into town.

"You all set?" he asked, taking the front porch steps two at a time. Telie was sitting outside in the rocker waiting for him. She was dressed in a gauzy pale-yellow skirt and loose white cotton blouse. Her hair was pulled back into a ponytail at the base of her neck; it swished slightly as she turned her head toward the bayou.

"Yes, I'm ready. I've just been watching a blue heron over in the marsh grass fishing for his breakfast." Her golden-brown eyes turned and peered up at him. A shaft of early morning light caught and illuminated her features.

His breath caught momentarily before he could reply. "Yeah, this place is full of life. I bet you had a hard time getting to sleep last night? The sounds from the bayou can be deafening."

"Not at all, that's my favorite way to go to sleep. I have a CD with nature sounds on it…won't ever need it here, though. I have my own symphony just outside my window," she said, gesturing with her hand.

Joe was probably right. Telie must be some kind of "treehugger," Michael surmised. Gone was the dirty tomboy of yesterday. She now looked every bit the naturalist, artsy and whimsical.

Uncomfortable with the silence and the way Michael was appraising her, she said, "I'd offer you coffee, but that's on my list of things I need to pick up today. I'm ready if you are. I'm sure you have better things to do than haul me around all day." Standing, she grabbed her purse and followed him down the steps as the movement from the vacated chair slowly came to a halt.

The truck creaked and squeaked and bounced Telie around on the seat as they drove down the rutted dirt road toward town. Her gathered hair began to come away from the loose ponytail as the truck jarred her small frame. Wispy strands of honey-blond hair fell around her face, catching in the upturned corner of her mouth.

"Were you frightened last night?" he asked. He glanced at her quickly, and then turned his attention back to the road.

"Uh...I don't get scared," she said, lightly brushing away the wayward strands from her face. "I'm not afraid of anything," she stated confidently.

Hiding his amusement, he turned toward her. "So, the bogeyman doesn't scare you?"

"Please." She dismissed his comment with a wave of her hand.

The truck bumped as it pulled onto pavement, smoothing out the roughness. She let go of the seat cushion, her knuckles white, and settled back into the seat. As they drove along, nearing the town of Moss Bay, she saw crayon-colored houses and old brick buildings perched side by side down Main Street; wrought-iron balconies in curved designs graced the fronts of many buildings. Grand homes surrounded by intricate iron fences bid the eye to look.

"What is it about wrought-iron fences that makes you want to peek to see what's behind them?" she asked, looking at a gate near an especially interesting home. The house was barely visible behind the vine-covered fence, but what could be glimpsed was impressive.

"That's a mystery." He reached over his head and pulled down the visor. A package of skinny cigars slid down into his fingers. He freed one and stuck the end of it in his mouth, rolling it over with his tongue until it lodged in his cheek. "My wife Emily talked me into putting a wrought-iron fence around our place," he said, between clenched teeth. "It has this massive iron gate that curves at the top and kind of butterflies open. I've always thought it looked pretentious, but she loved it."

"Sounds beautiful," Telie said, wistfully peering out at the passing houses.

"You're right about people though. They would walk by our house, stop and stare through the fence, like there must be something fascinating in there. I got tired of it after awhile, brought a few vines home from work and planted them around...it's pretty much all covered up now, thank goodness. Oh," he said, "I almost forgot." He spotted the bank remembering her request to find one. Pulling up to the curb, he said, "I think you'll be happy with this bank. Everyone is very friendly; come on, I'll introduce you."

Michael was right. The people at the bank could not have been nicer. She opened an account and deposited her savings. After they left the bank, he let her out at the town's only grocery store and waited patiently in the truck for her to finish shopping. Watching her push the cart toward the truck, he got out and helped her unload the bags of groceries. He covered them with a tarp and secured them down tightly. "It looks like we might get wet before we get back," he said, indicating with his head toward the west, while his arms pulled the rope tightly.

She glanced over her shoulder at the approaching storm clouds all black and ominous. A sudden wind lifted her hair, freeing it from the clasp as it dropped to the pavement. She bent over to retrieve the clasp, gathering her hair in one hand; she loosely secured it to the back of her neck. "Looks like we're in for it," she said, smiling.

True enough, they passed through the summer squall as they headed back to the cottage. Rain hammered the roof and hood of the truck with a relentless beat. It showed no sign of letting up. Michael eased off the road, deciding to wait it out. Looking out, they could see the trees bend with the strong winds and disappear behind a silver sheet of rain.

Raising his voice over the noise of the rain, Michael asked, "Do you like seafood?" He was trying to distract her from the storm.

"No, not really, to be honest...I've never had that much of it. Where I come from it's all about the barbeque," she answered in the same louder than usual tone.

"Coldwater's not that far from Memphis, is it?" Michael was looking out at the storm as he talked. He remembered how terrified his wife Emily had been of storms and assumed Telie might feel the same way. He was trying to keep the conversation going, hoping to keep her mind on something besides the raging elements. "Tell me about Coldwater. What makes it special?"

"It's beautiful too, only in a different way from Moss Bay. The Tennessee River runs through the whole area. Let's see...we have riverboats instead of shrimp boats, mountains

39

and bluffs instead of bayous and marshes, and barbeque instead of fresh seafood!"

A sudden streak of lightning flashed as thunder pealed through the air, vibrating and rattling the entire truck! Michael reached for her instinctively, pulling her across the seat near him with one arm. She surprised him by grinning, her wide eyes dancing with excitement. "That was close," she said, clearly enjoying the thrill of it.

"Yes...it was. I think it must have been right on top of us," he said, looking down at her bewildered. He released her, apologizing, "I'm sorry...I'm used to my wife being terrified of storms. I grabbed you out of habit."

"I understand...anyway," she continued, sliding back over to her side of the vehicle. "To answer your question, Memphis is only a two-hour drive from Coldwater. I'm not sure about the distance. I measure everything by hours, not miles," she laughed. "We're stuck up in the Northwest corner of the state, wedged close to Mississippi and Tennessee. But you know that already, don't you?" She understood then that he had merely been trying to distract her from the storm.

"I guess I forgot. I love the mountains up there, especially in the fall, and the way the river runs along the valley. It's beautiful. Did you grow up on the river?"

"You could say that *everybody* in Coldwater grows up on the river. It's impossible to get away from it. Two things you can't get away from in Coldwater, trains and the river! Sooner or later a train will catch you. My first night in the bunkroom I kept wondering why I couldn't sleep, what was missing? It was so quiet. Then it hit me: train whistles. I guess that's something you don't miss 'til you don't hear them anymore. You could set your clock by that whistle. I never needed an alarm clock...I knew it was 6:30 by the train whistle. That's something I probably should have picked up in town, an alarm clock. I just now thought about it." Continuing to stare out the window, she chided herself for rambling on and on. *He probably thinks I'm an idiot*, she thought, but the excitement of the storm had her feeling alive and chatty.

"I'll see if I can get some of the local shrimp boats to come by Bell Forest and sound their horns for you each morning. We wouldn't want you to get homesick or anything," he said, grinning.

She laughed. "Arrange that for me, would you?"

"I'll bet you're a really good swimmer, having lived near the river and all." He removed the chewed-up cigar from his mouth and tossed it into the ashtray.

"Swimming in the river makes me uneasy. I've seen fishermen pull up catfish as big as their boat! I never kick my feet too much in the water; that makes me feel like bait."

Michael was enjoying the easy flow of conversation and wasn't ready for it to end. "I've got an idea. Why don't we stop by Pap's Cove? I want you to try their famous pecan-crusted gulf fish; that's what they're known for. And if you know of a better chocolate brownie anywhere, you let me know."

"That convinces me...let's go," she said, looking like a little girl staring out of the front windshield, excitedly.

The windshield wipers slammed back and forth furiously as they drove down the road. They pulled up to a rundown-looking shack of a place. She wondered if Michael had missed his turn.

"Stay put," he said. "I'll run around and get you." He reached behind the truck seat and grabbed the umbrella, snapping it up as he walked around to the passenger door. Helping her out, he gathered her under his arm securely with one hand, firmly holding the umbrella handle with the other. Swinging wide the door, they stepped inside, shaking off the rain. Michael stomped his boots on the rug, raking his hair back with his hand.

Looking around, Telie was surprised at the warmth of the place. It had an unexpected charm. The aroma of coffee permeated the air. Each table was set with white linen tablecloths with flickering candles in small votives.

A pretty petite woman approached them wearing a glowing smile. "Michael, it's good to see you. Where have you been keeping yourself? We've missed you."

Telie thought the hostess was a little *too* comfortable flirting with a married man. She wondered if she treated all men that way or if she was selective. A thought hit her. *What was she doing having lunch with a married man!* Her face suddenly flushed at the thought. She moved her hand to her throat to hide the rising embarrassment.

"Hello Caroline, it's nice to see you, too. Caroline, this is Telie," he said, looking down at her, smiling. "She has never had your famous fish so I thought I'd treat her today while we wait out this storm."

"Hello Telie, we're happy to have you with us. Come on, I'll seat you somewhere near the windows." They followed her as she made her way around the tables to a quiet area that overlooked the marina. A small white candle flickered in a sparkling clear votive while soft music played in the background, giving a relaxed feeling to the place.

The rain continued to pour as the wind and waves tossed the boats around in the harbor like bathtub toys. Telie felt ashamed of herself for enjoying his company. *I would be livid if my husband took another woman to lunch without me!*

"What to drink?" Caroline asked, looking at Michael. "Telie?" Michael gestured to her.

"I'll have unsweetened tea, please."

"Make that two." Michael studied Telie, watching her eyes take in the surroundings. He was finding himself fascinated by this young girl. What was it about her that he found so interesting? He'd certainly been around beautiful women before...it wasn't that. He just had never met anyone quite like her.

Caroline was back with the drinks and ready to take their order.

"We'll have two pecan-crusted fish and a small bowl of your shrimp and grits. You've got to try them," Michael remarked, looking over at Telie. "Oh, and we'll have one of your brownies for dessert."

"Two spoons?" the waitress asked, curiously.

"No, just one...thanks," he said, handing back the menus.

"Let me know, Michael, if there is anything else I can get you." She flashed a flirty smile, then disappeared through the swinging kitchen door.

Telie couldn't believe the nerve of the girl! How could she be so bold as to openly flirt with a married man! *There's no excuse for her behavior,* she thought, outraged at the waitress.

"You know, this is my favorite time of day," Michael said. "I love to come here and watch the fishing boats come in and go out. You see that point over there?" He leaned down with both elbows on the table and pointed to a narrow strip of land jutting out into the bay. "Legend has it that an old Spanish vessel, supposedly a remnant of Hernando de Soto's expedition, made its way into the bay and ran aground

43

in the shallows, right over there. It was during a fierce storm, a lot like this one I'd imagine, back in the early 1500s."

One long-armed live oak formed an eerie frame as it jutted out from the bank, allowing the point to come into focus. "Did anyone die?" Telie asked, her golden-brown eyes wide with intrigue.

"Several," he added. It amused him to see the expression on her face. She looked spooked but fascinated. Her eyes caught movement from the dock as a few fishermen made their way up the rain-soaked dock toward the restaurant. They looked dark and foreboding in their slick rain gear. Telie shivered.

"Are you cold?" Michael asked, showing concern but knowing the real reason for her shivering. He knew she was probably thinking of how the fishermen looked like long-lost spirits, spit out from the depths of the sea. He bit his lip to keep from smiling. This brave-talking girl who had just pronounced she wasn't afraid of anything had the look of a frightened child.

She kept her eyes fastened on them, saying, "No, I'm fine."

"Well, here it is," said Caroline, placing the fish down in front of them. "Who gets the shrimp and grits?"

Michael pointed to Telie.

"Enjoy," she said, winking at Michael, as she left them to their dinner.

Digging into the crispy fish, Telie took a large bite. "Umm, this is delicious. So...do you bring your wife here often?" Telie asked, smiling. She suddenly felt like sticking up for his Emily in the face of the blatant flirtation going on by the waitress.

"Yes, I used to...my wife died three years ago," Michael stated, looking down, as he cut into his fish.

Telie was stunned. She'd had no idea. Hadn't he talked about his wife that afternoon as if she were just across town or even at home? She'd thought earlier how understanding she must be to allow her husband to drive her around all afternoon. Feeling suddenly awkward, she said, "I'm sorry, Michael, I didn't know." Changing the subject, she remarked, "I see why you love this place, the fish is really delicious. I'm not sure what to make of the shrimp and grits though. I love grits...I'm just trying to get used to having shrimp float around in them."

"Yeah, it's an acquired taste. But you're right about this place, it's great. Not many tourists know about it yet. It's our local secret. It's about the last place you can go and not have to wait in line for an hour, especially during tourist season."

"My lips are sealed. You'd probably have to tie me up and throw me into the sea if I were to go around blabbing local secrets."

"Yeah, probably, that's where those guys have been," he indicated with his eyes toward the fishermen walking up from the dock. "They've been out doing away with loud mouths." They both laughed with ease.

After they finished dinner, Caroline brought out the biggest brownie Telie had ever laid eyes on. It was topped with vanilla ice cream and soaked in a warm butterscotch sauce. Michael laughed out loud when he saw her mouth drop open.

"Here ya go," Caroline said, giving them each a spoon. Michael put his spoon down, then ordered coffee. He was clearly enjoying himself watching Telie slowly dip her spoon into the dessert, not taking her eyes off of it. Moving the spoon to her open mouth, she closed her eyes, savoring it. He sipped his coffee as he watched her. He had never seen anyone over the age of twelve get that excited over dessert. At any moment he expected her to start humming and swinging her feet.

"You've got to try this, Michael…I mean this is the best thing I've ever put in my mouth. Take a bite." She offered her spoon to him.

To pacify her, he picked up his spoon and dipped it down into the brownie. Taking a bite, he rolled his eyes in pleasure. "You're right…this *is* unbelievable!" He pulled the bowl toward him, pretending to dive into it again.

She pinched the lip of the bowl with her fingers and moved it back toward her slowly. "Not so fast."

His heart was melting as fast as the ice cream on the warm brownie. Amused by her playfully aggravated expression, he couldn't wipe the smile off his face.

An attractive girl approached their table, wearing *too* tight blue jeans and a low-cut T-shirt with the name Pap's Cove stamped across her ample bust. Her light brown hair was long with the slightest wave of curls around her soft features. Her lips were full, her frame small and curvy. She spoke softly, placing a hand on Michael's shoulder, "Michael! I thought that was you. How've you been? I thought you'd run off or something. I haven't seen you in awhile."

Telie could tell the girl was delighted to see him. Her pale blue eyes lit up the moment he turned to face her.

She let Michael handle his acquaintance; he obviously wasn't going to make introductions so she turned her attention back to the brownie. The girl never even glanced at her but gazed at Michael like she was looking into the face of an angel. He listened to her intently as she went on with her story, nodding every now and then. After what seemed like an hour, Telie placed her spoon down and looked up at them. Michael met her gaze. A smile tugged at her lips when she noticed his raised eyebrows and a hint of a wink in his eyes. Finally the girl said, "Oh, I didn't mean to interrupt your meal. I'll let you get back to your lunch. Don't be such a stranger." Patting his shoulder she wandered back over to the bar area.

"Long story," he said, evenly.

"I didn't ask," she responded.

Chapter 6

After Michael dropped Telie off at the cottage, he pulled up next door, across the bayou, at St. Thomas Monastery.

"Michael, good to see you...it's been such a long time!" Brother Lawrence grabbed Michael by the shoulders and shook him. His face beamed. "Tell me, what brings you out to see us this evening?"

"Well, I've got a favor to ask of you Brother Lawrence." Taking a seat in the study, he leaned back against the chair and exhaled.

"Sure, sure, what can I do for you, son?" Brother Lawrence walked around to his desk and sat down, leaning forward with his hands clasped. "Is there something wrong, Michael?"

"Oh no, nothing like that." Michael shook his head reassuringly. "I've hired a young girl from one of our suppliers up north, North Alabama," he clarified. "She's away from home and doesn't know very many people. I told her she could stay at Bell Forest for a while. I would really appreciate it if you would kind of keep an eye on her. I'm not all that comfortable with the arrangement."

"Oh, of course, Michael, you mean she'll be staying there all alone?"

"Yes, well…yes, I'm not crazy about the idea…but it's the lesser of two evils. You see, she had her mind made up to stay out at the old French Camp. I offered her the cottage to keep her from going out there. Sort of thought she'd be safer next to ya'll."

"Oh, I see…I see," he nodded, understanding. "She must be a tough young girl not to mind living alone way out here."

Shaking his head, Michael said, "Have you ever seen a kitten try to act like a tiger?"

"I think I know what you mean." They both laughed as Brother Lawrence reassured him. "I'll watch out for her and call you if anything comes up. I'll let the others know, so we all can keep an eye on her."

Turning to go, Michael paused at the door. "One more thing. Please don't tell her I talked to you. I wouldn't want to make that tiger mad at me," he said with a wink.

"It will be our secret."

Telie stepped into the hot bath and sighed from relief. Her body ached as she sunk down deep into the water. Lathering her skin with the huge bar of soap Michael had placed on her bed, she smirked remembering his comment about the boxcar. *That big-mouth Joe*, she thought, relaxing back into the warm suds.

Everything about Moss Bay appealed to her: the lazy rhythms, the salty air, even the people. They seemed different from what she was accustomed to, less rushed maybe. *They're certainly colorful*, she thought, thinking of June and the women at Pap's Cove.

Climbing into bed, she lay there listening to the strange night sounds surrounding her, tree frogs and crickets, along with the gentle sound of lapping water on the nearby shore. It was evident the bayou was near by the earthy smell coming into her room from the marsh. Pulling the comforter up and under her chin, she snuggled deep into the soft folds. Her hair lifted softly as the oscillating fan pulled fresh air in from the open window. The night sounds soon lulled her to sleep with their gentle rhythms.

Sunday morning came bright and clear with birds singing outside her window. The first thought to cross her mind upon awakening was of June. She had invited her to church. *What to wear?* Opening a box of clothes, she began lifting out pieces and placing them on the bed. She had never been much of a shopper, and it showed. She ran her hand over the soft fabric of a pale blue sundress. "This will just have to do…now for shoes," she said. She rummaged around in the box until she found a pair of sandals. After taking a quick shower, she lifted her hair into a French twist, securing it with pins. Sticking her finger into a little pot of lip-gloss, she smoothed it around her full lips. After applying blush and mascara, she picked up her purse and headed out the door.

A few women whispered behind their hands as June and Telie entered the church. Making their way down the aisle, several people stopped talking and turned to stare at them. *Wouldn't you know it*, she thought, *June would have to sit on the front row. I feel like every eye is on the back of my head!* Reaching back she tucked a stray hair back inside the twist. Smoothing out her dress nervously, she felt another wispy strand fall across her forehead. *I'm coming apart!*

"By the way, dear," June commented, "you look beautiful this morning! You don't even resemble that dirty little orphan girl that left my house Friday!" she whispered.

"Thanks…I think," she said, smiling.

Michael stared in disbelief as Telie sashayed by. Her familiar citrus scent wafted behind her. Watching her take a seat with June, he was struck by the transformation. In the short time he has known her, most of that time she had been splattered with mud, soot or dirt. He thought back to the day before and how much he enjoyed spending time with her. She was easy to be around.

"Do you know that girl?" Mary Grace Adams asked Michael, as she picked up a hymnal, trying to act disinterested.

"Yeah, she works for me," he said, as he continued to stare.

"Well…who is she? Where does she come from?" Mary Grace demanded.

"Her name is Telie McCain, and she comes from up north."

"A Yankee?" she said in disgust. Her lips snarled as she placed the hymnal back in the holder.

"War's over, Mary Grace…and no, she's from the northern part of the state," he stated, looking put out by her ridiculous questions.

Mary Grace was a beauty, in the outward sense of the word. Her long chestnut-brown hair and tall slender form made her the envy of every girl in Moss Bay. All it took was one look into her pale green eyes and most men were sunk. She could have her pick of any man, but she only wanted one, Michael Christenberry. She pursued him with every ounce of strength and scheming ability she possessed, only to be shown little to no interest at all from Michael.

Mary Grace considered her small victories lately. *He had agreed to go with me to the company dinner party the other night,* she thought. *And he did agree to take me to the "White Grape" for brunch today. That's something.* She eyed Telie harshly, taking note of the sudden change in Michael and the attention he was giving this new girl.

The service began with an old familiar song as they stood. Telie raised her soft voice, feeling the power of the words of praise for her Savior. For the first time since leaving home, she felt a connection. She felt joined to the other believers through the one cord that held them all together, Jesus Christ.

The pastor made his way toward the pulpit, placing his Bible down; he turned to a passage and began reading. His voice was strong and deep, with an air of excitement to it. He was not at all what Telie had expected. He was young, probably in his thirties, and very muscular, rugged and outdoorsy. *He favors Michael in a way,* she thought, *only with darker hair. They could pass for brothers.*

Raising his voice as he preached, the church seemed to vibrate with joy. It seemed as if he were indeed sharing good news!

When the service was over, Telie remarked to June, "I really enjoyed the sermon…is he always so engaging?"

"Most of the time, dear, but on occasion he can get riled up with the best of them. He's not one to sugarcoat, I can tell you. That's what I like about him!" June pointed a bony finger at Telie with an all-knowing look in her eyes.

"Good morning, ladies." Michael greeted them as they drew near.

Surprised, Telie turned to the voice. He was walking out of the pew with a gorgeous woman who seemed to take possession of his right arm.

"Good morning," June said, waiting for them to step out into the aisle in front of them.

"It's amazing what a little soap and water can do to a person – wouldn't you agree, Miss June?" he said teasingly, looking at Telie.

"Oh, it can do wonders...too bad they can't come up with some kind of detergent for the inside of a person," she said sharply, looking toward Mary Grace.

"The blood of Jesus," Michael stated, matter-of-factly.

"Yes, oh yes, the blood of Jesus...makes us whiter than snow!" June professed.

"Aren't you going to introduce me to your new employee, Michael?" Mary Grace looked back and raked her eyes over Telie. She held Michael's arm in a vice grip.

"Oh sure, Mary Grace Adams, this is Telie McCain. She's really an asset to the company...wouldn't you agree, Miss June?" Michael winked at Telie.

"She's the best *you* have; that's for sure," June said, her meaning not lost on him.

"It's nice to meet you, Mary Grace," Telie said, in a soft cadence.

"Michael forgot to mention that he hired a new employee. Oh, that's men for you," she shrugged, eyeing Telie like a competitor. "I'd just love to stay and chat, Telie, but Michael and I are late for our brunch. I'm sure you understand. It was so nice to meet you too. I'm sure we'll meet again." She caught Michael's arm with a look of possession and tried to pull him away, but he didn't budge.

"Why don't you girls join us? We're going to the White Grape. You'll love it, Telie." He waited expectantly for their answer.

June blurted out, "Some other time...Telie and I have plans of our own. I thought I'd take her to the Blue Plate for a little chicken fried steak and lemon pie. Then we're headed out to do some exploring," she said, lifting both eyebrows. She had the look of an outlaw, shifting her eyes back and forth.

"Next time then," he said, disappointment shadowed his face.

As the church people filed out slowly, Pastor Nathan smiled as he shook Telie's hand. "Glad to have you with us this morning. I hope you'll come again soon," Nathan said, as he greeted Telie.

"I enjoyed your sermon very much," she said warmly. "I plan on coming back."

Michael came up behind Telie. "Nathan, this is Telie McCain. She's an expert landscaper and now a highly valued employee of Christenberry's. You might want to keep that in mind for our annual workday. That's coming up, isn't it?" He smiled knowingly over the top of Telie's head at Nathan.

"Yes, as a matter of fact, next month," he said excitedly. It was widely known that few things lit the eyes of the pastor as much as workday at the church. "I'll make sure to remind you of it, Telie. We could use someone with your skill around here. Tell me, do you live nearby?"

"Yes, I live out at Bell Forest."

He turned a questioning gaze toward Michael.

"She's fixing the place up in exchange for rent. I think she's getting the raw end of the deal though. I've let the place run down over the years."

"So Telie," Nathan asked, "aren't you frightened living way out there by yourself?" He cocked his head slightly as he observed her face.

"Oh no, it's just perfect, really. I don't get frightened that easily. I love the beauty and solitude of the place."

June reached down and took hold of Telie's hand, pulling her away from the men and their conversation. Telie shrugged at them as she was being led away by June's persistent hand.

Overhearing the conversation, Mary Grace began to fume. She couldn't believe what she'd heard. This girl was actually living in Michael's home! Mary Grace called after Telie's retreating figure in a raised voice. "Do you mean to tell me that you're living in Michael's house?" Mary Grace was glaring at her furiously.

June had Telie out the front door and down the front steps before she could answer.

Michael narrowed his eyes at Mary Grace. "What's wrong with earning your keep in an honest way, Mary Grace? Nothing," he stated bluntly. Turning back to Nathan, he said, "Now, if you'll excuse us, Nathan, we'd better go before I change my mind about having lunch. I seem to have lost my appetite." He shot Mary Grace an angry look as he walked past her and out the front door.

After lunch, Telie and June acted like two women on a mission. They headed straight for the edge of town armed with clippers, plastic bags, wet paper towels and a cooler. June held on tightly to the truck seat as she gave directions to Telie. They crossed over an old rickety one-lane bridge that seemed to mark the end of one world and the beginning of another.

"This is one of the oldest cemeteries in the county," June remarked as they rolled onto the grass. "It's perfect for rose rustling!"

As they stepped out of the truck, they felt the hush all around them. It was a melancholy place, isolated from the outside world, connected by an old wooden bridge. All you could hear was the sound of wind in the trees, softly howling. Not even a bird could be heard.

Glancing around, she spied several old and crumbling tombstones, long forgotten. Weeds and tall grass swayed slightly in the breeze, hiding the stones from onlookers in that part of the cemetery. "What a lonesome and forgotten place," she whispered. It had the feeling of sacred ground. She sensed the place in her spirit…it was calling to her, whispering its secrets. A chill ran up her spine as wind from out of nowhere passed through her, lifting her hair, but leaving the trees undisturbed.

"June, where are you?" Telie's voice called out, breaking the eerie silence. Looking around she saw a hand go up and wave behind a headstone. Making her way toward June, she tried not to seem spooked. "What have you found?" she asked, looking down.

"Just look at this, Telie; have you ever seen such a gorgeous rose in all of your life?" She cupped the fragile rose in her hand, inhaling deeply. The massive rosebush had clusters of soft yellow roses trailing across a fence and spilling over, swallowing a few headstones as it twined around between them. Surveying the area where the rosebush trailed, she glanced down at a few markers. "I think Michael's wife is buried somewhere near here…I can't remember exactly where."

Telie shot June a look of complete surprise. "Did you know her?"

"My goodness yes, and she was the sweetest thing, too. They were high school sweethearts, you know. You never saw one without the other. I don't think he'll ever get over losing her. They were perfect for each other. She was so mild mannered and fragile, not to mention beautiful, and Michael with all of his strength and…well, I'm getting carried away – aren't I?"

"How did she die?" she asked, as she searched the headstones more closely, running her fingers over the sun-warmed marble.

"It was a car accident. She ran off the road and hit a tree. I guess it's been about three years now." Her voice trailed off. "I thought Michael was going to grieve himself to death. Martha was worried sick over that boy! She thinks of Michael as her very own son, you know."

Telie spotted a grave marker with the name Christenberry carved across the back of it in bold letters. She moved closer, noticing two yellow roses dangling over the top of Emily Christenberry's headstone near her name. One rose was full and complete; the other, a small delicate bud. "Was she expecting a child?" Telie asked, never taking her eyes off the roses.

"They desperately wanted a child, but I guess the good Lord knows best about those kinds of things," she said somberly, remembering her own childlessness.

Long after she and June left the cemetery, with their clippings all sealed up tight in their moist bags, her mind kept going back to the grave of Emily Christenberry.

She planted that particular rose clipping beside the cottage steps.

Chapter 7

A sheen of perspiration glowed on Telie's face and a look of satisfaction sparkled from her eyes. "There, now that's just fine," she added, looking around at all of her plantings.

"Hello." An unfamiliar voice called to her from across the bayou.

"Hello," she answered back, wiping the perspiration from her brow, as she squinted in the direction of the voice.

"Planting roses, I see."

"Yes, stolen roses! I've been raiding the local cemetery this afternoon." Straightening up, she clapped her hands together to get rid of all the grit.

"Ah, so you're confessing to be a thief...and on the Lord's Day too, I might add!" he called out.

As he approached, she could detect a hint of mischief in his eyes.

"Come on over and I'll tell you how hopeless I really am," she said with a grin.

As he reached her, he extended his hand. Taking it, she found it warm and his smile engaging as he introduced himself.

"I'm Brother Raphael."

He was not at all what she thought a monk should look like. Where was his round belly and bald spot on top of his head? *That's twice today*, she thought to herself. *First with Pastor Nathan and now with this guy. I really need to get out more.*

He looked to be thirty-something with dark eyes and almost black hair. He looked Middle Eastern or maybe even Italian.

"I'm Telie," she said. "Would you like some lemonade? I could really use a break." She motioned toward the porch, dropping her spade down in the dirt.

The crickets and frogs had begun their afternoon symphony. Holding their drinks carefully as condensation trickled down the slick glass, they took a seat on the porch. Telie let out a sigh. "This place is enchanting – don't you think?"

"Yes." He agreed, with a look of appreciation.

"How long have you lived here?" Telie asked, watching the way he held his glass cupped in his hand from underneath.

"Oh, about ten years now," he replied, taking a sip of the lemonade.

"So, do you ever get tired of it…life at the monastery I mean?" Her curious eyes observed his every action.

"Not yet," he answered, amused at her directness. She had an innocent, honest face that intrigued him.

"What do you do exactly, Brother Raphael? I mean what does a monk do in general?"

It had been a long time since he was the object of so much attention and it made him smile. "I tend to the grounds mostly with time devoted to prayer. We all have our various responsibilities around the monastery. Some cook, some manage the accounts, others attend to our guests."

"Guests?" She lifted her eyes in surprise.

"Yes, we not only support each other in the community of brothers, but we try and help those who come to us as well. We're Benedictine monks, following the Rule of St. Benedict. He was a sixth-century Italian abbot...the leader of the Order. St. Benedict says in his Rule that all guests are to be received as Christ. We're really known for our hospitality." He took a long sip of his drink and looked back at Telie, wondering momentarily if Christ had led her to them.

"Do you have guests all the time?" Telie asked, intrigued.

"Well, we host several retreats a year and attend to a stray pilgrim from time to time," he said, enjoying his conversation with this inquisitive young girl. "Now, can I ask you a question?" he added, smiling.

"Oh sure, I guess that's only fair. I've asked you enough questions, haven't I?" A slight blush crept up her face when she realized how she'd been interrogating him.

"Why are you here, Telie?" He put his glass down on the table and waited for her to answer.

"That's a tough one. I'm not really sure...I guess I sort of need a do-over. I moved here from Coldwater, up in North Alabama."

"Were you married?" He pushed on the most obvious door. He thought perhaps she was running away from a bad relationship.

She looked surprised, and then answered him quickly. "No, nothing like that. I'm not running from a man. I've never needed a man."

"I've never needed a man." He repeated her words. "Man is not a need, Telie; he's a gift! Like children are gifts. We have only one need, relationally speaking that is, and that is a need for God."

"In that case I guess I stopped accepting gifts a long time ago." She looked out toward the bay. He had hit a nerve and they both knew it.

There was a brief moment of silence between them, and then Brother Raphael looked at his watch. "Well, I've enjoyed our visit, but I've got to go…it's time for evening prayers." He stood to leave and looked down once more on Telie, smiling. "You make excellent lemonade!"

"You'll have to try my cookies next time," she said. "I hope you like chocolate chip."

"Love them and deal," he said as he stuck out his hand, giving hers a gentle squeeze.

From that day on and over the next few weeks, Telie and Brother Raphael were like kindred spirits. They'd spend hours together working around the grounds, discussing everything from trees and plants to the different sounds coming from the bayou. They had even planted a kitchen garden next to the back porch complete with everything from mint to corn.

"Where did the name 'Bayou Bell' come from?" Telie asked one day while they were hoeing the garden. She straightened up from her bent position to wait for his answer.

Brother Raphael stopped his hoeing, wiped his brow with the back of his hand and leaned on his hoe. "It's an old legend, I suppose, but they say that during the battle of Mobile Bay, when the Union soldiers were trying to gain a stronghold, the plantation owners around here hid their valuables to keep them out of the hands of the Yankees." He took a deep breath, cutting his eyes to her, making sure he had her attention. "This land was once part of the Bennier Plantation. The owner instructed his slaves to hide his silver down here in the bayou, thinking the Yankees wouldn't risk getting snake bitten to look for the treasure. Anyway, one slave girl decided she would take down the bell used for calling the slaves to and from the fields. This bell was highly treasured by the mistress of the house. They say that the bell had been made with one hundred silver dollars melted into it and that it had a special ring quality that no other bell had, due to the silver content. Plus, it had come from the mistress's childhood home and had been given to them as a wedding gift from her father. Keeping up so far?"

"I'm with you," Telie said, enjoying the tale so far.

"This slave girl apparently saw her chance to get back at her mistress. She cut down the bell and loaded it in the back of a cart and pulled it down to the bayou. She rolled it into the murky water and watched it sink, all the way to the bottom…never to be seen again. When the master found out about it, he was so upset by what the girl had done that he ordered her to be thrown into the bayou, with her hands and feet bound."

"No!" Telie exclaimed.

"They say that on occasion you can hear the bell ringing, deep in the night, as the ghost of the slave girl struggles to drag the bell out of the bayou…restless until she can return it to her mistress."

"That's awful!" Telie said, shocked. "I won't sleep a wink after that story!"

"Ah…you know how it is with folklore," he said, enjoying the look of fear mixed with outrage on her face.

"You better not even think about ringing that bell ya'll have over there tonight!" she warned him. "Do you hear me?"

"I would never think of doing such a thing!" he said, looking shocked.

"Well, you've been warned," she said, eyeing him suspiciously.

Chapter 8

The workweek finally ended. Michael and most of the crew had been out working on a big landscaping project that kept them busy and out of the office for most of the week. That left Martha and Telie to run things around the compound. Feeling exhausted and short of breath, Telie was glad for the next two days off to rest.

Peering out of the kitchen window early that morning, she noticed the huge pile of brush she and Brother Raphael had accumulated. *The place looks good*, she thought. All of the limbs and branches that had cluttered the grounds had been piled up in a huge mass ready to burn. Thanks to the help of Brother Raphael, it had taken only a few weeks to get the place in good shape. *This is a good day to do a little burning, not too windy, not too hot.* Going outside, she grabbed the rake that was propped up next to the steps and made her way toward the brush pile. Clouds floated by, all puffy and white. The air was less humid, but she could tell that they were in for another scorcher.

The small flat-bottom boat drifted lazily through the marsh grasses, rocking slightly with the gentle swells. A breeze caught and slowly moved the boat down Bayou Bell.

As they passed, turtles slipped off nearby floating logs into the still water, making a plopping noise in the fresh morning air.

"Not much biting today," Nathan commented to Michael as he reeled in his line.

"No, but it sure is nice out here, peaceful. This is the first time I've relaxed all week. I feel as contented as that turtle sunning on that rock over there."

"Moved a lot of dirt this week?"

"You're not kidding," he said, as he rummaged in his tackle box for a lure. "I'm glad you called...I needed a little peace and quiet. I can still hear the sound of that bulldozer in my head! Still feel it too!"

A loud high-pitched scream shot through the air, breaking the serenity of the morning, frightening the birds into flight. They jerked their heads toward the sound and saw the commotion. A monk was running from the direction of the monastery toward Bell Forest yelling, "No Telie...stop!"

Michael and Nathan looked at each other for the briefest of seconds, then Nathan yanked the cord of the motor and they headed for shore. As they reached the pier, Michael jumped out and secured the boat quickly, wrapping the rope around a cleat. Their feet hit the boards of the pier hard as they ran toward the path. They stepped into the clearing just in time to see Telie pull back and pelt the monk in the back with what looked like a pinecone.

"You get out of here and take that hideous monster with you!" Telie screamed after him. They watched the monk carefully walk back toward the monastery, holding a long brown snake with both hands, grinning.

As they approached, Michael commented to Nathan, "You know, Nathan...I hear there's a special place in Hell designed specifically for people who throw things at monks."

Telie glanced over her shoulder to see Nathan and Michael walking toward her, huge grins pasted on their faces as they slowed their pace.

"Is that supposed to be funny?" she asked sternly.

"Careful how you answer that, Michael; she has a wild look in her eyes. She may be hiding another pinecone in her pocket." Nathan held his hands out in a defensive posture.

Telie narrowed her eyes at Nathan. "I just don't like anacondas, Preacher; that's all!"

"Anacondas?" He laughed. "What about that poor monk? He looked pretty traumatized to me." Nathan said, winking at Michael. "Would you have hit St. Francis of Assisi if he'd tried to save the life of one of God's own?"

"Brother Raphael is fine...for now." Glancing over her shoulder toward the monastery, she remarked, "I can't make any promises concerning his future though. He knows how I feel about snakes. This isn't the first one I've come across around here, you know. If I hear him say one more time that snakes are 'God's creatures' I think I'll choke him."

Nathan knew he was treading on thin ice, but he continued. "Who are we to say which creatures live or die?" His tone changed, reminding her of the voice he used in the pulpit.

"Yeah, well what about all those fish you plan to catch, Preacher? Aren't they 'God's creatures' too?"

"It's different if you plan on eating them. Were you planning on eating that snake, Telie?" Nathan questioned innocently.

"I planned on frying it up for potluck, Pastor!" she said defiantly, with her hands on her hips.

Michael stifled a laugh as he listened to them banter back and forth, and for the first time in a long while he felt lighter. The way Telie stood with her hands on her hips and her face set, he couldn't help but laugh. Soon Nathan and Telie joined him, breaking the tension.

Michael looked over the brush pile. "You've been busy, Telie." Surveying the property, he said, "I'm surprised you haven't come across a nest of snakes in this heap."

Telie shivered, looking down at her feet and all around the ground. "That's one thing that gets to me. I'll have nightmares for weeks. I just can't stand snakes!"

"Nathan?" Michael said forcefully, reaching into his shirt pocket, pulling out a slim cigar. "Leave me here. I'm going to set fire to this snake pit before any more trouble comes of it." Hiding his amusement, he put the cigar into the side of his mouth and bit down. He took the rake from Telie's hand and asked her to find a match.

Before turning to head back down to the boat, Nathan cautioned, "Tread lightly, my friend, she can be dangerous when provoked." He opened his hand. "Toss me your keys. I'll have Pete follow me back out here to drop off your truck."

Telie and Michael worked side by side, making small talk as they raked and tossed brush into the fire. Michael talked about his childhood growing up there, how he'd fish from the pier until way past dark. He said he always waited for his daddy to come look for him so they could spend extra time together before bedtime. He told of the many summer nights he'd spent in the woods near the bayou building forts and campsites pretending to be in a war and what a hero he had been back then.

The tension in Telie's shoulders relaxed. In fact, her whole body had. She'd learned long ago how to appreciate the small things in life: a cold glass of tea, a cool breeze on a stiffening hot day and the way you feel all tired and worn out after a hard day's work. She smiled with genuine pleasure.

"I found a collection of glass pieces in a box buried under that tree over there," she said, pointing to the nearby oak. "Was that some of your buried treasure from long ago?"

"No...that sounds more like something my mother would have done. Her 'treasures' are all over the place. Anything she found lying around she would say, 'Oh look what God sent us today.' She'd be thrilled with any little thing the bay washed up. That's probably sea glass, I'd imagine. She had a thing for sea glass and smooth stones."

"I'll show you when we go inside; there are some other things too. You might remember it when you see it." She stuck her lip out and blew her hair off her forehead as she tossed another branch on the fire.

"How did you find it?" Michael asked, turning to look at her. He noticed how her hair fell softly around her face in gold-colored strands.

"I was cutting down vines and undergrowth from around the base of the tree and my foot hit the corner of the metal lid. It was buried underneath a layer of dirt and leaves. When I saw all of those colorful pieces, I thought for sure I'd uncovered a hidden treasure," she said, smiling.

The sun warmed things up quickly. They kept tossing more and more limbs onto the fire, building up the flames. As the day wore on, evening turned soft and mellow. The firelight flickered all around them, casting shadows onto the surrounding grounds.

"Is that your phone?" Michael asked, cocking his head slightly to one side.

"Sounds like it." Quickly moving to the porch, she retrieved her phone and flipped it open. "Hello?"

"Telie?" The voice cracked on the other end of the line.

"Yes."

"It's me, Betsy." Her voice was strained.

"Oh Betsy, how are you?" Telie asked, sounding surprised. She was the last person she'd expected to hear from.

"I wish I was calling with better news, but I just had to tell you!" she cried, letting out a weary breath.

"What's wrong?" Telie asked, as panic gripped her throat. "Is everyone okay?"

"I tried to convince your mother to tell you, but she wouldn't." Betsy sobbed.

"Just tell me, Betsy, please. What is it?" Telie pressed the phone closer to her ear while holding her hand over the other ear.

Michael lifted two lawn chairs from the corner of the house and placed them near her. Leading her by the elbow, he sat her down.

Still dazed, she stared at the fire, waiting for the news.

"They cut down your tree, Telie! Those awful people cut down your magnolia tree!" She sobbed loudly, and then sniffled.

Relief washed over her the moment she realized that everyone was all right. Then sadness hit like a wave, the thought of her beloved tree, gone. The corners of her mouth began to pull down, her throat tightened. "Oh no," Telie whispered.

"I'm sorry to be the one to tell you, Telie; it just breaks my heart. They just piled it up next to the road to be hauled off like so much trash! I can't stand to see it there! All I think about is you, Telie…you and your tree!"

"I know…it's all right, Betsy. Things like this happen. I'm glad you told me, though. Now, you don't worry anymore about it, I'll be fine. Tell everyone hello for me, would ya, especially your mother?"

Closing the phone in her hand, she stared into the fire, silent for a moment. Michael pulled a chair up next to her, leaving her alone for a while, not wanting to intrude into her thoughts. Then he asked softly as he searched her eyes, "Are you okay, Telie?"

Turning to him with a warm half smile, she nodded. "Yeah…that was a neighbor from home. She called to let me know that my tree, I mean…an old magnolia tree on our property had been cut down. The people I sold my house to cut it down and hauled it to the side of the road." She grimaced at the thought and slowly shook her head. A lump tightened in her throat. "She said she thinks of me whenever she sees it."

Listening to her words, letting them sink in, he waited a minute, then asked, "So…this tree was special?"

"To me. I guess it's kind of pathetic really, but I spent half my childhood up in that old tree. People started associating me with it…isn't that sad?" she said, looking down at the ground, not wanting to meet his gaze.

"A loss is a loss, Telie, no matter what it is…if it means something to you, it hurts when you lose it." Reaching over he took her hand in his strong, calloused one and gave it a gentle squeeze.

She felt suddenly ashamed for getting so emotional over a tree, when the man next to her offering sympathy had lost much more. Looking at him, she smiled. "I'm fine...really. I just hadn't expected that to ever happen. Sometimes things just catch you off guard."

"Yes, they do," he said, watching the fire as it cracked and popped.

"Hey, I've got some homemade soup on the stove and a pan of cornbread, you hungry?" she asked.

"Starving." Michael was already on his feet. He reached down and pulled her up to stand in front of him.

"I guess we better go eat then."

Ladling the steaming soup into bowls, she placed one in front of Michael. "Want some cornbread to go with that?"

"Of course, you can't have soup without cornbread! You have any butter?" he asked.

"Of course...you can't have cornbread without butter!" she added, teasingly.

They ate their meal in silence, both famished, both lost in thought.

"May I ask you a question?" he said. After a long pause, he put his spoon down and looked at her.

"You can ask, but I'm not sure I've got an answer for you." She broke off a piece of cornbread and popped it in her mouth.

"Why did you move way down here?" Michael watched her, narrowing his eyes, as he waited for an answer.

Looking up from her soup, she said, "You're the second person to ask me that." Clearing her throat, she continued. "I'm not really sure. I just knew I needed a change. I was beginning to feel...caged, trapped."

"What made you feel that way?" he pressed.

"The sameness of everything...old ghosts, I felt stuck, like I wasn't going forward or backward...stuck in neutral, stuck to my past."

"Have you felt that way since you've been here?" he questioned, trying his best to understand.

Shaking her head, she said, "No...I haven't. I've fallen in love with the land here, and it's fast becoming a part of me. I feel free here. Sounds crazy, doesn't it?" She felt bound to the land somehow but at a loss to explain it clearly.

"Not at all, I feel the same way. That's why I do what I do for a living. I know what it means to love the land." Michael stopped, shook his head and laughed.

"What?" she asked, puzzled at his laughter.

"When it comes to being crazy, I think we're pretty evenly matched. Maybe we should get an outside opinion if we're questioning our sanity."

"True enough," she said without argument.

After finishing their meal, Michael stood to leave. "I'd better be going," he said. "Thank you for supper; it was delicious."

"Oh, you're welcome and thank you for burning up the snake pit. I feel so much better knowing there's not another hideous monster lurking under the brush."

He melted her with his smile.

Chapter 9

No doubt about it, Mary Grace Adams was stunning. She moved gracefully down the aisle, her head held high. It was hard for anyone to keep from staring at her. She wore a beautiful yellow linen suit that formed around her frame perfectly. Her chestnut hair was long and sleek, flowing down her back in one smooth wave.

Stepping past her, Telie reached the pew where June was seated, feeling a little plain in her two-year-old cotton dress. She smiled at June as she slid into her seat.

The pew rocked slightly as someone sat down next to her. Glancing beside her, she was surprised to see Michael. He opened his Bible, turned and smiled. "Good morning," he whispered. "Rest well? No nightmares about snakes, I hope."

"No, no…just pleasant dreams about dissecting them piece by piece." She didn't have to turn around; she could feel the heat from the glare Mary Grace was sending her way. *What on earth has happened between them?* She wondered. Being so distracted by his presence, she hardly heard a word of the sermon!

"In closing," Nathan said in his deep resonating voice, "I would like to remind you all of 'workday' coming up in two weeks. We'll have dinner on the grounds at noon, but we'll expect everyone here around 7:00 a.m." With that said, everyone stood to sing the closing hymn.

June kept cutting her eyes at Telie throughout the entire service. *She's really enjoying this,* Telie thought, *a little too much.*

Michael leaned over and asked, "Do you girls have plans for lunch today?"

Risking a glance up at him, Telie prayed he wouldn't notice the flush on her face. His expression was different… as if he were seeing her for the first time. "No, no we don't," she replied, looking over at June hesitantly.

June interrupted, clearing her throat, "Speak for yourself, missy. I have plans. But you two go on without me. Just don't forget about tomorrow, bright and early. I made strawberry pretzel salad for lunch," she said, patting Telie's arm as she departed.

"I won't forget, June. Will I need my clippers or am I working in the garden?" she inquired.

"Clippers, darling, clippers." She left the sanctuary with a wave of her hand.

"Looks like it's just the two of us," Michael announced, smiling down at her. "What sounds good to you?"

"Well, I was going for a carryout from the Blue Plate and then head back to Bell Forest." Telie sensed being observed by Mary Grace. She tried to keep her voice low without looking directly at Michael, not wishing to provoke Mary Grace.

"Sounds great, I'll go get dinner. Meet you at Bell Forest then. Oh yeah, what about dessert?" he asked, remembering her fondness for all things sweet.

"Uh…I made a peach pie?" she answered, sounding like a question.

"Even better," he agreed. "I'll meet you there in thirty minutes." He walked away with purpose in his steps as he headed out the church doors. He paused only briefly to shake hands with Nathan before quickly making his exit.

If looks could kill, Telie would have been mutilated! Mary Grace seethed as she watched them. Michael walked right by her without so much as a word, seemingly distracted. She waited in the pew to allow time for Telie to pass, and then spoke in a low sharp voice as she approached. "I suppose you think I don't know what you're doing." She pulled in her lips to form a straight line with her mouth. "You've got it all figured out, haven't you? You've wormed your way into his business, now his house. How convenient it must be for you. You don't fool me for one second. I know what you're up to!" Flipping her hair behind her shoulder, she brushed passed her and stormed out of the church.

The afternoon turned muggy. A haze settled with a silvery shadow swallowing everything in sight. The air was thick with humidity, making it hard to breathe or move around quickly. It was truly a lazy hazy afternoon.

"I seemed to have made your girlfriend mad," Telie stated, as Michael put the lunch plates down on the table outside. She'd arranged the small kitchen table and two chairs outside on the porch. A glass jar half filled with his mother's sea glass in colors of green and blue sat in the center of the table with a white candle placed down into the pieces. Candlelight reflected off the colorful glass and danced around the center of the table.

"Girlfriend…do you mean Mary Grace?" He cocked his head to the side, giving her a puzzled look.

"Uh huh," she said, as she busied herself setting the table and removing the food from the containers.

"She's not my girlfriend," he stated flatly, placing the forks next to the plates.

"Oh, I thought you two dated," she said nonchalantly, as she sipped her iced tea. "Well anyway, I seem to have upset her."

"Did she say something to you?" he questioned, squinting his eyes as he looked at her.

"You might say that. She seems to be under the impression that I'm after you." She smiled with genuine amusement. "As a matter of fact, she doesn't like it one bit that I'm living out here or even working for you for that matter."

"Oh…well, I'm sorry about that. Mary Grace is…different. I've gone out with her on occasion, when she has asked me. A dinner party or out to eat maybe…something like that, but we've never 'dated.' In fact, I just about have to make myself go when she asks."

"Then why do you go?" Her voice was smooth as she looked at him over the top of her tea glass, taking another sip.

"I guess some part of me wants to be normal again. I always think getting out might help." He shrugged.

"So…*do* you feel normal when you're out with her?" She watched his expression closely.

"Almost never, our conversations revolve around three topics: diet, exercise and shopping. You can't even enjoy your meal because she's too busy counting fat grams and squeezing the butter out of her shrimp with her napkin!"

Telie's lips twisted. "Personally, I'm glad she has to sacrifice something to look that good." She looked down at the fried chicken and mashed potatoes running over with gravy on her plate and said, "And speaking of diets, save room for some peach pie."

After dinner, they moved to the rockers, enjoying the afternoon. Boats passed by on the bay as a gentle breeze stirred the thick air. White sails floated by silently. An occasional bird landed on the lawn, prancing around in front of them as the afternoon lazily rolled by.

After helping her clear away the dishes from the table, he stood in the doorway of the kitchen and watched her. She had an apron tied around her waist as she busily washed the dishes. He took out a cigar from his pocket and rolled it around between his fingers. He couldn't help but feel he was missing something about her. Some part of her she wasn't showing or telling. Was she running away from something traumatic? Or was it like she'd said, she just needed a fresh start.

"Where did you learn to make a pie like that? It was delicious!" He thought she looked adorable in the oversized apron with its oversized pockets. It had belonged to his mother. She'd used it to hold all of the treasures she'd discovered near the bay and around the property.

"My mother, she's the best cook in three counties," she said, smiling back at him.

Her golden-brown eyes too easily distracted him. "Do you favor your mother?"

"We have the same eyes, but she has dark brown hair, almost black, not…whatever you call this color I have." She crinkled her nose, then continued. "When I was little, I thought my mother looked like the Sun-Maid girl on the raisin box." She smiled, glancing back at Michael, waiting for his reaction.

"She must be beautiful then. I distinctly remember having a crush on the Sun-Maiden." His eyes squinted as he smiled. Leaning in the doorway he hesitated briefly, and then said, "Well, I better get going." Placing the cigar between his teeth, he looked at her one last time.

"Do you ever smoke those things?" she asked, rinsing the suds off of a plate, as she looked at him over her shoulder.

"Of course not, smoking is bad for you, Telie! Don't you know that?" He sounded shocked, then winked, as he headed out the door.

Telie expected to feel relief when he left, but she didn't; she felt lonely instead…really lonely for the first time in a long while.

Chapter 10

The day was gorgeous and bright with large thunder-clouds building up near the horizon to the west. Making her way to the office coffee pot, she shouted, "Good morning, Martha!"

"Yeah, it's gonna be. We won't have to put up with Michael today. He won't get back until late tonight."

"Where'd he go?" Telie asked, trying not to sound disappointed or *too* interested.

"Up to your neck of the woods, he's delivering those pecan trees to Grayson."

The sound of papers being shuffled around followed by the slam of the filing cabinet told her that Martha was in for another busy day. Business had picked up recently. They barely found time to sit and have lunch these days.

Telie walked up to Martha, coffee in hand. "That's good. Mr. Grayson will be thrilled. Nothing excites him quite as much as getting a shipment of something." Taking a sip of her coffee, she saw a mischievous grin spread across Martha's face.

"You think you could manage to ship me up there, sweetie?" Martha asked. "Hold on, I'll go get the bubble wrap!"

"Yeah, I would like to see his face when he opened *that* package." Telie said, giggling.

Michael reached the outskirts of the town of Coldwater, amazed at how different everything looked to him. He traveled up a year ago, but this time everything seemed much more interesting. He watched the sun, already brushing the treetops, as it turned the Tennessee River a molten gold. He made his way across the river, his thoughts on Telie. He wondered how many times she'd crossed the bridge, how many times she had floated down the gently rolling river.

The river was majestic. It dipped down from Tennessee and ran across the northern part of Alabama, going from east to west. In this northwest corner of the state, it seemed to defy gravity by flowing north as it curved to cross over into Mississippi.

From the bridge you could see amber lights from a docked riverboat glowing softly as people strolled lazily up and down the walkway near the harbor. Music played from somewhere, filling the air. Michael rolled down his window, taking it all in.

He turned up a street that ran along the river's edge ending at Grayson's Nursery.

"Where do you want these blasted pecan trees?" Michael yelled, seeing Paul Grayson walking toward him.

"Well, if it ain't Michael; good to see you, boy!" Paul said, slapping him on the back as he eyed the shipment. "You just unload them right there, that's fine. How are the girls?" The excitement on his face was evident.

"Sassy as ever, especially that one *you* sent me!" he said with a laugh. "I can see it'll take a bigger man than me to do anything with that one."

"So she's getting to you already?"

"More than I'm willing to admit." Michael raised his eyebrows as he glanced at Paul.

They worked together unloading the shipment for an hour or so, talking about nothing in particular, then Michael asked, "Tell me something, Paul...is Telie's dad still living? I've only heard her mention her mother."

"Yeah...he's alive," Paul Grayson stated, flatly.

Michael could tell from the disgusted look on Paul's face that there was more to the story. "What sort of a man is he?" Michael asked.

"The sort that walks out on his family!" he answered sharply.

From his tone he could tell that Paul didn't have much use for the man.

"He left them when Telie was, oh about thirteen, I guess." Taking off his straw hat, he wiped his brow with the back of his hand. "Took off with some woman and her three kids to Texas and never looked back. Telie adored him, too. I don't think she's ever gotten over it."

"Has there ever been a man in her life...other than her father?" Michael put down the last tree and leaned against the truck, wiping at the sweat trickling down his face.

"Yeah, once, he was kinda what you'd call a control freak. She got rid of him soon enough. She'll tell you real quick she don't need a man." Paul smirked, thinking of how similar they were in that regard. "Don't get the wrong idea, she's had her opportunities. Every once in awhile some guy would show up, hang around and wait for a chance to talk to her. She'd make some excuse and head out back; you wouldn't see her again until closing. I was hoping that moving down there would do her some good. I hate to see her all alone. She would make some lucky man an excellent wife." Paul cast his eyes over to Michael, sheepishly.

Ignoring the look, Michael said, "I need to stop by her old house before I go back. She had a call the other day from a neighbor about losing something over there." He didn't want to go into detail; he just needed directions. "Can you tell me how to get there?"

"Oh sure, it's easy to find. I'll jot it down for you."

Michael removed his work gloves to shake hands with Paul. He noticed a movement over Paul's shoulder. A few ladies were giggling and staring from the office window. "I think you're needed in the office." He nodded toward the window.

As Paul turned to look, they scattered. "Bunch of shameless hussies!" he said, shaking his head, as he walked back toward the office.

Chapter 11

A fierce storm rolled in from the bay, hammering the cottage with rain and wind. The ground vibrated as thunder exploded in the afternoon heat. The sound of the rain on the metal roof was deafening. Telie didn't hear as Michael ran up behind her. She was down on her knees in the mud pushing the soft ground down around a rosebush. The wind whipped around the trees pelting water on them, as the storm intensified.

"What are you doing?" He yelled over the sound of the storm. "Get inside!" He reached down and pulled her up by the arms and led her up the steps. Swinging the door open, he turned around and waited for her to step inside. Michael closed the door against the wind, turned to her and asked, "What is so important out there for you to risk being blown away by the storm?" He shook his head like a wet dog, raking his hand through his hair.

Telie grabbed a couple of bath towels from the closet and handed one to Michael. Dabbing her face dry, she replied, "I was trying to save the rosebush. That last big gust of wind almost ripped it up and blew it away," she said, out of breath.

"Better it than you!" he said, scowling. He shook his head again after rubbing the towel through his hair.

"I'm just trying to give it a chance…it's special…you want some coffee?"

"You're changing the subject, but yes, I'd love some coffee." Pulling off his rain jacket, he felt aggravated at the sight of her wet, muddy clothes clinging to her. "You need to get out of those wet clothes before you get sick. Hasn't anyone ever told you not to play outside in the rain?"

She rolled her eyes at him. "I'll go change. I wouldn't want to catch a cold. I'd never hear the end of it." Stepping away, she closed the bedroom door behind her.

After a second, he heard the shower come on. "I'll put on the coffee," he yelled through the door. He stepped into the kitchen and began opening cabinet doors until he located the coffee. Filling the pot with water, he scooped out a generous portion of coffee and placed it in the filter. "I hope she likes it strong." The aroma filled the tiny cottage.

He sat down and waited for the coffee to finish brewing. Running his hand over the polished wood of the kitchen table, his mind went back to a time when he was younger, sitting at the very same table with his parents. On days just like this, they would play games, laugh and talk, as they watched it storm. He could almost smell his mother's freshly baked cookies as he gazed out of the window, watching the wind toss around the tops of the trees.

Telie emerged from the bedroom wearing a pair of white sweatpants and a light pink T-shirt. Smiling, she inhaled deeply. "That coffee smells wonderful…I've got just the thing to go with it too." Grabbing a chair, she moved it over to the hutch against the far wall. Standing on the chair, she reached up to the top shelf and pulled out a plastic zip bag full of chocolate chip cookies. "I have to hide these from myself." She stated matter-of-factly.

After pouring the coffee, she arranged the cookies on a plate. "I made these yesterday after I heard the weather forecast on the radio."

"Do you always celebrate the weather with cookies?" he asked, amused.

"Almost always." She took a bite and grinned.

Michael grabbed two from the plate. "So...tell me," he asked with his mouth full of cookies, "what makes your rosebush so special? It hardly looks worth the effort. I mean...it's just a stick with a few leaves on top."

"That's because it's a clipping. It's from a wild yellow rosebush we found growing in the cemetery. It's absolutely gorgeous! You need to baby them for the first few weeks until they're established."

"Cemetery?"

"Yeah, the old one across town."

He gave her a confused look.

"The one where your wife and baby are buried," she blurted out, not thinking of the impact of her words until it was too late. She cringed at the realization.

He couldn't have looked more stunned if she had slapped his face. Staring at her in shock for what seemed like an eternity, he quietly asked, "How did you know about the baby?" The pain was evident in his eyes as he searched hers for answers.

Sitting across from him, speechless, she made an apologetic gesture toward the rosebush through the rain-streaked window. Telie understood in an instant the implications of trespassing on forbidden territory. She felt trapped. All she could do was sit and endure his penetrating glare.

Not comprehending, Michael stared at her for a long moment. "Do you mean to say," he hesitated a moment, "that a rosebush told you?" His eyes narrowed and his throat tightened; he was losing control fast.

Shaking her head, she quickly added, "I'm sorry, Michael...I was just..."

"You were just what?" Michael raised his voice, never taking his eyes off of her. His hurt was quickly being replaced by anger.

"I was just there...at the cemetery, looking down at Emily's grave and..."

"And what!" he demanded. His expression left no doubt he was frustrated and angry.

A mixture of fear and sadness washed over her. She felt as if she'd swallowed a rock. "I just had this sense that there were two of them. I don't know...I can't explain it without sounding crazy." She took a deep breath. "I saw two roses... hanging over the headstone. One was perfect and complete; the other, just a small delicate bud." She looked down; an ache began deep inside her. She hated herself for causing him pain with her foolish notions. That's all it had been, a notion about the baby, but apparently her notion had been correct.

He backed away from the table and stood up, lifting his jacket from the back of the chair. His face looked so dejected, so sorrowful; she couldn't bear to look at him. He walked to the door, pulled it open and left in the rain.

Outside the confines of the cottage, Michael felt his anger slowly subside. Taking a deep breath, he turned his face toward heaven. The stinging rain cooled him as he walked to his truck. Once inside the cab of the truck, he leaned back, closing his eyes.

His mind drifted back to the day Emily died. *Three years ago now*, he thought, struggling with the deep emptiness he felt growing inside. *How had she known? No one knew about the baby, no one, but God alone.*

He remembered that day, that horrible day. He'd cried out to the Lord with unbelievable anguish when he'd first learned of the accident. Barely an hour before, Emily had called to tell him that they were expecting their first child. She'd been to Mobile for a doctor's appointment, and it was there she was told she was pregnant. Finally, the baby they had always wanted had become a reality. He could still hear the excitement in her voice as she squealed to him the good news. It had haunted him for years now, that happy joyful sound of an excited new mother.

"Why did I have to come here?" he spoke out loud. He felt numb. Loneliness and despair replaced all other feelings. Emptiness burned inside him.

Telie watched from the kitchen window, as Michael pulled away. She felt sick seeing the image of his torn and confused face. "What's the matter with me?" She walked to her bed, picked up her pillow and clutched it close, saying a quiet prayer for him.

Chapter 12

A polite silence developed between Michael and Telie. The mental picture of intruding into his life had plagued Telie's thoughts. She remembered his pain-stricken face whenever she saw him, a visual image she would give anything to erase.

Michael kept busy, away from her. Martha relayed messages between them. When he needed to tell her something or ask her to do something, he'd have Martha or Joe instruct her. Telie could tell they were curious, but not curious enough to ask what was going on.

Whenever Telie and Michael crossed paths, he would nod slightly, and then turn his attention away. The situation was beginning to wear on her emotionally. She dreaded coming to work. She knew exactly what she had to do to end this torture and find peace again.

Gathering her courage, Telie headed inside to speak with Michael. She carefully maneuvered around Mary Grace who seemed to have planted herself in Michael's office these days. "Can I talk to you for a minute, Michael?" Her voice sounded weak, shaky.

"Sure," he said, as he took the unlit cigar from his mouth. He removed his feet from the corner of his desk and got up from his chair. "Will you excuse us, Mary Grace?"

Mary Grace let out an exasperating sigh, then slowly stood, glancing toward Telie suspiciously. "Of course," she said, forcing a smile.

"Close the door on your way out." A look of concern played across his features. Sitting back down at his desk, he waited for Telie to speak. Noticing how flushed she looked, his apprehension started to build.

She took a seat across from him and began. "First of all…I want you to know how grateful I am that you hired me. This job has been more than I could ever have hoped for." She swallowed hard, then continued, "But, I think under the circumstances, it would be better if I leave. I've been offered another job with Inyard Landscapes, and I think I should probably take it. I'm giving you my two weeks' notice. I'll be out of Bell Forest by that time or sooner if you like."

His eyes narrowed. "What? Why?" Taken totally by surprise, he leaned forward on the desk, knocking over a silver-framed picture of Emily.

"It's easier this way, Michael." She took a deep breath, intending to continue.

"Easier?" he interrupted, propping his elbows on the desk, he lifted his hands to his forehead. He thought a moment before speaking. "I know things have been …strained between us lately, Telie, but I don't want it to stay that way. Is that why you want to leave, because of me…because of this…awkwardness between us?"

The pleading expression on his face caught her off guard. She'd been so sure he wanted her out of his life. "For the most part," she whispered. "I can't handle the pain I've caused you by meddling in your life. It's easier to leave."

"You said for the most part. Is there some other part, something else?" he asked, carefully watching her face, suddenly desperate to hang on to her.

She nodded, but wouldn't look at him. "Well...I don't feel right staying at the cottage without paying rent. There's been some talk about it, mostly whispers at church. June told me." She looked down at her hands. Heat crept up from her neck and ignited on her face. She kept her gaze down. After a long silence, she lifted her eyes to meet his. His expression held an emotion she couldn't read.

He stated calmly, "If anyone says anything else to you about that, tell me. I promise they'll not bother you again." The threat in his voice convinced her he meant it.

He knew who was behind the talk; he could almost swear it was Mary Grace. He was also sure she hadn't wasted any time spreading the rumor among her circle of friends at church. It infuriated him to think Christians would gossip, especially about Telie! An unexpected surge of emotions coursed through him. Regaining his composure, he spoke softly. "I want you to stay, Telie; we need you here. *I* need you here. Let's work this out, can we? As for the cottage, what about a six-month lease with a reasonable rent? I don't want to lose you as an employee or a tenant. Bell Forest is in the best shape it's been in for years. As for my behavior...I'm truly sorry."

Hesitating a moment, she searched her heart. "If you're sure," she said warmly. Inwardly she was relieved. She never wanted to leave; it would have broken her heart to go.

He narrowed his eyes, putting the cigar back into his mouth, "I'm sure."

Standing, Michael extended his hand. She clasped it and smiled.

A persistent knock sounded on the office door. "Am I interrupting anything?" Mary Grace peeked around the corner of the door as she opened it.

"No," they said simultaneously.

"Good," she said, with a mischievous grin on her face. "I just need to tell Telie that Lane Bennett is here for you. He asked me to tell you that he'll wait for you out front. I told him you were in a meeting."

"Oh, I almost forgot!" She stepped quickly to the door. "Mary Grace, will you please tell him to give me five minutes to wash up?" She turned back to Michael. "Thanks Michael, I'm glad we worked that out."

"Anytime." He stared after her as she hurried from the room.

Dashing to the back, after grabbing her bag off the table, she headed for the shower. A few minutes later, she emerged wearing a simple white summer dress. Small pearl earrings dangled from her ears.

Michael noticed the faint scent of lemons drift by as she hurried to the door. It always surprised him to see her look so lovely. One minute she was splattered with mud, her hair all wild around her face; the next, clean and sweet smelling and beautiful.

"Do you mind if I leave my truck here for a while, Michael?" She stopped at the door, waiting for his answer.

Losing his train of thought, he stammered, "No, no...that's fine. You can leave it here. No one will bother it."

She smiled before pushing the glass door open, making her exit. Slightly dazed, he watched her walk across the parking lot toward someone who seemed thrilled to see her. *Who wouldn't be,* he thought to himself.

Lane was waiting, leaning against his red jeep when Telie came out to meet him. "You look beautiful," he commented. A pleasantly surprised expression played on his face.

"Thank you, you're not so bad yourself," she said, as he helped her into the jeep. She took note of his white button-down shirt and slightly wrinkled khaki pants. *He's the kind of guy that looks good in anything*, she noted.

"Would you like for me to put the top up? I'm sorry I didn't think about your hair in the wind."

"No, please. I love the wind in my hair. I have my brush with me. I'm fine." Buckling up, she turned to smile at Lane as he got in. "I think I'd rather have a jeep than a boat."

"Really, why?"

She shrugged, "I guess I'm just a landlubber."

"Well, I'll just have to see if I can change your mind about that." Lane reached over and pulled her hand to his lips, gently kissing it.

Michael and Mary Grace watched the interaction through the office door. Turning to Mary Grace, he asked, "Do you know that guy?"

"Yeah, that's Lane Bennett. The artist from Mobile, you've heard of him, I know…or at least you've heard of his family. He's a Bennett, as in Bennett Shipbuilding…lucky girl," she said, under her breath. "His grandfather, Tom Bennett, lives next door to June in that big white house on the corner. Lane has made a name for himself. I can't imagine how Telie knows him. June must have introduced them." Mary Grace turned to Michael. "He certainly looked excited to see her, didn't he?"

Making a face, Michael spat the word "Artist." He mumbled something under his breath. Turning back to Mary Grace, feeling suddenly annoyed, he asked, "Did you need something, Mary Grace, or is this just another one of your daily social calls?"

"Just a social call," she answered, smiling with satisfaction.

Lane and Telie pulled up to the entrance of the gallery and hopped out. "I can't thank you enough for helping me out like this, Telie." He took her hand as they rushed toward the doors to the art gallery. "I hate these things...it's the worst part of being an artist."

"Oh, relax. It'll all be over in a few hours. Don't be so nervous. Remember, these people love and appreciate your work. What's so hard about walking around hearing people praise you all evening long? I wish people treated my work like that." She smiled, giving him a reassuring squeeze of her hand. "What I wouldn't give to hear someone say, 'Why Telie, ever since you touched my garden, people think they're at Bellingrath.'"

Lane laughed at her attempt to calm him. "I'm not feeling nervous, I'm feeling dread...there's a difference!" He took a deep breath and led the way inside.

The gallery had a soft glow about it. All of the artwork hung gracefully on the dark gray walls with accent lighting, bringing the pictures to life. There was an aura about the place, like a church or museum. Telie walked around the room in silence, fascinated by the paintings. Lane's name was scrawled beneath each one. She strolled all around, admiring the colors, shapes and subjects of his art. Stopping at a painting of a magnificent oak tree, she stood frozen by the sheer beauty of it. The branches of the giant oak dripped with moss, as they twisted and turned, displaying the glory of the tree. "You like that one?" Lane whispered in her ear, as he came up behind her.

"It's magnificent." She was seeing him in a new light. "I had no idea you were so talented. I thought you were just some annoying, ill-tempered neighbor Miss June had to put up with on occasion."

Throwing his hand up in protest, he said, "Oh please, your flattery is overwhelming." His eyes sparkled as he observed Telie. Her fascination with his painting pleased him.

Lane was a free spirit. His tousled blonde hair had unkemptness about it, as if he'd been beachcombing all day or just crawled out of bed. His smile was warm and engaging; his humor, dry. By anyone's standard he was adorable.

She thought back to the first time she'd met him. She was yanking down vines from a tree behind June's house. Struggling to free the tree from the choking vine, she lost her balance and fell flat on her backside. It was getting the best of her when she heard a calm voice say, "Are we a little frustrated today?"

Turning around, still holding a fistful of vines, she looked up and saw him staring down at her. He just stood there, grinning with his arms folded, clearly enjoying the moment. He didn't even offer to help her up off the ground!

"I was just sketching that particular tree, when I noticed parts of it kept disappearing." A smile tugged at the corners of his mouth. "I thought surely I'd find some logical explanation to the mystery of the vanishing tree, but instead, I find you. What are you…some kind of a wood nymph gone wild?"

Telie forced a smile. "Oh, that's very funny. I see you're a man of many skills…artist, comedian…what other talents do you possess…gentleman maybe?" She extended her hand up to him.

Reaching down, he took hold of her hand. With a gentle pull he lifted her to her feet. "Pardon me. I almost forgot my manners. By the way, I'm Lane Bennett," he said with a smile.

"Telie McCain," she said, dusting off the back of her jeans.

"So, tell me. Do you always go around destroying things…releasing your hostility on unsuspecting trees?" Lane pursed his lips, waiting for a reply.

"I pretty much vent my hostility on anything that annoys me," she said, pretending a smile.

He laughed and said, "Thanks for the warning. I'll just have to make sure I never annoy you."

"Too late," she stated flatly.

He searched her face, not sure what to make of this girl. Was she serious, or playing? "Is there a shred of grace in you, Miss McCain?"

Telie's face broke into a huge grin and she began to laugh. "Of course, I'm only teasing."

"Good, you had me worried for a minute. You're sort of intimidating when you're not smiling." He pretended to shiver. "After annoying you, the absolute least I can do is offer you a cup of coffee." He stuck his thumb out and motioned toward his back patio. Just over the hedge, she could see a small table and two chairs set on a large slab of stone. An easel and several canvas bags were propped up next to it.

"That sounds great. I really could use a break right now."

A friendship developed between them. Lane would seek her out each Monday while she was busy around the grounds at June's house. They became good friends. That's when he talked her into going with him to the showing.

She sensed Lane watching her, carefully evaluating her reaction to his work.

"As you can see, I do a lot of beach and ocean scenes, very few trees."

"I noticed. But the landscapes appeal to me," she said, not taking her eyes off the painting.

"Why does that not surprise me, you being such a landlubber and all, but people around here seem to be stuck on sand and water. You'd think they'd be sick to death of it." He shrugged his shoulders. "I get bored painting the same scenes over and over. I need more inspiration. Got any suggestions? Maybe you'd like to pose for me," he said teasingly.

"Well, as you may remember, I'm not from around here. I like trees. And as for your other suggestion, no, I have no intention of being painted by you. I can just imagine what you'd have in mind."

"Shy, or just no confidence in me?" he asked, smiling down at her. He felt warmth in her presence and enjoyed her company.

"Both."

It was sometime before midnight when Lane dropped Telie off at her truck. "I'll follow you home," he said.

She hopped down from the jeep and fumbled around in her purse for her keys. "I'll be fine; you go on home. I know you're tired. I'm about to drop myself."

"Don't be so annoying. I'm following you home!"

"Okay, okay." She held her hand up in protest.

Their headlights hit the trees as they pulled into the drive at Bell Forest. Leaving the jeep running, he got out and reached behind the seat, pulling out a large paper package. "Here," he said, handing the package to her. "This is for holding you hostage all night."

She took the package. "You don't have to give me anything, Lane. I really enjoyed myself tonight."

"Quit stalling and open it," he said, anxious for her reaction.

She tore the top off of the brown paper and gasped. "Oh! No Lane! You can't give this to me!" Her face lit up with joy. "You have no idea what you're doing. You could get a fortune for this!" Life came back into her tired eyes.

"I want *you* to have it. I saw the way you looked at it. I wish I could find someone to look at me the way you looked at that painting. It belongs with you. I want people to have my paintings that really love them."

"I adore it, Lane, and I will always treasure it. Thank you so much. I believe this is the nicest gift anyone has ever given me." Looking down at the painting, she snapped her fingers. "I have the perfect place for it too. Come on inside and I'll show you."

Opening the door, she walked over to the mantle and propped it up. "See...it's perfect, just like it was made for that spot." She turned around to face Lane, wrapping her arms around him, hugging him. He responded to her quickly. His arms came around her waist, and he crushed her to himself. "I think you can do better than that. I mean, you did say it was worth, what was it, a fortune. Yes, I believe you said a fortune."

For a split second she was anxious, but as his lips gently covered hers in a warm and tender kiss, she relaxed. He pulled away and smiled. "Now, that's better. But maybe next time, if you try really hard, you might think about kissing back." He smiled playfully into her eyes.

There was something absolutely adorable about him. Without thinking, she reached her hand around his head and grabbed a fistful of his wavy blond hair, bending his head down to hers. She returned his kiss with an intensity she'd never believed possible. She pulled his head back with her hand still securely wrapped in his hair and said, "Will that do?"

Speechless, he could only nod. Still a little dazed, he bit his lip trying not to smile, as Telie led the way to the door.

"I really enjoyed myself tonight, Lane. Thanks again for asking me and...thanks again for the painting."

"My pleasure, I'll see you soon."

After he had gone, Telie stood there, frozen to the floor. *What got into me?* She thought. *I've never done anything like that before. I mean it was just a kiss, right? So why do I feel like I've done something wrong?*

The look on Lane's face told her the answer. He had been shocked by her reaction, and truth be told, she was shocked by it too. Part of her knew she had done it for that very reason, to shock him and wipe that smug look off his face. But the other part of her knew it might be for another reason. Maybe she was interested in being more than just a friend to Lane.

Chapter 13

Telie had never given any guy much of a chance. She dated some in high school, but nothing serious. Once, she'd gotten pretty involved with a man she'd met while at work. He'd recently built a home and wanted Telie to help decide where the trees should be planted. He was attractive, charming and made a decent living working for the government. But he had a controlling nature and questioned everything she did. The final straw came when he timed how long it took her to get home from work. When she got home her cell phone was about to vibrate off the counter. She snatched it up and listened for ten minutes as he accused her of secretly meeting someone after work.

Sick of it and finally having enough, she simply said, "You caught me."

Stunned, he could only stammer, "What?"

She insisted it would be better for him to forget about her and find somebody trustworthier. After that, she preferred to be alone.

Lying in bed, restless, she got up and walked out on the porch. The familiar sounds of the night surrounded her, soothing her as she took a deep breath of the cool night air.

Her mind was filled with thoughts of Lane. What was it about him that appealed to her? Was it his easygoing carefree ways? Of course he was attractive, very attractive in a boyish kind of way. But there was something undefined, something else about him that she found appealing. *Maybe I'm just lonely,* she thought.

The sound of a distant chime brought her back to reality. Her heartbeat quickened as she thought about the slave girl and the silver bell down in the bayou. "Oh...I wish Brother Raphael had never told me that story. My ears are always listening for that stupid bell!"

Telie wasn't the only one not sleeping that night. Across town, Michael tossed and turned. His mind was on nothing but Telie. He pounded his pillow with his fist and shot up out of bed. "Enough of this, I'm going crazy!" he said, with clenched teeth. Walking over to the window, he looked out at the clear bright night and wondered, *Where is she? What is she doing?*

Something strange stirred inside him. He hadn't felt this way before, not even with Emily. He and Emily had been together since grade school. There had never been anyone else. All they had ever experienced, they'd experienced together. Jealousy was never part of their relationship. Each one trusted the other completely. But this...this was new and almost unbearable.

"Why does it bother me that she's out on a date? She's a young pretty girl; why wouldn't she be dating?" Michael leaned his forehead into the cool glass window. *What is it about her I find so interesting? She's nothing like Emily.*

At some point in the long night, he wandered back to bed. "I've got to talk to Nathan!" he said out loud. Throwing the covers back he collapsed on the bed, pushing the thoughts of Telie out of his head.

Michael got out of bed early, determined to find Nathan. He'd had a fitful night's sleep. After showering, he dressed, then grabbed his cell phone from the counter and dialed Nathan. "Nathan...you up?" He held his cell phone close to his ear.

"Yeah, I'm down at the dock," he yelled over the sound of a boat motor sputtering next to him. "I'm headed out; wanna come along?"

"Hold on, I'll be right there." He closed his phone and slid the truck keys off the kitchen counter. Making his way toward the truck, he remembered his fishing gear back in the garage. "Can't fish without a pole," he chided himself.

Nathan watched as Michael bounded down the pier. Even from a distance he could tell he looked beat. His face was scruffy and shadowed, and his eyes were tired and red.

"You look fresh as a daisy," Nathan said teasingly.

"Yeah, that's exactly how I feel, too. I know I don't look it, but I am clean...just in case you're worried about being downwind of me," he answered back.

They loaded up and stepped into the boat as it rocked and wobbled underneath their weight. Nathan yanked the cord and they headed out into the bay. The fresh morning air did little to help revive Michael.

"Here, have some coffee." Nathan offered his thermos to Michael who took it, putting it between his legs as he unscrewed the top. He carefully poured it out into a mug he had stashed away in his bag.

"Thanks," he yelled over the sound of the motor as he handed back the thermos.

Nathan steered toward his favorite fishing hole and cut the motor, letting it drift along the grasses near the shore.

Tossing his line, he asked without looking up, "What's eating you?"

"Telie McCain," he answered firmly, never taking his eyes off the line as he made a cast.

"What has she done now? Nothing else to that poor monk, I hope." Smiling over at Michael, he couldn't help but be concerned when he observed his friend.

"No…not that I know of anyway." He returned his smile. "I'm not sure how to explain it. I don't know how to put it into words."

"Just try, I'll hang on." Nathan fumbled with another lure in his tackle box, giving Michael a chance to form his thoughts.

"Remember when that bad storm blew in a few weeks ago?"

Nathan nodded once. He'd learned years ago to listen more than talk.

"Well, I drove out to Bell Forest to check on Telie. When I got there, I saw her down on her knees in the mud…right in the middle of the storm. She was pushing dirt around a rosebush, trying to save it. To make a long story short, I asked her why that particular bush was so important. Do you know what she told me?"

"No idea."

"She told me that she'd gotten the rosebush from the cemetery where my wife and child are buried." He stopped talking, looked up at Nathan and waited for that to sink in.

"I'm not following you…what child?" Nathan asked, confused.

Placing the end of his pole securely under his seat, Michael explained. "Emily was expecting our child when she died. She'd called me with the news about an hour before the accident. I've never told anyone." Michael was not able to keep the edge out of his voice. He looked down and waited for Nathan to say something.

That he had never told anyone about the baby hadn't surprised Nathan. Emily was sacred ground and no one ever dared walk on it, not even him. "I see...then how did Telie know?" Nathan asked, giving his full attention to Michael as he placed his rod beside him.

"This part gets strange. She told me she was looking down at Emily's headstone when she noticed two yellow roses. According to her, one was full and complete, and the other, just a bud." He opened his hands and shrugged. "That's what she said, believe it or not."

"That's interesting. So...how did you respond to that?"

Taking in a deep breath, he said, "Like an idiot. I got angry, yelled at her and left." Clearly upset, Michael shook his head, disgusted. "I don't know why, but I've been brooding over it for weeks, barely even speaking to her."

"So, how are things between you now?"

"Like I said, we haven't really talked since that day...until yesterday."

"What happened yesterday?" Nathan leaned forward, hanging on every word.

"She asked to speak with me. We've worked side by side all this time, been polite to each other, but it's been, for lack of a better word, strained. Yesterday she told me she was offered another job and would be leaving. She said it would be easier for her to leave than to keep going like we were going. I convinced her to stay and we worked it out."

Raising his eyebrows, Nathan said, "That's good…so what's the problem?"

"Good question." He ran a hand through his hair and sighed deeply. "Well, after our talk…this guy pulls up. They have a date."

"I'm listening." Nathan said.

"It bothers me…a lot. When I got home last night I couldn't eat, sleep or think about anything else. It's about to drive me crazy! What the heck is happening to me? Why am I feeling this way about a girl I've only known for a few short months?" Puzzled, Michael waited for his response.

"I'll tell you why, if that's what you're asking. You have feelings for her. You may even love her."

"What? I love Emily," he stated sharply.

"Yes, and you always will. But that doesn't mean you'll never love anyone else ever again. It doesn't work that way, Michael. You were blessed with an incredible wife. Emily is not here though; she's already made it. Marriage is strictly for earthbound creatures, like us, not heavenly ones. That's why we pledge in our vows 'Till death do us part.'"

Nathan knew he was touching a tender spot, but he had wanted to say that to Michael for a long time. God had just given him an opportunity and he would not let the chance pass him by.

Picking up his pole, Michael tossed his line, reeling it in slowly.

Nathan could tell there was a struggle going on inside of him, but he remained quiet, giving him space. He wouldn't bring up the subject again unless Michael did.

"I've been such a fool," Michael finally said, "hanging on to something that will never come back to me. I mean, she would never even want to, not after being in heaven for Pete's sake!"

"Yeah, that reminds me of what King David said when his baby died. He said, 'He can't come back to me, but I'll one day go to him.' That's the goal of every believer, Michael, to be where Emily and the baby are now."

Michael stared out at the water for a while, and then asked, "Now what? I mean...how am I supposed to treat her now?"

"Oh that's easy; you treat her as your friend." Nathan relaxed a little as he picked up his pole again, tugging on the line.

"That'll be easy enough. I've never known anyone like her, Nathan; she kind of gets to you." A smile spread across his face slowly.

Nathan was glad to see the light come back into his friend's eyes. When he talked about Telie, his whole face lit up. "Yeah, you got it bad," Nathan said, fumbling around in his tackle box again.

"I hope she had an awful time last night," Michael said, waiting for Nathan to jump on him. "I know, I know, don't look at me that way. I'm just sharing how I feel, save the sermon for Sunday!"

"Yeah, I believe that falls under the category of envy or jealousy, one of the big ten."

"Figures, now if I could just get my sanity back, I think I might be all right."

"You'll have to go over my head for that one," Nathan teased. "But I'll be glad to make an intercession for you."

Chapter 14

Brother Raphael ran down the path that led to the cottage, gripping his robe to avoid tripping. Out of breath, he hastily rapped on the door. "Telie, come out. I need you!"

Wiping her hands dry on a dishtowel, she quickly opened the door. Panic washed over her face. "What's the matter?"

"I need your help! We've just been informed that we're expecting company in the morning, a sudden change of plans. It's all so unexpected and I only have this afternoon to make the front entrance presentable. Will you help me?" he asked, with hopeful expectation. His brown eyes sparkled with excitement.

"Oh, of course, is that all? You scared the life out of me. Now calm down, it's just company." She walked to the little table on the back porch and picked up her work gloves. "Let's go."

"It's not *just* company, Telie. It's the abbot."

She turned back to look at him and thought she saw him cross himself. "Oh, well in that case, let's get rolling!" she said, smiling. She had never seen Brother Raphael so beside himself. It was kinda funny. She didn't know what an "abbot" was, but he certainly must be important.

After working so closely together all summer, they could anticipate what the other one needed without words. Telie began tugging weeds in the flowerbed next to the monastery while Brother Raphael scooped mulch, spreading it carefully around the plants.

The old monastery was ancient looking, medieval almost. It was made largely of smooth honey-colored stones, warmed from the sun. Rounded archways led to the interior courtyard with corridors that wound around in both directions, connecting the buildings. Beautifully kept gardens were everywhere. There were fountains and quiet spots for reflection; stone benches and arbors draped with sweet smelling vines dotted the grounds.

"I've never seen anyone pull weeds as fast as you, Telie, and with such rhythm. Where did you learn to do that?" he asked, impressed.

"It's a highly developed skill," she said, grinning. "My dad taught me. He had a machete in my hand by the time I was eight!"

"Impressive," he added, gathering up the discarded weeds and tossing them in a bucket. "Remind me to steer clear of you if I ever see a machete in your hand."

"I'll give you fair warning," she shot back.

"So...what did you clear with your machete?" he asked, making small talk.

"Whatever piece of mosquito-infested swampland my daddy bought. We'd clear all but the mature trees. He had a thing for trees. I guess that's where I get it. He could tell you everything there was to know about them." Wiping her brow with the back of her hand, she swatted what she thought was a mosquito on her arm.

"What would he do with the land after you cleared it?"

"Sell it." She laughed at the startled look on his face. "Yeah, I think he used me for cheap child labor. He always made a nice profit."

"How did that make you feel? Did you ever feel used?" Brother Raphael looked at her sympathetically.

"Oh no, I got paid, just not with money. I was paid with exercise and knowledge of the land," she said sarcastically. "That's what Daddy would always say."

"Oh, he was good. Do you have brothers and sisters?" Brother Raphael stopped what he was doing and looked at her until she answered. The heat of the day was showing on his reddened face.

"No, but I do have lots of cousins, boys all of them. They lived next door to us when I was growing up."

"I'm beginning to understand you better. That must be where you get all of your tomboy ways," he joked, holding up a handful of weeds before dumping them in the bucket. "Practice does make perfect in your case."

"Yeah well, everyone has their God-given talents, right? Mine just happens to be weeds." She broke out in a huge grin.

"You remind me of my sister," he said wistfully as he noticed her smile.

"She must be an incredibly interesting person then." Turning, she noticed a sadness pulling at the corners of his mouth.

He half smiled, then his eyes turned sad again.

"Do you see her often?" she asked, thinking that must be the reason behind his sadness.

"I haven't seen her in many years now." He kept raking up weeds with his hand but looked a million miles away.

"That's not right. Won't they let you take a vacation around here? I mean, come on." She looked perturbed, thinking how much she didn't understand about the life of a monk.

"It's not that...you don't understand," he said, continuing to gather and dump weeds into the bucket.

"Well, enlighten me."

"It's simple. I'm dead to my family, Telie." His voice sounded hollow.

"What?" Telie stopped what she was doing and turned to him, waiting for an explanation.

He took a shallow breath. "You see, in my culture when a person gives his life to Christ, some very dangerous repercussions come from that decision. Some have even lost their lives, martyred because of their faith. With me, I was just pronounced dead by my father, so I no longer exist to my family."

Telie's mouth dropped open, unable to speak as she listened to his explanation.

"He forbids any of my family members to contact me... including my sister. No one would ever think of disobeying my father. Not even my mother."

Telie sat back on her heels and stared at him in disbelief. She went back to yanking weeds, harder this time. She thought about all he must have suffered and was still suffering. She wondered if he had any regrets. "How do you feel about your father now?"

"Oh, I love him and pray for him daily, all of them in fact. But truly, my earthly father doesn't begin to compare to the joy I've experienced in the presence of my heavenly Father. You see, when I became a Christian, I found a whole new family, a new life rich with meaning and purpose. Old things passed away, and all things became new. My heavenly Father will never leave me. He will never forsake me." Joy was evident on his face as he spoke. He meant every word.

"I know what it's like to lose a father," Telie said softly.

Brother Raphael said nothing, afraid it might stop her from speaking. He'd wanted to know what had caused his young friend to isolate herself from the world. He knew he was about to find out.

"He didn't disown me outright, but he might as well have. He left us and moved to Texas with his new wife and her three kids, girls all of them." Her throat tightened at the memory and the still raw wound.

Soothingly, Brother Raphael said, "Yes...our earthly fathers can fail us, leave us, reject us, disappoint us and even die on us. Only God remains unfailing and He loves us with an everlasting love. He knows us intimately and loves us immensely."

"Don't you ever just miss them though, your family?" Her brown eyes squinted in the sun as she looked at him.

"Of course I do. God knows and cares how I feel. He looks out for me. I've been surrounded with the most wonderful people, Telie, and I'm so grateful to Him for that. After all, He sent you here, didn't He? Now I have a new sister."

"Well, I am your sister in Christ, you know," she said, coughing slightly, then winked.

"Yes, and every bit as annoying as my earthly sister too!" he said, dodging the grass Telie threw at him. "Come on," Brother Raphael said, wiping the dirt from his hands, "let's go inside. You can wait for me while I go to evening prayers, then you can dine with us."

"Oh no, that's okay, I'll go on home."

"Nonsense, I want you to see the monastery and meet the others. We have a chapel on the first floor that you are welcome to use. Better is a handful of quietness than two hands full of toil, Ecclesiastes 4:6," he quoted, with a smile.

Telie got up and dusted off, following Brother Raphael inside.

Upon entering, she had an overwhelming sense of awe. A cool silence filled the enormous entry hall. The rich earthy scent of wood, polish and old books filled her senses.

"The chapel is down the hall on the left. It's just past the library."

Telie watched as Brother Raphael walked down the long corridor in the opposite direction without a sound. She listened for his footsteps and other noises from the occupants but found only silence. She felt the need to tiptoe as she walked toward the chapel, stopping occasionally to admire some work of art on the dark paneled walls. As she reached the chapel door, she hesitated a moment, then turned the knob and entered.

The chapel was cloaked in darkness. The only source of light emanated from a small metal candle stand toward the front of the chapel. Six rows of tiny candles, each row stacked slightly higher than the previous, flickered, dispelling the thick cool blackness. The light from the candles cast moving shadows around the room, illuminating the figure of Jesus on the cross.

Stepping inside, she felt the mystery of the place envelope her. Taking a seat near the front, she closed her eyes and drank deeply of her surroundings. *God is here,* she thought. *His presence is in this holy place.*

Time disappeared. All she wanted to do was be bathed in His love, His peace and His presence.

She felt rather than heard the door open behind her. Afraid of losing the holy moment, she sat still, not wanting it to vanish.

Brother Raphael slipped in beside her and waited, saying nothing. Telie reached for his hand. "He's here," she said quietly.

Once outside the chapel, he spoke, "So, I see you've discovered *my* thunderstorm."

"Thunderstorm?" she questioned.

"You once told me that you felt close to God when you watched a thunderstorm. God is everywhere, Telie, in the storm, in the chapel, even in everyday life. It's up to us to quiet down enough to notice Him."

Chapter 15

Brother Lawrence sat at his desk, sorting papers, preparing for the abbot's arrival. Brother Simeon, an elderly monk, rapped lightly on the office door.

Brother Simeon was small of frame, with snow-white hair the consistency of cotton candy. His faded blue eyes still held a twinkle. He had a slight shuffle to his steps. You could hear his approach as his slippers swished slowly across the polished stone floor. His thick Irish brogue made everything he said sound like music. Stepping inside the office, he announced, "Beggin' your pardon, Brother Lawrence, but all seems to be in order for the arrival of the abbot."

"Wonderful…thank you for supervising everything for me, Brother Simeon. I can always count on you to oversee these kinds of affairs." Brother Lawrence never looked up, busily arranging the papers on his desk.

"Yes, well, I do what I can. But another matter needs your attention, sir. If I may be explainin' to ya," the old monk's voice held concern.

Looking up this time, he stopped what he was doing and waited for Brother Simeon to explain.

"The young Miss Telie has us all a bit worried, Brother Lawrence. It's not like her to be stayin' inside the cottage up into the day and on such a fine day as this. She failed to appear on her porch last evening when the storm blew up. As you may well know, it's her habit to watch these storms as they come into the bay. After mentioning my concern to Brother Raphael, he went over to check on her, but she did not come to the door. I thought it might interest you to know." Looking over the top of his glasses at Brother Lawrence, he waited for a response.

"Thank you for telling me, Brother Simeon. As always, I can count on you to keep me informed about the goings-on. I'll call Michael right away. He'll know what to do."

Brother Simeon nodded and turned to shuffle out of the room. But before he left, he called back. "If you don't mind, Brother Lawrence, please be letting me know what Michael finds out. Poor Brother Raphael is a bit troubled. He noticed she looked a little pale last evening at dinner."

Shutting the door behind him, Brother Simeon eased down the corridor. Brother Raphael rushed to his side and asked, "Well, what did he say?"

"He will be calling Michael, son. Now you don't be worrying yourself about it. I'm sure she's fine. I'll settle myself on the glass porch and keep an eye out. I'll let you know if I see a sign of her. Michael will probably come and tell us what he finds out, I'm sure of it." Patting Brother Raphael's crossed arms, he said, "You go on now...about your duties. I'll find you when I hear of anything worth mentioning."

Picking up the phone, Brother Lawrence dialed Michael's number, flipping the card with Michael's number on it with his thumb as he waited for him to answer. He had placed the card with his phone number on it directly under a small statue of Michael the Archangel, to make sure he wouldn't forget his promise to look after Telie.

The phone rang several times before Michael answered. "Hello."

"Michael? Brother Lawrence. I hate to trouble you, especially on Sunday, but we have a concern here."

"You're not troubling me. What's the matter?" he asked, a little impatiently.

"The concern is Telie. The Brothers here tell me that it's not like her to stay in the cottage without making an appearance this late in the day."

Without a hesitation, Michael retrieved his boots from the doorway and yanked them on. "I'm on my way."

"It may be nothing, but we would all feel better to know if...Michael?" The phone buzzed, obviously disconnected. Brother Lawrence smiled as he placed the receiver back in place.

Michael hung up the phone, grabbed his keys, slamming the back door shut as he took off toward the truck. Mary Grace was pulling up, as he backed out, flying past her. He sped down the road toward Bell Forest.

He knocked repeatedly on the door, no answer, no sound, nothing. "Telie!" he called loudly. For a brief moment he wondered if she was alone. *Maybe that artist guy is with her.* He pushed the thought from his mind and tried the door. To his surprise it opened. "Telie!" he called again, stepping cautiously in the direction of the bedroom.

He froze in the doorway of her bedroom. Lying there like a crumpled rag doll in the center of the bed was Telie. He could see the sheet rise and fall with her breath. Her damp hair stuck to her face in matted strands. He eased near her, pressing the flat of his hand against her forehead. She stirred slightly at his touch, moaning through chattering teeth. She was burning with fever and shaking all over.

"Telie," he said tenderly.

Slowly opening her eyes, she saw Michael and smiled. "Hey," she said in a whisper, "what are you doing here?"

"I was gonna ask you the same question. What hurts?" he asked, watching her face intently, looking for signs that might give him a clue about her illness.

She closed her eyes, moving her head from side to side. "Everything, I have bronchitis," she choked out in a dry cough.

"Are you sure it's bronchitis?" he questioned, not really sure if he should trust her judgment. She might be delirious with fever.

"Yeah...happens to me every year." Her raspy voice let him know that she struggled to breathe. "I know the symptoms well."

"What have you taken for it – anything?" He smoothed her hair away from her face, resisting the urge to gather her into his arms and take the chill away from her shaking body. Looking around the room, he saw a quilt in a heap at the foot of the bed. Retrieving it, he spread it out, tucking it around her. His lips curved into a half smile when he recognized the quilt. It was the same one his mother had used for him on cool nights and feverish days.

Rolling over onto her side, she pointed to the nightstand and the cough medicine, a sticky red-coated spoon propped up next to it.

He picked up the bottle to examine it closely. "I'll be right back," he said, tapping the bed. Reaching in his pocket he pulled out his cell phone, flipped it open and dialed Dr. Allen.

"Doc, this is Michael. Sorry to bother you on a Sunday afternoon...I'll make this brief. I'm down at the cottage with a sick girl. You may remember Telie, she goes to church with us...comes with June."

"Yes, I remember her. What's the problem?" Dr. Allen asked.

"She has a fever and a dry cough. Tells me it's bronchitis, and she has it every year, but I don't know. I hate when people diagnose themselves; what if she's wrong?"

"Who's taking care of her?" he asked, then cleared his throat. He was probably in the middle of Sunday dinner from the sound of his muffled voice.

"She rents the cottage from me." Michael hesitated momentarily. "She doesn't have family here so I'm looking after her."

Without hesitation, he said, "Watch her, and if she gets worse or her fever continues, bring her in. In the meantime make sure she drinks plenty of liquids. An over-the-counter pain medication will be fine for the fever. Keep her in bed, she needs rest." He paused, then added, "People who are prone to bronchitis usually recognize the symptoms. Going in and out from hot air to cold air can sometimes bring it on this time of year."

"Well, she certainly does that." He thought about the ice-cold office and the sweltering heat of the grounds. "Doc...thanks. I really appreciate your help."

"Anytime, call me if you need me and watch that fever."

Walking back to her bedside, he fumbled around on the nightstand picking up bottles looking for pain relievers. Finding a small bottle of Advil, he asked, "How long since you've had this?" He held the bottle up for her inspection.

"I can't remember, maybe this morning. What time is it anyway?"

"Around three." He stepped into the kitchen and filled a glass of water. Placing the medicine in the palm of her hand, he said, "Take this and drink all of it, doctor's orders." Holding the glass to her lips, she placed the pill on her tongue and swallowed down the cool water, finishing about half. He eyed her suspiciously. "All means all."

She cut her eyes at him, wanting to protest but didn't have the strength. Tipping the glass up, she drank it down and handed him the empty glass.

Telie began to shake as her fever climbed. Seeing her reaction, he went to the closet and pulled down another quilt. He smoothed it over the top of the other quilt, patting it down around her, rubbing her legs.

As she slept, he walked through the grass, across the yard toward the monastery. Walking up the path, a movement caught his eye from a tall window. He saw a small gray-haired monk standing in the window with his hands behind his back. He seemed as if he expected him. As he rounded the corner toward the back entrance, the door was standing open. The elderly monk motioned for him to enter. Michael recognized him to be Brother Simeon.

"Come in, come in, Michael," Brother Simeon said, eyes twinkling.

Michael walked in as Brother Simeon waved to the chair next to him. "Sit down, sit down, young man, tell me now, how is our girl?" Peering over his glasses, Brother Simeon fixed his gaze on Michael.

"She's sick, Brother Simeon. We think she has bronchitis. I called Doctor Allen and he said to watch her. If she doesn't improve, I'm to bring her in to his office. She's sleeping now."

The old monk nodded his head while Michael briefed him. "I knew something was wrong. I just knew it. I got concerned when the storm came through last night and I didn't see her."

"The storm?" Michael questioned, trying to understand. "What does the storm have to do with Telie?"

"Oh, she's like an unfettered spirit that one, coming out when the weather rages. She sits and rocks away watching the storms approach. That's when I got worried, knew something was wrong. I told Brother Raphael my concerns and he went right over. When she didn't respond, we called you." He shook his head, his leathery face looked grieved. "A young girl like that living all alone." He looked away, lost in thought.

Michael agreed with Brother Simeon. It wasn't right for a young girl like Telie to be living alone. "Thank you for looking after her so well, Brother Simeon. I feel so much better knowing you're here." Michael stuck out his hand as he stood.

"My pleasure, son, anything I can do to help, you just let me know." With a look of satisfaction in his eyes, he gripped Michael's hand. "We've grown kinda fond of Miss Telie around here, ya know. Why, she even had dinner with us last evening."

Michael smiled at the old monk, thinking what a bright spot Telie must have been around their dinner table. Closing the door, he made his way down the path and back to the cottage. He stopped dead in his tracks. Mary Grace's silver BMW was parked beside his truck. *Can't that woman ever give it a rest*, he thought, quickening his pace. He didn't trust her to be near Telie when she was well, much less when she was sick and defenseless.

Coming up behind Mary Grace, he startled her. He motioned for her to step into the living room, trying to maneuver her away from the bedroom door where she'd been standing, staring at Telie's sleeping form.

Feeling suddenly protective, he asked, "What brings you out this way?" He eyed her suspiciously.

"I saw how you flew around me in a hurry, I was worried. I thought something was on fire," she said, flirting. She rested her hand on his chest, fingering a button. "But now I see that it's nothing. What's the matter with her anyway – she looks awful."

Forever the shallow, self-centered prima donna, he thought. Her lack of compassion still surprised him. He'd only seen her upset over one loss and that was the loss of her freshly manicured fingernail.

"Something *is* on fire," he shot back. "It's Telie. She has a fever, maybe even a highly contagious disease, Mary Grace. I don't think you really need to be here. It's not safe."

"I'm sure," she responded sarcastically. She walked around the room, appraising everything. "So this is where she lives…kinda primitive, isn't it?"

"You mean simple and…unpretentious." He glared at her wishing she would go away. "That's what I love about the place."

"Oh!" she said, raising her eyebrows as she glided over to the fireplace. She looked up at the mantle, gazing at the picture of the magnificent tree. "I see her boyfriend gave her one of his paintings." She ran a finger across the bottom of the frame, and then turned around to see his reaction.

Glancing up at the picture above the mantle, he stated, "So it seems." Trying to act disinterested, he turned back to the couch and sat down, picking up a book from the coffee table. He leafed through the pages one at a time without really noticing, determined to wait her out. His annoyance continued to mount.

"Shouldn't we call Lane and let him know that she's sick? I mean I would want you to know if I were sick." She slipped down next to him on the couch, crossing her legs as she leaned in to him. "I could slip in there and get her cell phone and find his number," she whispered.

"I'll ask her when she wakes up. You don't need to do anything, Mary Grace. As a matter of fact, I can see you're getting bored here. Why don't you go shopping? I hear there's a sale going on over at the outlet mall."

She got up and moved to the bedroom door. "Oh, she's awake! How are you feeling? I've been so worried about you." Mary Grace's voice was smooth, dripping with concern.

The color drained out of Telie's face as she recognized Mary Grace, standing in the doorway.

Michael shot up from the couch to stand behind Mary Grace. He saw the shocked look in Telie's eyes and some other emotion he couldn't identify. She looked frightened. With both of his hands firmly on Mary Grace's shoulders, he removed her from the doorway. Coming near the side of the bed, he bent down and whispered, "Don't worry, I'll protect you." The grin on his face told her he was teasing, but the look on her face told him he'd better! Michael lifted his hand to her forehead. "I'm glad to see you've finally decided to wake up. You've been sleeping for hours. Fever's down too…good."

Mary Grace was seething. She struggled to keep her temper under control as she watched Michael tenderly care for Telie. *She's probably faking all of this just to get his attention!* Moving closer she said, "Michael and I were just discussing whether or not to call Lane and let him know about your illness. Would you like for us to call him for you?

We wouldn't want to upset him or have him mad at us for not telling him about you."

"No, please, it's not necessary," she responded weakly. "Lane is busy in Mobile."

"Okay then…I'll just have to stay and nurse you back to health. We'll let him know how sick you've been after you've recovered." Mary Grace brushed the front of her beige linen pantsuit and plopped down in the rocker next to the bed. She picked up a book from the nightstand, feigning interest, as she flipped the pages.

Michael had to bite his lip to keep from laughing at the expression on Telie's face. It was somewhere between terror and nausea. She looked at him, pleading with her eyes.

Michael cleared his throat. "I don't think that will be necessary, Mary Grace. But the thought is touching." He slowly removed the book from her hand and placed it back on the nightstand. Taking hold of her hand, he lifted her up and out of the rocker.

"Well, *you* certainly can't stay! What would people say?" she said, sounding shocked and horrified. "Her reputation is bad enough already. People are assuming the worst with her living out here in your cottage…not paying rent…with cash I mean!"

Her insinuation did not go unnoticed. That did it. His patience had finally run out. Anger rose to the surface, exploding on his face as he spoke in slow measured words. "It's time for you to go, Mary Grace." He spit out the words carefully. "I'll show you to the door." His eyes flared with controlled anger.

The expression on his face told Mary Grace all she needed to know. She had crossed a line. She didn't push it; she stood up, glared at Telie and walked out.

Exhaling slowly, Telie felt relief at once. She had not even realized she'd been holding her breath.

Moments later Michael came back into the room, the lines had smoothed out from his face, as if the dark cloud had suddenly lifted and the sun was shining again. "I think it's time for something to eat. What sounds good to you – how about soup?" Michael said cheerfully.

"Sounds good," she said, not wanting to spoil his cheerful mood. She'd seen him angry before, even with her, but this was different. It was more like controlled rage. The way his face set like steel and his jaw clenched together, she shuddered briefly, not sure if it was from the fever or the thought of Michael's temper.

She listened as he rattled pots and pans around in the kitchen, whistling. She must have dozed off because the next thing she remembered was seeing Michael holding out his hand with an Advil and a glass of water. She saw a tray with soup and crackers on the nightstand beside the bed. Smiling, she gestured toward the tray. "Is that for me?" She took the pill from his hand and swallowed it down with a cool sip of water.

"Sure is," he said, picking up the tray. He took the spoon and dipped it into the soup, stirring.

"That smells good. I'm starving." She pulled up slightly. He reached around and gently lifted her to a sitting position. She felt his muscles tighten behind her. His nearness caused her heart to pound in her chest. Afraid he would hear it, she coughed, trying to cover it up. His scent, masculine and outdoorsy, like leather, soap and tobacco all mixed together, left her dizzy. *Is it his nearness or the fact that I've been in bed all day?* She really couldn't tell.

"Seems like you're always taking care of me," she said, feeling awkward and embarrassed all at the same time. She tucked a loose strand of hair behind her ear. "How did you know I was sick?"

"Myrtle told me."

"Myrtle?" she whispered, with a questioning look.

"Yeah, crepe myrtle. I guess you think rosebushes are the only things that talk around here." Michael grinned mischievously.

"Funny," she said sarcastically.

Michael dipped the spoon into the soup, trying hard not to laugh.

"You know, you don't have to spoon-feed me. I think I'm capable of finding my mouth," Telie said smoothly, taking the spoon from his hand.

Easing back in the rocker, he left her to feed herself. "Who looked after you before I came along...your mother?" He rocked back in the chair, waiting for her answer.

"She probably would have if I'd ever let her." She took a long steady sip of soup from the spoon and dipped it back down, catching more noodles than soup.

"Why wouldn't you let her? Isn't that what mothers are for, to nurse their children back to health?" he questioned, mystified.

"It was just...easier. I like to take care of myself."

He shook his head. "Why does everything have to be easy with you, Telie? I would really like to know. Have you ever considered that it just might give some people pleasure to take care of you?"

"I like to rely on myself when I can and not trouble others with my problems. I'm sure there are more important things for you to do on a Sunday afternoon than look after me. You could be fishing right now."

"Like I said, it's a pleasure to take care of you. By the way, this is way more fun than fishing," he added playfully.

Chapter 16

The night passed quietly. Telie slept, waking only when Michael nudged her to take her medication. He watched her sleep. *She looks so sweet and pretty, even with her matted hair all over the place*, he thought. Picking up her collection of books from the nightstand, he read each title, curious to know what interested her. He whispered the titles, "*Pilgrims Progress* by John Bunyan." He placed the book back down on the nightstand and turned over the next book in his lap. "*Pilgrim at Tinker Creek* by Annie Dillard. Uh-huh…I think I see a pattern." He reached for her Bible and leafed through it, stopping on the passages she had highlighted. "I am the vine, you are the branches, if a man remains in me and I in him, he will bear much fruit; apart from me you can do nothing," he whispered as he scanned the page. *She not only highlighted this passage, but also underlined it. This must be one of her favorite verses,* he thought, thumbing through the rest of her Bible. He paused on a page with a dried, pressed rose stuck into the seam. *I wonder who gave this to her? Probably someone she loved?* He closed the Bible, placing it back on the nightstand. A feeling of melancholy came over him at the thought of her loving someone. Studying her intently, he watched as her lips pursed, then relaxed in her sleep.

A gray dawn light filtered through the window, landing in irregular patterns on the crumpled bed. Michael raised his stiff neck from the back of the rocker. Looking at Telie, he noticed she was breathing easier. He made his way to the kitchen and put on some coffee.

Telie moved around in the bed, tossing the covers back. The smell of coffee wafted through the door; she was confused for a minute, then remembered...Michael. Looking around, she saw his boots on the floor. His cell phone and a set of keys were placed neatly beside her books. *He must have stayed here all night.* Something stirred inside her at the thought. Her eyes moved to the other side of the rocker where she saw a quilt and a pillow on the floor. *Did he sleep in the chair?* She wondered.

"Good morning," he said, leaning in the doorway, both hands on the frame. His smile melted her. Stepping back, he disappeared only to return a moment later with a cup of steaming coffee. "Did you sleep well?"

"I must've because I can't remember a thing."

A teasing glint came into his eyes. "I can't imagine how you can sleep with the racket you make. You snore like a buzz saw!"

"Oh, I do not!" Her face flamed red. "Do I?"

Deciding to let her off the hook, he shook his head. "Nah, I'm just teasing...but you do gab a lot."

She stared at him with wide eyes. "So I've been told. What did I say? Nothing too embarrassing, I hope."

"Something about snakes...and I think you were flying through the air or something. You looked like you were enjoying it."

"I'm really not that complicated, am I?" She smiled at him, hoping and praying that was all she'd said. "When I leave this world I hope I get to fly around for awhile. I've always wanted to. I must've been testing my wings."

"Ready for some coffee?" he asked, putting his cup down on the nightstand.

"I'd love some juice if it's not too much trouble. I feel pretty dry."

Smiling, he added, "All that flying around can really work up a thirst." Pausing in the doorway, he turned around. "By the way, you look much better this morning. You could stand a shower though; I've never seen hair stand up on end like that before. And like I said…you're no trouble."

Running her hands through her hair, she made a face and stuck out her tongue.

Michael handed her the juice and felt her head. "You're good to go…no fever. Make sure you take it slow." Relieved there was no fever, he went back to the kitchen to make breakfast. "Yell if you need me."

"Uh, I don't think I'll need you in the shower," she said, to no one in particular as she stepped into the bathroom. The hot steamy water felt good on her achy muscles. She lathered up, washing every bit of the last two days of sickness away.

After the shower, she wrapped her bathrobe securely around her and headed to the kitchen. She sat down at the table and smiled at Michael, feeling a little self-conscious being with him in her pajamas. "I wonder what Mary Grace would say if she saw us like this," she said, slightly amused.

"Let's not spoil our morning by bringing up Mary Grace." He glanced over his shoulder as he turned the bacon in the pan. "You shouldn't worry too much about what Mary Grace thinks. I'm sure she went out shopping last night and has long forgotten about us. Shopping seems to cure most female troubles." He poured her a cup of coffee, placing it in front of her.

"I'd break out in hives if I was forced to go shopping." She sipped her coffee slowly.

"What?" he asked quizzically.

"I hate shopping. My eyes glaze over and my body shuts down when I enter a department store. It overwhelms me... always has," she shuddered.

"I stand corrected. And here I am thinking I know women." He smiled, thinking how very little he knew about this particular woman. "So...if you hate shopping, how do you always manage to look so nice? You looked especially pretty for your date the other night."

"Thank you." She smiled at the compliment. "I'm a catalog shopper when I can afford it. I'm like a kid when it comes to getting a package in the mail. I buy only what I like and what feels good on my skin. Most of the things I wear are several years old and have been washed a hundred times. It'd be safe to say that I'm no slave to fashion." She held her cup of coffee with both hands as if it might escape, then took a sip.

Brushing the biscuits with melted butter, he placed them back in the oven to brown further. "I like my biscuits extra brown, how 'bout you?"

"Definitely, I've got some molasses over on the hutch. I bought it at Davis's store the other day. Boy, you weren't kidding about Mrs. Davis. I felt like I was being interrogated! She kept asking me where I lived, and then answered her own question by telling *me* where I lived. She asked if I was related to you. Thankfully someone butted in before I could answer her question. I saw my chance and made my escape. I'm not used to being the object of so much attention."

"I don't believe that," Michael stated, grinning. "You sure seem to be getting a lot of attention from me these days."

Getting up from her chair, she eased over to the hutch. She opened the cabinet door and lifted out a glass jar of molasses. Looking down she noticed the silver spoon she'd found in the garden. "Oh, I almost forgot about this." She handed him the silver spoon. "Here, I found this in the garden after the storm the other night. We must have unearthed it when we tilled up the soil for our garden. I guess the rain caused it to perk to the top."

He wiped his hands dry with the dishtowel, tossing it over his shoulder as he took the spoon from her hand. "Looks like a teaspoon," he said. He ran it under hot water, then rubbed it down with the towel, examining it.

"Was that one of your mother's?" she asked, sitting back down at the table.

"Oh no, we never had the good stuff down here. This must be silver from the Bennier Plantation. They hid some of it near the bayou during the war."

"I heard about that. Brother Raphael told me a little bit about the legend of Bayou Bell."

He raised one eye. "How much?"

"Oh, not much, just the part that keeps me up half the night listening for the sound of that stupid bell!"

"No, he didn't!" He gave her a skeptical look. Raising his eyebrows, he shrugged, "I underestimated Brother Raphael. He must have decided it was time for payback. That's one way to do it."

"Payback for what?" she asked, looking and sounding innocent.

"Surely you haven't forgotten the 'pinecone' incident. Maybe he thought it was time you did a little penance for your trespasses."

She waved her hand in dismissal. "Please."

He handed the spoon to her. "See, look at all of the detail. The etchings are beautiful...simple, but beautiful. I'll bet there's more out there somewhere." A smile played at the corners of his mouth. "Hopefully that slave girl won't come looking for it."

Handing the spoon back to him she said, "That's a nice thought. Thanks for sharing it with me." She swatted at a pesky fly as it circled around her face.

He laughed, sticking the spoon in his pocket. "Well, let's eat. Somebody's got to get to work today."

"This is really good, Michael. I had no idea you could cook! What else can you do that I'm not aware of?"

He smirked at her over his coffee. "Cooking is just one of many talents."

"You certainly have a talent for getting rid of someone." She shuddered, thinking of his temper.

"Mary Grace has a way of pushing the wrong buttons with me." He studied her for a moment, wondering if she was afraid of him. He hated the thought. "I do have a terrible temper. Just when I think I'm doing better, I'm tested on it and I usually fail. I've prayed about it more times than I care to remember. God must be fed up with hearing my repeated pleas for help in controlling that part of me."

Telie nodded. "I've failed a few tests of my own lately. I'm just glad God is longsuffering and doesn't give up on us too easily."

After breakfast she was given strict orders to stay inside and rest. Michael told her to call him if she needed anything and that he would come by after work to check on her. Before he walked out the door, he said, smirking, "I'll call Lane when I get to my office and let him know we spent the night together. But don't worry…I'll tell him that you looked absolutely radiant this morning."

"Oh that's low." She threw her napkin at him. "Why don't you call Mary Grace and tell her the same thing?"

He dodged the napkin, laughing, and closed the door.

Chapter 17

Mary Grace didn't waste any time. After driving out to Bell Forest earlier that morning to confirm her suspicions, she called Pastor Nathan to share the news with him.

"I'm just so concerned, Pastor Nathan," Mary Grace said, spewing worry. "I really think you need to speak to Michael. He stayed with Telie at Bell Forest all night! And Telie, bless her heart, her good will be evil spoken of...isn't that what the Bible warns us to never let happen? Not to mention the fact that Michael is a deacon in the church. If our members hear of this, well, I guess you know what kind of trouble that will cause," she said, with a hint of threat in her tone.

Sighing deeply Nathan replied, "I'll look into it, Mary Grace. I appreciate your concern. Knowing Michael, I'm sure there's a good reason for his behavior. You don't worry about it, I'll handle it." Hanging up the phone, he shook his head. He knew better than to trust Mary Grace. He also knew her history; she was one of the church's biggest troublemakers. It seemed as if he was always putting out fires caused by her careless words and insinuations. *I feel a sermon coming on about those who cause discord among the brethren!* He thought a moment, and then lifted the receiver, dialing Michael's cell-phone number.

"Hey Michael," Nathan said, dreading the reason for his call.

"Nathan! How's it going?" Michael wiped the sweat off his brow and backed away from the noise of the backhoe.

"Oh...same old stuff really. I just got a call from Mary Grace a few minutes ago." He waited, hoping he would volunteer the information.

"Don't tell me, let me guess. She's just so worried about what's going on with Telie and me, right? And I'll also bet that she never mentioned the fact that Telie is sick with bronchitis either."

"That's about right. She's worried about Telie's reputation since you spent the night out there last night." An uncomfortable silence followed as he waited for a response.

Michael laughed. "I've got to hand it to her, she sure didn't waste time letting you know, did she? What did she do – park down the road and stake us out all night? Unbelievable," he said, shaking his head. "Well, this is what's going on, Nathan. I got a call yesterday from Brother Lawrence telling me that they were concerned because they hadn't seen Telie all day. I knew she'd missed church that morning, but I really wasn't concerned...I thought maybe she'd overslept or something. Anyway, when they said they couldn't get her to come to the door, I began to worry. I went down to check on her and found her in bed, burning up with fever. I called Doctor Allen and he told me what to do. She has bronchitis. Mary Grace followed me out there. She knows good and well that Telie is sick and had a high fever. I can't believe she's stirring up trouble like this." He hesitated a moment, then added, "I guess I probably should have asked Martha to come down and stay with her last night instead of staying myself...but I just couldn't leave her. She looked so helpless.

I guess you of all people know why I chose to stay." His voice whispered the last words. "Nathan, nothing's going on between us. I understand my judgment on this is…well, not the best. But I can't lie and tell you it didn't feel good to take care of her. She needed me, Nathan."

Nathan cleared his throat, touched by the emotion he heard in Michael's voice. "So you stayed all night taking care of Telie?"

"Yes."

"Doctor Allen and the monks can vouch for your intentions then," he stated.

"Yes, they certainly can."

"Good, end of story. I'll just warn you though, Michael, Mary Grace is not through causing trouble. I've seen her operate before. You can handle her, I know, but what about Telie? Is she tough enough to weather it?" The question in Nathan's voice let him know that his concern was for Telie.

"She's tough. I believe she can take whatever Mary Grace dishes out."

"Good. I'll handle my end; you handle yours. Let me know if anything else comes up. Tell Telie that I hope she feels better soon. I'll pray for a quick recovery."

"Thanks, Nathan. I'll let her know."

It took a moment for Michael to pull himself together. In a few quick strides he was inside his office. Martha saw the look on his face and decided to follow him and find out what was going on.

"Michael, what's the matter?" Martha stood facing him, looking him squarely in the eye.

"What makes you think something's the matter?" Running a hand through his hair, he glanced at her, forcing a smile.

"Don't play games with me, boy, I know you," she said, aggravated by his little game.

"In a word, or two...Mary Grace, that's what's the matter." He sighed deeply.

"What's she done this time?" Martha rolled her eyes in exasperation.

"She's causing trouble, that's what she's doing." He dug around in his desk until he found a skinny cigar. Biting down on it, he said, "It's nothing I can't handle. She's just up to her old tricks. I should have never gotten involved with that woman, period!"

"She caught you at a weak moment," Martha shrugged. "Don't worry about it. You just let me know if I need to get involved," she threatened. "I would love the chance to tell that girl a thing or two, starting with the way she runs all over people to get what she wants. Unfortunately, you're what she wants and pity the person who gets in her way!"

Michael watched as she strutted back to her desk. He twisted his lips to keep from smiling. She was small but feisty. When she got mad, you'd better look out. He thought better of telling her the whole story, but the fewer people to know, the better for Telie.

"Before I forget," he hollered, "Telie won't be coming in today; she has bronchitis."

"What did you say about Telie? I thought I heard you say she was sick." Martha was at Michael's door again. Gone was the attitude from a second ago, replaced with genuine concern.

"She's better today. Her fever broke last night."

136

"Oh the poor dear, I wish I had known…I could have made some soup for her." Martha walked quickly back to her desk, grabbed the phone and began dialing June's number. She spoke back to Michael, "June will be furious if she's the last to know about Telie."

The other phone line began to ring. "Michael, line one," Martha called out. He picked up the phone and was surprised to hear the voice on the other end of the line.

"Michael, this is Lane, Lane Bennett."

"Oh, hey Lane, what can I do for you?"

"You can tell me about Telie. How is she doing?" Lane's voice was full of concern.

"Telie has a little bronchitis, that's all. Her fever broke last night and she's much better today." Michael prepared to answer the inevitable question as to why he had not been informed sooner. If the shoe had been on the other foot, he would have been furious.

"When Mary Grace called, she sounded frantic! I thought Telie was on her deathbed or something. I was so worried," he said, sounding relieved. "She said to call you, that you were taking care of her, I hope you don't mind. Do you think I need to come down? I'm in Mobile, but I could drive over tonight if you think I need to. She doesn't really have anybody here, you know, all of her family is up north."

"Oh, let me put your mind at ease about that, Lane. Mary Grace tends to exaggerate. Telie is fine, I promise. I'm keeping an eye on her. Martha and June are fixing her up with plenty to eat, so you don't need to worry; she's in good hands. I'm going to stop by after work and check on her. I promise to call you if anything changes."

"Thanks, Michael. I feel better knowing you're there to look after her. Please tell her to call me when she feels up to it. She must have her phone turned off. I haven't been able to reach her for days. Will you call me after you see her this afternoon to let me know how she's doing?"

"I promise." *He seems like a nice enough guy,* Michael thought, fighting the guilt that assaulted him from out of nowhere. *Why couldn't he be a jerk?* Something bothered Michael. Was it the fact that he didn't really want anyone, including Telie's boyfriend, around her? The thought annoyed him. *What's wrong with me!*

"Hey boss," Joe hollered inside the door. "Can you come here for a second?"

"Close the door, Joe; you're letting out all the bought air!" Martha yelled, and then turned around to answer the phone.

Michael got up from his desk and walked toward the door. As he neared, he recognized Sonny standing next to Joe. And a little girl with straight long brown hair and big chocolate brown eyes smiled up at him as he walked out of the door.

Nathan had introduced Michael to Sonny a few months back. He'd thought it odd how she always sat in the back of the church, observing from a distance. *She's really very attractive,* Michael thought. "Sonny, good to see you...and who is this beautiful young lady with you?"

"This is my daughter, Mary Amelia. Mary Amelia, say hello to Mr. Christenberry."

Mary Amelia stuck out her hand. "Nice to meet you, Mr. Chris'berry." She looked at her mother for approval, as if to say, "Did I do that right, Mama?"

Michael was instantly charmed. "My goodness, you have very good manners. Who taught you to be so polite, your mother?"

"Yes, sir." She batted her eyes at Michael.

"Tell Mr. Christenberry how old you are today." Sonny watched her daughter as she held up four fingers.

She clearly favors her mother, just like a miniature replica, Michael thought. "Four, well now that calls for something special, doesn't it?" Michael motioned for Joe, leaning over, he whispered something to him.

Joe ambled off in the direction of the pond supplies. He returned shortly, water splashing over the rim of a glass bowl with a goldfish inside. Taking it from Joe, Michael bent down to Mary Amelia and said, "If it's all right with your mother, I'd love for you to have a new friend for your birthday." He looked at Sonny to see if she would allow her daughter to have the gift.

Mary Amelia looked at her mother with pleading eyes. "Can I, Mama…please, I'm so 'cited about havin' a fish of my very own."

"If you promise to take good care of it, you know that's a big responsibility." Sonny nodded her approval. "Now, what do you say to Mr. Christenberry?"

Mary Amelia reached out with both hands to take the bowl, saying, "Thank you, Mr. Chris'berry. I'll do my best at takin' care of him."

"You're welcome. Your mother's right, you know; you need to take special care of living creatures. So, what are you going to name him?"

Mary Amelia thought about that for a minute, furrowing her brow, then said, "Nate, like Pastor Nathan, he's my friend."

Michael twisted his lips to keep from smiling. "Well, I hope I can be your friend, too." He patted Mary Amelia on the head. She beamed up at him.

Sonny smiled at the two of them, briefly embarrassed at her outspoken daughter. "Speaking of Nathan, that's why I'm here. He told me about Telie this morning. Is she feeling any better? I made a casserole..."

"And some brownies!" Mary Amelia interrupted.

"And some brownies?" Michael questioned with a hint of playfulness in his bluish-green eyes. "Oh, I'm sure Miss Telie will love that. She's a chocolate lover, you know!"

Sonny grinned as she reached over to take her daughter's hand. "If you don't mind, Michael, I'd appreciate it if you would drop it off for me. I've got to take Mary Amelia to the dentist and I'm not sure how long it will take us." She walked over to her car and opened the rear door, picking up a box with several dishes covered in aluminum foil. "There's enough here for you, too." She cast a knowing glance toward Michael.

"Thank you, Sonny. I know Telie will appreciate it. She might share her dinner, but I'll have to get my brownie out now if I want one. It's hard for her to share chocolate," he said, laughing.

As they pulled out to leave, Michael thought how blessed his friend Nathan was to have such a wonderful friend like Sonny. He hadn't heard if they were seeing each other "officially," but he'd noticed the way Nathan looked at her, like she was the most incredible person he'd ever met. Considering all the "talk" his pastor would have to endure, he understood his reluctance to move too fast.

Chapter 18

The next few days crept by at a snail's pace. Every time Telie tried to do anything even slightly strenuous, she fell across her bed in exhaustion.

"Knock-knock," Brother Raphael said. He held up a fresh loaf of bread in one hand and homemade soup in a plastic bowl in the other. A small brown sack sat on top of the bowl. "Brother Simeon sends chocolate," he said, indicating the brown bag.

Telie lifted the bag off the soup bowl. "Finally… someone who understands the healing properties of chocolate." She took the other items from his hands and went inside.

"The beauty of nature…there's something profoundly healing about that too," he commented. He sat down in his favorite chair on the porch, speaking to her through the screen door. "Isn't this a glorious day?"

"I guess that's why we send flowers to the sick and grieving. It soothes the soul somehow and we know it instinctively." She placed the food on the counter. "Want some tea?"

"No thanks, I'm fine. Come...talk with me," he said, patting the chair beside him.

"Oh all right, I'm just trying to be a good hostess." Telie walked to her rocker and sat down.

"So, are you beginning to heal physically?" Brother Raphael asked, lifting his eyebrows.

"Yes. Do I need to heal any other way?" She laughed at her question.

"Most definitely." He looked into her eyes without smiling.

"I guess you mean mentally...funny." She rocked back in her chair, ready to banter back and forth as was their custom.

"No, I mean your heart."

An eerie silence settled over everything as thunder clouds rolled in. After what seemed like an eternal moment, Telie turned to him and asked, "So what do you think is wrong with my heart?"

"It's broken."

She considered his words. "What do you see when you look at me?" She immediately regretted asking the question. Brother Raphael was painfully honest, and she wasn't sure she was ready to hear the truth.

He took her hand in his before replying. "I see a woman who has been wounded. Who thinks she's replaceable. I see a girl trying to live a self-protected life, an empty life that protects her heart. But that same heart aches for intimacy. It's a struggle for her. Like most people, she fears abandonment and rejection. She is lonely and wants to trust her heart to love again, but fear holds her back."

Telie ran her free hand smoothly down the arm of her chair.

He squeezed her hand, and then released it. "Ask God to touch those hurting places and heal your heart. He loves you so much and wants you to be restored. He wants an intimate relationship with you, Telie. He will never leave you."

"How have you gotten to be so intimate with Him?"

"God said to draw near to Him, and He would draw near to you."

Telie wanted to draw closer to God. She felt the distance between them and knew she had only herself to blame.

Brother Raphael asked her a startling question. "Who is sitting on the throne of your heart?"

What a strange question, she thought. *How do I respond to that?* Then it suddenly dawned on her. "My father, my father sits there and has always occupied that place in my heart!" The realization hit her hard. *Mack McCain had her heart...he was occupying a stolen throne! God's throne!* Her mind raced with the implication of what she'd just realized. *How could I be so stupid! How could I do that to my Savior! After all He has done for me! No mere mortal should ever be placed on His throne! I'm the one who put him there, too!*

"You know where I'll be if you need me." He patted the top of her head before walking down the steps.

After a long inhale and exhale she got down on her knees facing her rocker and called out to God. "Oh Father! Please forgive me. How could I have been so wrong, so blind, and so stupid? Give me your wisdom and your guidance to never let anyone ever again take the place that belongs only to you." She placed her face down on her arms, feeling the warmth of an embrace wrap around her. She heard a voice in her spirit saying, "Now forgive him and let go of it forever."

How long she remained there she didn't know, but when she got up, a wave of peace covered her from head to toe. She had dethroned her earthly father and put her heavenly Father in His rightful place, on the throne of her heart.

For the first time in many years Telie felt light, almost buoyant. The heavy burden of carrying around the past and not releasing it had weighed her down. She'd been living a guarded life, not allowing anything to get through her wall of defense. Now the wall felt cracked and weakened.

The evening fell softly with shades of purple and pink streaked across the sky. An easy playful breeze stirred the marsh grasses blowing up warm from the bayou. Sitting in her favorite rocker, sipping tea, she thanked God for His love, His protection and His strength. For the first time in a long time, she felt totally alive.

Gravel crunched under the wheels of Michael's truck as he pulled up to the cottage. Shutting off the engine, he stepped out, lifting a bag from behind his seat. Taking the porch steps in his familiar stride, two at a time, he said, "You certainly look better than the last time I saw you."

"I feel good, too!" She couldn't suppress the smile that spread across her face displaying the joy in her heart. "If I'd known I had to get sick to feel this good, I'd do it all over again," she teased. The wind rose, pulling her hair in different directions all at once, sending her citrus scent past him. Tucking her hair behind her ears, she smiled up at him. "What's in the bag, a surprise for me?"

He came near her, bent down and whispered in her ear, "Chocolate ice cream."

The sound of his deep masculine voice in her ear caused her to shiver.

"Wow...I should have known you'd have a reaction like that to chocolate," he teased.

Hiding her embarrassment, she stood up fast and reached for the bag. "Have a seat. I'll dip some out for us, and we'll have a little sunset party." The screen door slapped against the doorframe behind her as she made her way to the kitchen.

Something is different about her, Michael thought. *I can't put my finger on it. Is it her face? Her hair?*

"Here you go, enjoy," she said, handing a bowl full of chocolate ice cream covered with pecan pieces to Michael.

"Pecans?"

"Uh, yeah…that's the way I like it; I thought you might like it that way too."

Scooping out a spoonful, he took a bite, "Umm… excellent, good combination."

A smile of satisfaction crossed her lips. "Stick with me, Michael, and I'll show you how to squeeze the good out of this life."

Chapter 19

Workday at church had finally arrived, and Pastor Nathan could barely contain his joy. Church members teasingly accused him of enjoying this annual event even more than Christmas! Making the announcement months in advance he had done everything humanly possible to muster up support.

The morning sky was clear, with no threat of rain. White tablecloths flapped in the breeze as ladies arranged dishes of food on the tables outside under shady trees. Platters of biscuits and donuts and jars of jam were scattered across the tables. A large coffee pot covered one table with Styrofoam cups, cream and sugar. Everything was ready for the first round of workers. Around eleven, the breakfast tables would be cleared away and replaced with dinner dishes.

The women manned their stations with warrior zeal as they fought the never-ending battle of the flies. The younger girls tended to the babies, placing them on colorful quilts fanned out on the ground. It was a picture-perfect day.

Telie arrived carrying her work gloves in her hand. Walking past a few ladies, she smiled and said good morning. Heads came together in whispers but she pretended not to notice. Nothing could disturb her today. She felt light and free.

Michael noticed. He'd watched her pull up and get out, walking by the women, smiling and saying hello. It angered him to see how they ignored her. He knew Mary Grace was behind it. "Thank goodness for June," he said under his breath. He watched June make her way over to the girls who were still whispering, and for the first time he really appreciated her bold directness. Whatever she'd said to them put them in their place. Telie was her pet baby, and she was not going to stand for anyone mistreating her!

About halfway through the morning, with sweat trickling down her neck, Telie looked up as a shadow moved across her face.

"May I join you? You look like you're having all the fun."

Telie rested back on her heels and looked at the woman in front of her. She was dressed in an old pair of torn jeans and a T-shirt. Her light brown hair was pulled back from her face with a wide headband; it shimmered in the light. "Sure, I wouldn't want to be accused of having all the fun. I'm Telie McCain," she said, offering a hand and a smile.

"Nice to finally meet you, I'm Sonny Dante." Smiling warmly, she took Telie's hand and firmly shook it.

"I see you're dressed for work. I like your boots," Telie said, admiringly.

"Thanks. I figured I might need to actually work on workday." They both laughed.

Telie recognized her name as the woman who sent food earlier in the week. "By the way, thanks for dinner the other night; it was delicious, especially the brownies. That's probably why I'm back on feet so soon. Chocolate cures all, you know!"

"So I've been told." She sat down Indian style next to Telie and started yanking up weeds. "I am glad you're feeling better. Nathan was so excited about having you helping out this year. Michael sold him on you. But please don't overdo it. I wouldn't want you to have a relapse."

"Don't worry about me. I've never felt better." Telie smiled and it reached her eyes.

Looking into her eyes, Sonny thought it must be true. "I've been inside cleaning the bathrooms and I can honestly say the tile floor is much cooler."

"Maybe…but I'll bet it smells better out here. They just fired up the grill a few minutes ago, and whatever it is they're cooking, it smells wonderful!"

"I don't know about you, but I'm starving. All this manual labor really works up an appetite." Sonny took in a deep breath.

"Do you go to church here?" Telie asked. She didn't remember seeing her, but she hadn't been going long enough to know everyone. That was one of the drawbacks of sitting on the front row. You couldn't scan the pews for new faces.

"Sort of, I guess…well, I'm Catholic." She waited for the usual response but it didn't come. Looking over at Telie curiously, she asked, "Aren't you going to ask me why I'm here? Do I worship Mary, that kind of thing?"

"No." A smile played at her lips. "Why would I do that? You have every right to be here if you want to be," she answered. "I'd like to visit a Catholic church sometime. One of my best friends is a monk from St. Thomas, and I'm just dying to know more about his beliefs. I've been trying to figure out what makes that guy tick for months now."

The shovel speared into a pile of white rocks, making a crunching sound. Michael lifted the heavy load, gripping the wooden handle securely with both hands, tossing the contents into a hole in the parking lot.

"One of these days, Michael, mark my word, we'll have a paved parking lot, Lord willing. And all of this white chalky dust won't get all over everything, including me!" Nathan slapped the chalk from his hands. He glanced over at Sonny and Telie, glad they seemed to be enjoying each other's company.

"We can only hope. I'm sure the ladies around here wouldn't mind it either. I've heard more than a few complaints about what these rocks do to their new shoes." He remembered hearing Mary Grace gripe about that for years.

"Maybe we should start passing out sandals, you know, like Jesus wore. We could have a foot washing just inside the door each Sunday," Nathan said, teasingly.

"Sounds good, Nathan. Let's do it!" Michael glanced over at Telie. It had bothered him that no one had approached her since she'd arrived. But he breathed a sigh of relief when he saw Sonny plop down next to her.

"Tell me about, Sonny," Michael asked, sounding protective.

"Relax. She's a really sweet girl."

He turned his attention away from the girls to look at Nathan, picking up on something different in his voice. "Why does she sit at the back of the church like she's ready to jump and run at any given moment?"

Nathan shrugged. "I don't blame her for sitting in the back near the door." Nathan took the shovel out of Michael's hand and started scooping up gravel.

He looked as if he wanted to avoid the conversation entirely. But that only made Michael all the more interested in finding out why. He had never seen Nathan act this way, without his "holy composure."

"Should she be afraid of God, or of you?" Michael asked, grinning.

Nathan understood the meaning in Michael's words. "Neither...she's Catholic," he blurted out. "That's why she's a little uncomfortable."

"So...is she married?" he asked, facing him square on.

Nathan's face turned a shade darker. "Divorced...with a three-year-old little girl." Never taking his eyes off of the gravel in his shovel, he kept working.

"Four."

"What?" Nathan stopped what he was doing and squinted at him.

"Four. Mary Amelia is four."

"Oh yeah, that's right, she's four." He looked up suddenly, eyeing him suspiciously. "How did you know that?"

"She told me." A smile played across Michael's face. "If I didn't know you better, I'd say you were jealous!"

"How do *you* know so much about them?" Nathan asked. He looked closely at Michael, cocking his head to the side.

"She came by to see me the other day." The look on Nathan's face made him struggle to keep from laughing. Deciding to let him off the hook he added, "And like all good Christian ladies in the south, she'd made dinner for

Telie when she'd heard she was sick." Seeing the relief on Nathan's face caused him to laugh out loud. "Now the question is how do *you* know so much about her?"

"She came by my office a few months back, seeking counsel." He didn't offer any more information.

"Oh?" Michael raised his eyebrows.

"It's not like that, Michael. My secretary Mildred was with us. You know me better than to think I'd ever be that stupid. It's just…well…I don't know. I really just don't know what to think, or why I feel this way." He stretched the handle of the shovel out and leaned on it with both hands, staring at Michael. "I just like her, that's all. She's a good person."

"You want to know why you feel that way? I'll tell you why." Michael enjoyed having the tables turned on his friend. It was rare to ever get the upper hand on Nathan.

"Seems like I've heard that somewhere before." They both grinned. "Just pray for me, man. I need guidance. Sonny doesn't have a clue how I feel. All I know is this: she's an incredible woman. I'm sure God will direct me in all of this."

"Forgive me for being a little shocked, Nathan. It's just that I've always thought you were somehow immune to the effects of women. Many have tried to nab you; still, you've always managed to elude them. I've been impressed, but now?" Slapping Nathan's back and smiling, he reached in his front pocket and took out a cigar. He looked at it and decided to not tempt Nathan too much with his patience. He put it back in his pocket and said, "You know I'll pray for you, my friend. Heaven help us both."

They announced dinner and everyone gradually made their way over to the tables. A welcoming breeze stirred the air as the aroma of grilled onions and hamburgers wafted through the air.

Mary Grace stood behind the first table that held the plates, forks and napkins. Fanning herself with a paper plate, she looked down her nose in disgust as Telie and Sonny approached. "You girls need to clean up before you eat, don't you think? I mean just look at you…all covered in dirt and sweat."

Sonny responded cheerfully, "What's the point of workday if you're not going to work? Besides, I've got some cleansing wipes in my purse; that's all we'll need until we get back at it." Picking up a plate and a fork, she disregarded the snide remark.

Michael and Nathan had walked up to the line in time to hear Mary Grace's comment and the reply from Sonny. Michael turned to Nathan and whispered, "I'm beginning to like that girl myself."

After filling their plates, Telie and Sonny found a shady spot under a tree and sat down. "Wait here, I've got a quilt in my car," Sonny said. She returned with a small pink and green quilt with baby bunnies jumping all over it. "This belongs to my daughter. I don't think she'll mind if we use it. Oh here, grab a wipe. I wouldn't want you to get dirt on your fork or anything." Handing Telie the round tub of cleansing wipes, she sat down and breathed a sigh of relief.

"Are you married?" Telie asked, wiping her hands, then the back of her neck with the wipe.

"Not anymore. I'm divorced. But I do have the most adorable little four-year-old girl you've ever laid eyes on. She's with my mother today. Mom promised her a tea party this afternoon." Sonny took a bite of her burger, chewing slowly and savoring it.

"What's her name?" Telie asked, sipping the ice-cold lemonade June had fixed for her.

"Mary Amelia."

"What a beautiful name. Is it a family name?"

"Why yes. You know every good southern woman has a family name. What about your name? It sounds like a name that has been passed down from dear old grandmother."

"Six generations. I'm Telie the sixth." She batted her eyes haughtily.

"I could tell you were well bred when I saw you wipe your nose with your sleeve earlier."

"That was because a ladybug landed on my nose," she said, covering her mouth as she chewed a cookie. "Whoever made these chocolate chip cookies owns me." Taking another bite she prodded Sonny with her elbow. "Why don't you go and get some more for us before they're all gone?"

"I see how it is...let me look like the dirty, sweaty, gluttonous pig," Sonny chided. "Mildred made them. I helped put them out, so I'm pretty sure I could convince her to sneak us a few more."

"Do it!" Telie poked her. "Which one is Mildred?"

"She's wearing the blue shirt and white apron. I really like her. She's the church secretary, you know." She looked at Mildred with tenderness.

"She has a kind face, doesn't she? Kindness seems to ooze out of her," Telie noted. The affection Sonny held for Mildred was evident on her face.

"She's helped me so much. I've had my struggles. But she's been there for me, so has Pastor Nathan. I don't know what I'd do without them. That's why I'm here, you know, because of those two. I see the love of Christ in them. It's a powerful draw."

"Yes, it is. I've experienced that myself," Telie replied, thinking of Brother Raphael and his Christ-like ways.

Michael and Nathan approached the girls, as they were finishing up their meal. "Looks like we have a few loafers on our hands, Nathan," Michael teased. "Don't they realize we're burning daylight?"

"Well, you always have a few people that come to these things just to be seen and eat up all the food." Nathan winked at Michael, then dodged the grape Telie threw at him.

"Seriously Telie, that's all for you today," Michael said sternly. "You're still recovering from your illness."

"Michael, I feel fine, really," Telie protested. "In fact, I've never felt better in my entire life." Telie stood up and lifted her face to him, smiling.

"End of discussion." He grabbed the shovel out of Nathan's hand and walked back toward the gravel parking lot.

"Well, I guess you heard that, didn't you?" Nathan said, firmly. "Now you girls go on inside and get out of this heat. If you insist on doing something, the bulletin boards could sure use some work. I don't think Michael will mind as long as you're not doing anything strenuous, Telie."

"Okay Nathan," Sonny replied. "Tell Michael I'll watch her like a mother hen." As she looked at Nathan a smile spread across her face.

The current that ran between Nathan and Sonny was so strong you could feel it in the air around you. Telie smiled as she watched the obvious attraction they had for each other play outright in front of her. She laughed to herself as she thought about the impact that would have on a few eligible females in the church. She had noticed the attention young girls paid to her pastor. Bringing pies and cakes to him and inviting him to dinner. He always seemed genuinely grateful, but she had never seen anyone have the kind of effect Sonny had on him.

The long day had finally come to an end. Everyone started packing up. Telie thanked Sonny for spending time with her all day. "I've really enjoyed your company today, Sonny. You're a good partner. You'll have to come out and visit me soon and bring Mary Amelia; I want to meet her."

"We'd love to. Here's my number. You just call me and we'll be there," she said. "I hope we can be friends."

"As far as I'm concerned, we already are."

Chapter 20

Joe spotted Telie near the Bradford pear trees. He meandered his way near her, dragging his water hose behind.

"Hey Joe." She pushed a bucket full of soil out into the path.

"Need some help with that?" Joe asked, as he hiked his hat up higher on his head.

"No, I've got it. I'm just going to re-pot that pitiful looking Jackson vine over there in the corner." Pointing to the vine with its pitiful leaves all wilted and dangling, she shook her head once. "It looks like it needs life support."

"How do you like living out at Bell Forest? You ever get scared?" Joe asked.

"I love it, and no, I don't get scared. Not even after Brother Raphael told me about the legend of Bayou Bell. Have you ever heard that story?"

"Oh man, yeah. That gives me chills just thinkin' about it." He shook once and the water hose turned on Telie, splashing across her face and down the front of her cotton shirt.

"Oh man, Telie, I'm sorry…I bet that was cold too. You know this is well water and it's always cold."

Shaking her head, she said, "It actually felt pretty good, Joe; here, let me show you." She wrestled the hose away from him and turned the nozzle on him full blast, drenching him from head to toe. She bent over laughing as he dodged the spray and screamed. She jerked on the hose to get more slack and yelled, "You scream like a little girl, Joe! Joe? Where'd you go?" Looking around she couldn't see him anywhere. Joe had disappeared.

The bell on the office door clanged. Turning, she saw Michael walking slowly toward her. There was an air of confidence and command about him. He walked with purpose in his stride. Her heart pounded, not from fright but from sheer admiration as she watched him approach. She was certain Joe had seen him coming and took off. *That chicken Joe,* she thought.

When he reached her he paused, taking in her appearance. She was wet and dirty with bits of mulch stuck to her skin. She stood frozen, guilty.

"You're very quiet suddenly," he noted.

It was impossible to read the expression on his face. She didn't know what to say, so she just stood there, dripping, looking helpless.

He was painfully aware of how much he wanted to brush her hair back away from her face and tuck it behind her ear. "Do you have anything to say for yourself?" His eyes moved over her as he observed her disheveled appearance. Strangely, she had never looked more endearing.

She shook her head and looked down. "I'll clean up my mess, Michael." With her eyes still on the ground, she said, "I'm sorry about this. I don't know what got into me." She began the work of winding up the hose, pulling on the long wet muddy line, wrapping it around her elbow and arm in short neat circles.

Michael turned away, aware of his ever-increasing heartbeat. Walking back to the office, he yelled over his shoulder, "Do me a favor, Telie, and try to control your impulse to torture poor Joe, would you?"

Telie's cell phone buzzed from the back pocket of her jeans. Noticing the number, she hurried to answer it. It was her mother calling from home. After the first excited hellos, she found herself trying to convince her mother that she was fine and happy.

"What do you mean, Momma? Nothing's wrong and you don't hear anything unusual in my voice. I'm sorry I haven't called lately; I've just been so busy adjusting to life here."

Telie's mom, Mila, had recently met someone and had been preoccupied with her new relationship, but she really missed her daughter. "Are you happy, Telie?" her mother finally asked.

"I am. I really am."

Then she lowered her voice, adding, "Needless to say, if you should ever want to come home, I'm always here for you. You know that, don't you sweetie?"

"I've never doubted that, Momma," Telie said, before hanging up.

Michael stopped at the door and looked back at Telie. She seemed to be deep in conversation. Sitting cross-legged on the ground while she talked, she was making circles with her finger in the sandy soil. *Probably Lane*, he figured.

"That was quite a show!" Martha said, coming up behind Michael. "I can see Telie is feeling better. I like seeing her playful side. I laughed my head off when she told Joe he screamed like a little girl! I can understand now why June and Telie get along so well; they both love to torture poor Joe!"

"He deserves most of what happens to him," Michael said, unsympathetically.

Martha gazed out the door. "This South Alabama living sure agrees with her, doesn't it? Look at her hair; it's tawny and gold, just like her skin and eyes!"

"Yeah...I've noticed." He turned and walked into his office. "I've got to pull myself together," he mumbled under his breath. "I've got a business to run...acting like some kind of..." he let his voice trail off.

The door opened and Telie walked in, pulling on her shirt to keep the cold material away from her skin. "That Joe is such a chicken. He saw Michael coming and just vanished. I've never seen him move so fast. I still can't find him!"

Martha shook her head. "Too bad Michael had to break it up. It was just beginning to get interesting. I haven't seen a good water fight in a long time. My money was on you," she said with a wink, biting down on the end of her pen.

Leaning on the doorframe watching them, Michael commented, "I'm trying my best to run a professional outfit here. That's why I had to remove 'water fights' from the job description." He grinned. "And for heaven sakes, will you please go change clothes? All we need is for you to get sick again."

Telie slumped forward slightly and shivered. "I don't have anything to change into."

"Not a problem. I've got an extra shirt in the bunkroom." He turned and walked back to his desk. "Oh and Telie," he called out, "do something with your hair while you're back there, will you? We don't want to frighten away the customers!"

She stuck her tongue out in the direction of his opened door.

Martha giggled. "Michael," she called, "you better go and find Joe, get him a dry shirt. He's probably licking his wounds in the tractor shed." She turned to Telie. "Michael's the only parent that poor boy has."

"What happened to Joe's parents?" Telie asked, concerned.

"His daddy is no count, and his mother is just like a dollar, she goes from hand to hand," Martha's deep voice declared.

"Oh, I see." Telie's voice betrayed her sympathy. She walked toward the back thinking of poor Joe and what he must have endured.

The bunkroom smelled like a man, some combination of tobacco, diesel fuel and dirt. Pulling open the top drawer of the old pine dresser, she saw a small stack of T-shirts all of which had the Christenberry logo stamped on the upper left-hand corner. Lifting a dark blue shirt off the top of the stack, she quickly removed her wet clothing and put on the large oversized T-shirt. It fell just below her knees and past her elbows. Adjusting the sleeves, she began rolling them in tight little bands just above her elbows. Gathering up the bottom of the tee, she tied it in a knot and let it hang to the side. "Not bad," she remarked, looking in the mirror over the dresser. She took her brush out of her purse and began brushing her hair into a smooth wave, then twisted it up to secure on top of her head, allowing pieces to fall softly on her neck.

"Well if it ain't the homecoming queen!" Martha stated looking up from her papers. Telie made a mock pageant entrance into the room. "I'll bet you *were* homecoming queen too; weren't you, girl?"

Telie waved her hand in dismissal. "Please, not even close. I wasn't a cheerleader either; they always got on my nerves."

Michael stepped from his office and eyed Telie up and down. "You're right once again, Martha; she does have that royal air about her. I'll tell you what; you can be queen of Christenberry's for the day!"

"Why thank you. What an honor. Where is my corsage?" Telie sat down across from Martha and smiled. "I was wondering when the mums and pumpkins would start coming in. Fall is just around the corner."

Michael answered, "Our growing season lasts a little longer here than what you're accustomed to. Our first shipment of mums should arrive next month. Think you'll miss seeing the fall colors this year?"

Telie shrugged. "I haven't given it much thought. They really are pretty though. We have lots of sugar maples in Coldwater. How cold does it get here in the winter?"

"Oh, it varies. On average I'd say our coldest night might hover somewhere around forty degrees. That reminds me; I'll split some wood for your fireplace at Bell Forest. You'll enjoy having a fire this winter. Maybe that will keep you from getting too homesick." Michael watched her expression waiting for any sign of sadness to cross her face. When none appeared he continued, "Is football big up in your part of the state?"

"It's almost a religion. I'm talking about *high school football,* you understand."

"Yeah, it's the same here."

Martha chimed in. "Well, you happen to be talking to a famous Moss Bay star quarterback, Miss Telie, and I never missed a game."

Michael rolled his eyes. "Martha is one of those fanatical fans we were just mentioning."

Telie looked at Michael. "I bet you also dated the home-coming queen."

"Married her," Michael replied quietly.

Chapter 21

Telie worked in and around the garden at Bell Forest, enjoying her simplistic life. Lane usually called in the afternoons, and they whiled away the evening hours with small talk about the day's events. She knew he was absorbed in his art but desperately needed the diversion their chitchat provided. He had gone back to Mobile to complete a commissioned job his heart just wasn't into. He'd told her as soon as it was finished he was coming to get her for a night on the town.

Men just complicate things, she thought one particularly lonesome afternoon. *All I really need is a dog*. Hopping into her truck, she headed into town to find the nearest animal shelter. It wasn't hard to find anything in Moss Bay. Most businesses were within a one-mile radius. She pushed through the doors of the shelter and stepped inside.

"That one," she said, pointing to a big brown-eyed mixed-breed dog. He had soulful eyes. He wasn't jumping around all over the place like most of the other dogs. While older than many of the other dogs, he had a calm demeanor that appealed to her. He looked as if he couldn't be rattled easily. "He's the one," she said to the attendant.

The dog jumped into the front seat of the truck, and they pulled out, headed back to Bell Forest. "McKeever, that's what I'm going to call you. You just look like a McKeever." Sticking his head out of the truck window, his ears flapping behind him in the wind, he panted excitedly. He looked as if he'd just been released from prison. Every now and then he would close his mouth, raise his ears and follow some interesting distraction from the side of the road.

As the days passed, McKeever turned out to be a wonderful companion. He seemed to know instinctively how to behave and was a pretty good judge of character, too. He announced Brother Raphael each morning as he made his way down the path toward the kitchen garden. He even escorted him home afterwards. On more than one occasion he would appear at the back door, begging for Telie to join him. The only person he didn't seem to like was the mail carrier, Mr. Summers. He would bare his teeth at the man, daring him to step outside of his vehicle. Mr. Summers would honk his horn, yelling unspeakable things. The dislike was apparently mutual.

Michael stopped by to warn Telie of a tropical storm brewing in the gulf. As soon as he got out of his truck, McKeever pounced on him, jumping and wagging his tail with excitement.

"Whoa boy, where did you come from?" he questioned, scratching the back of the dog's ears roughly.

Telie stepped outside when she heard the commotion and walked to the end of the porch. "How do you like the reception committee?"

"I wish everybody got that excited to see me!" Michael said, patting the dog on his side.

"That's McKeever. I picked him out of a crowd of questionable breeds."

Michael laughed, throwing his head back. "Oh, I can see you certainly have a trained eye for good dog breeding." McKeever followed close on Michael's heels every step of the way, down the path and up to the cottage.

"Want some coffee? I just made some."

"Coffee would be great." Taking the steps two at a time, he plopped down in the old willow chair. "I came by to give you a heads-up about the weather. I think we're in for some pretty nasty stuff," he said, rubbing the back of McKeever's head. "A tropical storm warning has been issued."

"Oh...I've been warned." She stuck her thumb out motioning in the direction of the monastery. "Brother Simeon sent word to me about an hour ago. He makes certain I never miss the good ones." She felt pleased by the attention Michael was paying to her dog. She watched the way his strong hand slid over his shaggy fur. The gold band around his finger caught her eye as it gleamed. *Funny...I've never noticed that before,* she thought. *He still wears his wedding ring.* Something ached in the pit of her stomach.

A low rumble sounded in the distance. Trying to convince herself it didn't bother her that he still wore his wedding ring, she stepped inside to get the coffee.

The sky was a dark boiling gray. You could see lightning displayed in random patterns all charged and sharp inside the ominous clouds. Peering out of the kitchen window, she was reminded once again of how God's mighty work couldn't easily be replicated. Not even by an artist as capable as her friend Lane. Pulling out a few cookies from a sealed bag, she arranged them on a plate and placed them on the tray with the coffee. Bumping her hip against the screened door she pushed it open, placing the tray down beside Michael on the small wicker table. She handed him a cup of steaming coffee.

"Want to see my guardian?" Telie inquired, sitting down next to Michael as she took a sip of steaming hot coffee.

"You have a guardian?" he questioned.

She turned to him and mouthed the words. "Glance up slowly toward the monastery and find the glass window facing this way."

Taking a sip of coffee, he raised his eyes past her and almost spewed his coffee. Brother Simeon looked protectively down on them. His hands were behind his back as his eyes stared over the top of his glasses. Regret washed through Michael. He knew he was to blame for the close supervision. He pursed his lips. "From the look I'm getting he may have the wrong idea about the reason for my visit. I bet that kind of scrutiny cuts down drastically on your social life, huh?"

"One day you may realize that being sociable is not my strongest quality," she said with a smirk.

He wondered about Lane and how he played into her social life. She never talked about him, but that didn't mean he wasn't involved with her. It annoyed him every time he caught a glimpse of the painting that hung over the mantle.

In the short time Telie had been at the cottage, she had put her stamp on it, so to speak. He could see into the house from his chair. A pot of colorful daisies sat perched on the kitchen windowsill. She had arranged a wicker rocker that she must've lugged from the back porch to sit next to the front window. A vase of soft roses from the yard sat neatly on a nearby round table near the door, giving fragrance to the entire cottage and spilling out onto the porch. The place had life and warmth, and he loved the serenity of it, just like when his mother lived there.

"I'm impressed with your dog," Michael said, turning his attention back to McKeever. "That's what I call self-control.

You put the plate of cookies down right in front of him and he hasn't flinched."

Telie beamed proudly.

"You can certainly tell he has a fine pedigree. Why, if he were a common everyday mutt, he wouldn't have manners like that." He grinned and sipped his coffee, looking out over the bay at the approaching storm.

"He seems to like you," she commented. "He doesn't feel that way about everybody."

"I seem to have that effect on animals," he mused.

"And some women...I've noticed."

Lifting an eyebrow, he glanced at her. "What do you mean?" he asked curiously.

"Oh, let me see. There's Mary Grace, of course, and a certain woman from Pap's Cove if I remember correctly." She looked at him with an impish grin.

He let out a deep breath. "That was a low point in my life. I'm not proud of it, I can assure you." He hesitated, not sure if he should continue.

"I'm listening," she encouraged. She felt he needed to open up about it, or maybe it was just her curiosity. She'd been told all of her life that confession was good for the soul. She was willing to even use that excuse if it would get him to tell her about the attractive girl from Pap's Cove.

He sat back in his chair. "Not long after the accident I was having trouble sleeping. That was the case most nights, but this...was different. It was Emily's birthday. I couldn't stand being in the house; it felt like the walls were closing in." He ran his hand through his hair, sweeping it back away from his forehead. "I left the house and ended up at Pap's Cove. Let me explain," he hesitated. "Pap's is very different at night. It's one of the few places still open late. The night scene there is…well, you can imagine."

"Seedy?"

He nodded in agreement. "Anyway, I went in. That's when…" there was a pause. Speaking carefully, he said. "I lost it…basically…the grip I'd always had on my life. It just slipped out of my hands. I began to drink, heavily. That's when I met Elle. She came on shift bartending and saw how messed up I was and started paying attention to me. She talked to me as I sat there, miserable and drunk. I kept begging her for another drink but she refused. I'm ashamed to admit it, but I thought I was going to lose my mind that night. I was out of control. I am *never* out of control." He straightened his legs out in front of him and continued. "Elle drove me home after closing. How she found out where I lived, I'll never know. She helped me inside and put me to bed. I passed out and don't remember anything else. She was gone the next morning." He took a deep breath and let it out slowly. "Once I sobered up I vowed to God that I would never let myself sink that low again. I didn't introduce you to her out of sheer embarrassment. I have no idea what I did with her or said to her that night. Only she knows for sure and I've never had the nerve to ask."

"I wish I'd known that story the afternoon we went to Pap's. I would have insisted you introduce me. She could have saved your life, you know. What if you had tried to drive home? You could have killed yourself or someone else!"

"I know, I've thought about that. I've tried to think of some way to thank her, but I've let embarrassment stop me. That's why whenever I see her she gets my undivided attention. I know she's a little rough around the edges, but she has a good heart." He shook his head. "It embarrasses me to think of how I must have acted. I can't even remember what I said to her. I'm sure it wasn't…good."

"I understand. She saw you at your lowest and is still willing to be your friend." Telie stated.

The clouds moved in angrily and the winds picked up, bending heavy tree branches, howling a low mournful sound. "I guess we better go inside or we'll be soaked to the skin." Telie picked up her cup.

McKeever followed closely behind as they walked inside and sat down on the couch. He brushed passed them to arrange himself near the fireplace, circling twice before dropping onto the rug in front of the stone hearth.

Telie pulled her legs up on the couch, tucking them under her. Loosening the small throw from the back of the couch, Michael covered Telie's feet with it.

"How long have you known Nathan? You two seem so close, like brothers." Telie glanced out of the window as the wind howled around the corner of the house. She pulled the throw closer, finding comfort in the warmth of the faded and worn cotton blanket.

"Three years, give or take. We got him fresh out of seminary."

Telie nodded, then smiled. "So, you two hit it off from the start."

"He got here just before my wife passed away. I don't know what I would have done without him. If it hadn't been for him, I'd probably be dead or in an insane asylum right now." Michael stared out the window, lost in thought.

Telie understood without explanation.

"Does Nathan ever date?" Telie asked, straightforwardly.

"Not that I'm aware of. He hasn't shown interest...not until recently that is." Michael realized too late he might have said too much.

"Any chance it's Sonny? She's such a sweetheart." Raising her eyebrows, she waited for an answer.

"He'd kill me if he knew I said anything, but yeah, if it's anybody, it's Sonny." Michael shifted his weight and patted his pocket, looking for a cigar. "I hope things work out for him. I'd hate to think that someone from church would cause trouble about it."

"Why on earth would they do that? You mean they don't want their pastor to date?"

"It's not that simple, not for a pastor. Sonny's been married before. I don't know the circumstances but Nathan knows and I trust his judgment."

"Yeah, she told me she was divorced and about her daughter, Mary Amelia."

Michael's eyes lit up. "Oh, Mary Amelia is a little doll. She was so 'cited over a goldfish I gave her for her birthday."

"Who wouldn't be 'cited over a goldfish!" Telie remarked. "Want some more coffee?"

"Oh no, I'm fine." He covered his cup with his hand.

Telie sat her cup down on the table, then reached for his. Their hands touched briefly causing her stomach to flutter as she placed his cup beside hers. "I know Sonny thinks the world of Nathan *and* his secretary Mildred. She said she didn't know what she would have done without them."

"Nathan never counsels women alone in his office; that's where Mildred comes in. She's invaluable to him, possessing the rare quality of mouth control," Michael said, smiling.

"I hate to admit it, but that's rare even in the church," Telie said, thinking of all the trouble Mary Grace has caused her lately. Telie pursed her lips. "He doesn't strike me as the type to care too much about what other people think."

"You're so right. He only cares about one opinion and that's God's."

"I need to remember that the next time I get a dirty look from someone in church."

His face registered sorrow. "Telie," there was always something affectionate about the way he referred to her, "I'm sorry you're being treated so badly. I wish I had an explanation for why certain people, who claim to be Christ followers, are mean and hurtful, but I don't. Please don't let those few malicious women cause you to think badly of everyone else. Even the Lord told us to leave the weeds alone and let them grow up together with the wheat. He will do the separating in the end."

"I know, Michael, and I won't let them get to me. Thanks for reminding me of that. I never thought about it before, but the *Lord* is the master weed puller."

Chapter 22

Early in the evening the following day, in hopes of catching a sunset over the bay, Telie wandered down the path that led to the shore. A breeze blowing in from the gulf drew her to the water. Strolling along the narrow beach, she looked back at the cottage, tucked back among the trees. *My home,* she thought, *however temporary. It doesn't seem to matter how long you stay in a place; once you claim it for your own, it becomes a part of you somehow, whether through memories or through the giving of ourselves to it, it becomes part of us in a mysterious way.*

Something caught her eye, shining in the garden behind the house. Curious, she walked around the bend and back up the path to the garden in the direction of the shiny object. As she approached, she saw a silver handle jutting out of the ground. Reaching down, she gently pulled out a long silver teaspoon. Wiping off as much dirt as possible, she ran her fingers over the handle. *Hmm, just like the other one, I wonder how many of these are going to come up! I wish my corn would pop up as fast as all of this silver,* she mused.

Lane Bennett didn't have a reputation for being easily accessible. He was a recluse by nature. Michael pulled up in front of Tom Bennett's home and got out, taking the front steps to the door. "I'm impressed," he mumbled, looking over the place. "Nothing flamboyant but reeks of old money." After a brisk rap on the door, a few seconds later an elderly gentleman opened the large wooded door and peered out at Michael suspiciously. "May I help you?" he asked abruptly.

"I hope so, I'm Michael Christenberry."

The old man's eyes lit up, taking in Michael's face. "Yes, son," he said excitedly, as he grasped Michael's hand in a firm shake, "I'm Tom Bennett; how may I help you?"

Tom Bennett was a stately man somewhere in his seventies. He was broad in the shoulders but lean in build. His gray hair was neat and trim; there was a hard elegance about him.

Michael couldn't help but notice how his tone changed. He seemed welcoming all of a sudden. "I'm here to see Lane, if he's not too busy. I was told that I could find him here."

"Oh sure, sure, wait right...oh never mind, follow me." The old man kept glancing back at Michael as they moved through the house toward the back. The expression in the old man's eyes made him feel uncomfortable. He led him out to a sun porch at the back of the house where Lane was seated with his back to them, working on a painting of some sort.

"Lane, this is Michael Christenberry," Tom announced, smiling softly. "He wishes to see you."

Lane turned his head, pushing his chair back with his legs as he stood up. "Michael, good to see you; is everything okay – Telie?" he asked, looking worried. He put down his paintbrush and wiped his hands down the side of his shirt, taking Michael's hand.

"Yes, she's fine, mean as ever." He looked over at Tom Bennett who stood smiling, appraising Michael's height.

"Please then, have a seat," Lane said, gesturing to a patio chair.

Tom Bennett excused himself reluctantly to give them privacy, but before he left, he said, "Michael, please stay and have dinner with us."

"Oh, no thank you, Mr. Bennett. I apologize for barging in on you at dinnertime. I'll make this as brief as possible."

Tom furrowed his brow. "Not at all, dinner is not for another two hours. I was just hoping you'd stay awhile and visit. Please reconsider." With that, he smiled warmly, turned and left the room.

Michael stared after the man briefly, not sure what to make of Tom Bennett. He decided he was just a gracious host, a gentleman from another era. "I have a little business for you, if you're interested, Lane. I was told by my sources that you work in silver from time to time." He reached into his pocket and pulled out the silver teaspoon. "Telie found this on the property at Bell Forest. I think it came from the old Bennier Plantation, part of the silver they buried there during the war."

Lane took the piece from Michael and examined it. He ran his fingers over the intricate design of the etching. "This is exquisite," he said, intrigued. "What do you have in mind?"

"I was thinking of a bracelet. Can you fashion one from it? Is there enough to work with?"

Measuring it with his eyes, he placed it down on the table, tilting his head slightly. "Easily…as a matter of fact, there should be room enough for an engraving on it also." He pointed to where the spoon head rested on the table. I'll form it to make it slender and then make a little silver tag from the spoon head. How does that sound?"

"That would be great. Can you put Telie's name on the tag?"

"I see no problem with that. I should even have room for another word or two or perhaps the date. Maybe Bell Forest, if you like."

"Perfect...Bell Forest it is. Now, I've got another favor to ask of you. I want you to give it to her. It will mean so much more to her if you do." Michael didn't look at Lane; he kept his eyes fixed on the spoon.

"Oh no, I couldn't." Lane's voice was the kind you could trust, sincere.

"I want her to have it. She found it and it belongs to her. I know you two are friends and she will love the thought that you made it for her." He stood to leave. "Just let me know how much I owe you when you finish, and I'll drop by and pay you for it."

Lane picked up the spoon from the table, tapping it in the palm of his hand. "No charge. That's my condition. It will be a pleasure to do this for Telie."

"I really appreciate that, Lane. She'll be thrilled. I know how time consuming things like this can be. I don't work in silver, but I do work in wood occasionally. I'd feel better if you'd let me pay you for it. An artist's time is very valuable."

Lane shook his head. "No."

Just then a cough came from behind them as Tom Bennett appeared. He'd apparently choked. Regaining his composure, he offered Michael a drink. "Let me get a drink for you, son; what's your pleasure?"

"No thank you, Mr. Bennett. I've taken up enough of your time already. I can see my way out." He shook hands with both men and turned to leave the room. Tom Bennett stared after him.

"Have you met Michael before, Granddad?" Lane questioned, seeing the attention he was paying to him and thinking it odd behavior, even for him.

"A few times, but never up close; he's a fine boy, don't you think? He's done well for himself at that landscaping business of his." He paused, wistful for a moment, then added, "I knew his mother."

"Uh, in the biblical sense, Granddad?" Lane inquired, and then laughed at the absurdity.

Tom Bennett spoke calmly. "It's a bit late to be concerned about my past, Lane, my boy."

Chapter 23

Lane worked on the bracelet on and off for a week or so. When it was finally complete, he called Michael.

"Michael, this is Lane. I just wanted to tell you that I've finished the bracelet, and I have to say, it's more beautiful than I ever expected!"

"That's wonderful. When are you going to give it to her?" he asked, excitedly.

"I was thinking of this afternoon. I'll be going back to Mobile in the morning. So, if you're sure you don't want to give it to her, I'll have to give it to her sometime tonight."

"Tonight is good."

"Great. Is she around so I can firm up our plans?"

"No, the last time I saw her she was around back yanking on some vine that's trying to take over the shed."

"That sounds like her, always yanking on something. That's how we met, you know. She was yanking down a vine that had twisted around a tree in June's backyard. I happened to be painting that particular tree at the time of its destruction. I found out quickly that once she gets a hold of something, she doesn't let go easily!"

"Yeah, that's her all right," Michael agreed.

"Would you like to see it first, before I give it to her?"

"I'd love to. I'll stop by this afternoon."

"I'll look forward to seeing you again, Michael."

After the first knock, with Michael's hand still in midair, the door swung open wide. Tom Bennett stood in the doorway, smiling. "Michael, come in, come in, son; it's good to see you." The reception this time was remarkably different from the first. *He probably thought I was a salesman or something the last time I was here*, he thought to himself.

"Sit down, Michael. Can I offer you a drink? Beer, Coke, tea...you name it."

"Tea would be great, if it's not too much trouble," he said, accepting the offer this time. *He must not have guests very often,* he thought, as he sat down on the couch. *Lane seems to be pretty much a loner, absorbed in his art. He couldn't provide much companionship for the old man.*

"Here you go, nice and cold. Julia, our cook, puts in a little mint, I hope you don't mind." Tom handed the glass of tea to Michael. He sat down next to him, observing him intently.

Feeling a little self-conscious, Michael lifted the frosty glass to his lips and gulped down a few swigs. "I'm sorry I'm so dirty. I just got off work. I've been moving dirt around all day. I think half of it stuck to me." He took another big swig of the tea and set it down on his knee, feeling awkward at all of the undivided attention the man was giving him.

"Do you enjoy your work, Michael?" Tom asked, in a manner that said he was really interested to know.

"Yes, more than a man has a right to. It's all I've ever known. I love the land, working with my hands."

"You mentioned you enjoy woodworking. What types of things do you make?"

"Oh I just play around with it mostly. I've made a few tables, benches, things like that. It's really more of a therapy for me. I find it relaxing."

Lane appeared in the arched doorway. "Michael, I didn't know you were here. I'll go get the bracelet." He stopped, turned back and added, "Granddad tells me he knew your mother...small world, isn't it? I'm sure he has plenty of stories to tell you."

"Oh?" Michael raised his eyebrows, waiting for Tom to explain.

Tom's face flushed. He lifted his hands in a gesture of futility. "It was long ago...she was not the kind of person you could easily forget. You favor her, you know, especially in the eyes." Taking out a cigar from a carved wooden box on the table, he offered it to Michael. "Care for one?"

Michael shook his head and raised his fingers to decline the offer. "No thanks." Moving to the edge of his seat, he waited for Tom to continue.

"I remember they had a way of turning from green to blue with her moods. A pale green color when she was mad," he said smiling. "And a deep blue when...," he hesitated a moment, "when she was not." Lighting his cigar, he looked away from Michael, took a puff or two and dropped the match in the ashtray.

Michael felt uncomfortable with the way the conversation had turned. He didn't like the thought of this man, or any other man for that matter, knowing so much about his mother. His mother, Joy, had married late in life and must have had a life before his father entered the picture. But, he certainly didn't want to think about it, not now, not ever. "Sounds like you knew her well," he murmured under his breath.

Tom cleared his throat and said, "Yes, well, that was a long time ago, son. You certainly could never forget someone like your mother. She was a remarkable woman. Tell me, did she ever find time to work on her beach glass creations? I remember walking with her along the beach hunting bits of colored glass. She would get so excited when we stumbled upon one, even though she had buckets and buckets of them: green, blue, white, pink. I can still see her now..." He let his voice trail off, as he looked up through the cigar smoke, lost in thought.

The look on Tom Bennett's face caused heat to rise in Michael. He wasn't accustomed to his mother being the object of another man's interest. His parents had had him late in life; his mother was in her thirties, and his father, in his forties. Trying his best to keep the aggravation out of his voice, he asked, "Did you know my father as well, Mr. Bennett?"

"No," he sighed, "unfortunately I did not. He must've been a fine man. I'd always heard he was a hard worker with a good head for business...and that he adored your mother. He was older than your mother, wasn't he?"

"Twelve years. I remember my mother telling me that it's better to be an old man's darling than a young man's fool. She was certainly his darling." Still not completely comfortable with the conversation, Michael changed the subject and asked, "So, how many children do you have, Mr. Bennett?"

Lane spoke from the doorway, interrupting, as he walked to the couch. "I hope you like it, Michael. I think it turned out really well...excellent silver," he added, handing the bracelet over to him.

Michael turned it around in his hand, admiring the beauty of the piece. "You've outdone yourself, Lane. Telie will love it. It suits her, don't you think?"

"I certainly do. The understated beauty is just like her, authentic and pure." Lane smiled, knowing they both understood the real treasure was not the bracelet.

"You've got a good eye, Lane, and you're very perceptive." Michael handed the bracelet back to him. "Well, I can't thank you enough, now please let me pay you for it."

"Absolutely not," Tom chimed in. "This is a gift for Telie. Money should never enter into it!" Both men turned and stared at him, surprised at the intensity of his words.

"Granddad is absolutely right. It was a pleasure to do this for Telie and a very good idea. I can't wait to give it to her tonight," Lane said.

Michael shook hands with the Bennett men and assured Tom Bennett that he would drop by again.

Tom gave Michael a hearty slap on his back. "I'm holding you to that, son."

As he pulled away Michael shook his head as he looked back at the house from his rearview mirror. The thought of that old man being so infatuated with his mother was hard to take. "I must really favor her for him to get that worked up!" he said out loud.

Chapter 24

A trail of white dust followed after Michael's truck as it came to a stop in front of Telie. She was watering flowers near the parking lot as Michael hopped out of his truck.

"I don't know about you, but I sure could use a shower," she said, as she put down the hose and walked with him toward the office. He held open the door as she lowered her head and walked under his arm. "Have we finished for the day?"

"Yes, are you in a hurry to leave? Got a big date lined up or something?"

"Kind of, Lane called and asked if he could stop by. I think he's going back to Mobile tonight."

"In that case, why don't you go on home? I'll stay behind and help Martha lock up," he said, slapping Martha's desk as he passed.

"Okay. Good night. I'll see you both in the morning." She grabbed her bag off the table and walked out, humming the tune to some old blues song that had been stuck in her head all day.

Arriving home, she hopped in the shower. After the first initial sting on her partially sunburned arms, the warm water felt good. Lathering up, she scrubbed away the day's dirt and grime. Pouring a generous amount of lemon shower gel on a sponge, she massaged it over her entire body, making bubbly circles with the smooth fragrant liquid. After rinsing, she dried off, and worked her hair into a French braid. She put on a white cotton skirt paired with a loose lavender blouse. The warning bark of McKeever told her Lane had probably arrived.

Lane looked as adorable as ever, dressed in jeans and a white button-down shirt. "Come on in, Lane," she yelled out to him.

"Nice dog. What's his name?" he asked, patting the top of McKeever's head.

Standing in the doorway, Telie smirked. "McKeever, but like most well-bred dogs, he's kind of high strung." Telie twisted her lips to hide her smile.

"Oh sure, that's how it is with well-bred dogs." He laughed. McKeever flopped down on the porch, thumping his tail slowly as if knowing he was the object of their attention.

"Come on in, Lane, have a seat. Can I get you a drink?"

"Please, I'll take anything, as long as it's wet."

"How about iced tea with lemon?"

"Sure," Lane said, sitting down on the couch. He noticed his painting on the mantle. "Looks like it was made for that spot," he commented, looking up at the painting.

Handing the glass to Lane, she looked up. "It does, doesn't it?"

Lane took a long drink of his tea, then placed the glass down on the coffee table. He reached into his shirt pocket and pulled out a small silver wrapped box with a tiny pink bow. "Here, sit down." He patted the cushion beside him. "This is for you," he said, watching her face light up. He couldn't keep from smiling; she looked so childlike at times.

"For me?" she said, sitting down next to him. She took the gift from his hand and looked up at him, then down at the box again.

"Well open it!" he said impatiently.

Tearing off the paper, she gently lifted the lid on the box. "Oh my goodness!" she exclaimed. "It's beautiful!" Telie blushed as she searched Lane's face. Casting her eyes to the bracelet again she noted, "I know this design…is this the silver spoon I found on the property?"

"Yes, that's Bennier silver. Michael brought it to me to fashion a bracelet for you. See, I engraved your name and Bell Forest underneath." He pointed to the delicate lettering on the smooth clasp.

"Michael?" she asked, with a puzzled expression.

"Uh huh, he thought you should have it since you found it. He'd heard from somewhere that I worked in silver and asked if I could do it. I really enjoyed the process. That's some of the finest silver I've seen in a while. Just look at the intricate design of the carving…the way it glows," he said, as he ran a finger over the piece. "Put it on."

She opened the clasp and slid her hand through the delicate circle. "It's breathtaking…thank you so much. I'll treasure it always. I can't wait to show Michael how it turned out. He'll be so surprised."

"Oh, he came by this afternoon to see it. He was pleased. I think he was more excited to think of your reaction. I told him I knew you'd love it."

"I certainly do. I can't get over how beautiful it is," she muttered, thinking of Michael. She felt warm at the thought of his attention to the gift and his thoughtfulness.

"Just how grateful are you this time? I hope at least as much as the last time I gave you a gift." He turned his attention away from the bracelet and on to her.

She tore her eyes away from the bracelet and noticed him, waiting expectantly. Leaning over, she planted a brief kiss on his lips. "How's that?"

"I would say fine, but I know you can do so much better."

"How about—"

Her last suggestion was lost as his lips found hers. For a fleeting moment she wondered what it would feel like to be kissed by Michael, but quickly chased the thought away. Lane's lips were soft and warm and intense. She relaxed into his arms as they encircled her, pulling her close. He leaned into her, moving her back until she felt the seat cushion of the couch pressing into her back. She wrapped her arms around his neck, loving the way he felt powerful to her.

Lane pulled away from her lips, then trailed soft and slow kisses across her cheek and down the side of her neck.

Her reaction was swift. Taking both hands, she pushed at his chest trying to break the spell of desire she was under. This feeling threatened to overtake her resolve.

Pretending not to notice the stress Telie was under or how she was trying to catch her breath, he asked, "Why don't we go into town and have dinner." He stood up, reached for her hand and placed a soft kiss on the back of it.

Helping her to her feet, she put her hand on his arm for support.

"I'm a little dizzy," she said shyly.

"Of course you are. You're hungry after working hard all day out in the hot sun. Come on, let's go before you pass out and I try to take advantage of you," he teased.

They sat on the patio of the White Grape under the shade of an old willow tree, branches swaying slightly in the breeze. Soft jazz music played from some hidden place in the landscaping. From the sidewalk, passersby tossed coins into the gurgling fountain, making wishes and dreaming dreams.

Each wrought-iron table had a crisp white tablecloth with colorful green glass jars filled with a handful of flowers, fresh and lightly scented. As the evening progressed, soft white lights glowed all around them, lending a magical feel.

"Enjoying your meal?" Lane asked, as he sipped his wine. He studied her over the top of his upturned glass.

"Yes, almost as much as I'm enjoying the company and the atmosphere of this place."

"The White Grape is famous for quiet repose. I sometimes come here for inspiration," he remarked. "I painted this very courtyard once, but I could never capture the ambiance with my brush." The conversation quickly turned to art and the commissioned job he was working on in Mobile. "I hate to say it, but I'm really finding it difficult to get interested in my latest work."

"Oh," she raised her eyebrows, "what's the subject?"

"A lady and her...cat," he spit the last word out in disgust.

"And you don't like cats." It was a statement, not a question.

"I can't stand them," he stated harshly. "I have even less tolerance for those who treat their animals like they're human. You know the type, they're in the vet's office each week with Pinkie and the pimple that popped up on her bottom...so troubled and stressed that poor Pinkie might be suffering." He shook his head, sipped his wine again. "Are you sure you don't want a glass of wine? It might relax you."

"I'm sure and *I am* relaxed," she emphasized. "You know, Lane, some people are just lonely. People need companionship and something to love, something to take care of. They need to reach outside of themselves, to give of themselves. Maybe that's all your client is trying to do...to simply love."

He shrugged. "Maybe you're right. I've never thought of it that way." He looked at Telie, noticing the soft glow around her hair and the sweet way her lips curled up at the corners, all glossy and pink. Contemplating something carefully in his mind, he asked, "Would you like to go to Mobile with me for the weekend?"

She jerked her hand up so quickly it knocked over her tea glass. A liquid pool of tea ran across the table and onto the stone patio, making a splash. She backed away from the table and bent down, mopping up the spill with her napkin. Without looking up she replied, "To answer your question, Lane, no, no thank you." *What had she done to give him the impression she'd be interested in spending the weekend with him?* Thinking back to the kiss they'd shared, her face went hot. Now she was paying the price for giving the wrong impression.

He grabbed his napkin and began helping her wipe up the spill. "Just so you'll know, I'm not in the habit of inviting women to stay with me often. I just thought you might enjoy some time away." His sandy hair moved in the slight breeze. A charming smile played across his lips, signaling that he really was a good person, no matter what she believed at the moment. "If you change your mind, call me. I'll come and get you whenever you like. No one will know, no strings attached," he continued, "we're similar, I think. We both like our privacy and our freedom. But that doesn't mean we can't enjoy each other on occasion. It does get lonely sometimes."

"Is that the kind of impression I give you," she asked horrified, "like I'm some kind of self-centered pleasure-hungry woman without the ability to handle a long-term relationship!" She could feel the heat rising from her neck, not knowing if she was angry, hurt or just plain embarrassed.

Lane watched her, puzzled, confused by her response.

She stretched out her arms, pushing back her chair and the offer at the same time. Grabbing the edge of the table, she stood facing him square on. "I'm sorry, Lane. Contrary to my earlier behavior, I'm not like that at all. I'm sorry I've misled you. I'm so ashamed of myself for giving you the wrong impression. You see, I'm a poor example of what a Christian is supposed to be. You didn't even know that about me, did you?"

Straightening up, he stepped near her, gently holding her elbow as he looked down into her eyes. The look on her face made him melt. He wanted to bend down and kiss her for how fragile and hurt she looked, but he didn't. "No, I'm the one that's sorry, Telie. I know what kind of girl you are and I've offended you terribly. I could blame it on the wine, but that's really not the source for my thoughtlessness. I hope you can forgive me."

"Of course I forgive you, Lane. I'm responsible for my behavior." Trying to make her voice steady she said, "But if it's all the same to you, I think I'll stay in town awhile. I want to see June before I go home. She can drive me home later."

"I understand," he sighed deeply. In a second, his arms folded around her and they stayed like that for a long moment, locked in a true embrace. His hands moved up and down her back. "I'm so sorry, Telie. Please don't hold this against me. I don't want to lose our friendship."

She moved away from him, speaking softly. "I'm not going to let a little thing like you propositioning me get in the way of our friendship, Lane." She dismissed his concern. "Sometimes desire has a way of doing that to us without caring about the rules we live by. It's only natural. Our friendship will survive."

Telie sighed deeply as she watched the taillights of Lane's jeep disappear around the corner. Wandering down the street, looking in the windows of the quaint shops along Main Street, she was lost in thought. An overwhelming sense of loneliness washed over her, causing her knees to weaken. Crossing her arms, she tried to keep her emotions intact, holding back the tears. She kept walking toward June's house. Everything became a blur. Her eyes stung from the hot tears that finally broke loose, streaming down her face. Overwhelmed, she thought, *How can I live the rest of my life like this, so alone, without anyone?* She doubled over, grabbing her stomach, feeling sick. She kept walking, faster now, determined to get to her destination.

She passed unfamiliar houses, realizing she had made a wrong turn. *Maybe the next block will look familiar,* she thought. The streetlights cast an eerie glow surrounding everything in shadows. People passed, looking curiously at her, but didn't interfere; they let her pass without comment. Frantic, her pace quickened. She stepped around a corner. A massive iron fence covered in vines sent chills up her spine as she walked next to it. She expected at any moment for hands to reach through and grab her. Shivering, she rubbed her arms. Even that small movement felt heavy and difficult. Her breathing became labored as a panic overtook her. The street looked abandoned, only a fine mist hovered over the damp pavement. She looked behind her, sensing someone's approach. She saw a figure standing there and halted her steps, frozen in fear. The silhouette of a man stood facing her, outlined in the streetlight. Without taking her eyes off him, ready to run if he took one step toward her, her mind raced as she tried to think what to do. *Don't faint, breathe,* she told herself.

The stranger walked toward her. Telie bolted, out into the street. The figure lunged forward, grabbing her around the waist. He picked her up off the ground effortlessly, as if she was made entirely of air. She wailed, kicking and punching him as she struggled to get free.

Still holding tightly to her, he backed onto the sidewalk, turning his face away from her flailing arms. "Telie, Telie! It's me, Michael!"

The initial shock of his revelation paralyzed her briefly, and then she collapsed, sliding down his side. He lifted her into his arms, carefully stepping passed the hydrangeas that flanked the gated entrance to his house. Turning the knob on the front door, he moved inside, cradling her against his chest. Walking toward his bedroom, he released her gently onto his bed.

The room was decidedly masculine. The huge bed, covered in a dark gray comforter, felt thick and firm beneath her. The walls reflected a lighter version of the same gray with wide moldings trimmed out in white. Massive furniture in deep mahogany was placed throughout the room. But the fragrance of Michael, tobacco and spice, permeated everything.

He stepped away, returning a short time later with a warm, wet washcloth. He sat down next to her and gently began wiping her face. "It's all right...I just scared you, that's all." He stroked her face lightly. "You're safe."

His very nearness calmed her. Letting out a shudder sigh, she began to feel herself relax.

He sensed her body relaxing. "Now, do you want to tell me why you're out wandering the streets in the middle of the night?" He raised his eyebrows, waiting for her response.

She thought of what she should say. For some unknown reason, she didn't want to betray Lane. But, she also knew she wasn't going to lie to Michael either. Taking a deep breath, she said, "I was having dinner with Lane at the White Grape, and he made a suggestion that I didn't particularly care for. So, I told him I wanted to stay in town and that I'd walk to June's and have her drive me home. I guess I was sort of upset and got lost and that's when you found me," she said, her breath catching as she inhaled.

"I see." Michael winced, but smoothed his expression. "Do you mind telling me what he said to upset you?"

"It was just a big misunderstanding," she said, dismissingly. Casting her eyes at Michael, she hoped he would drop the subject.

He saw the sadness in her eyes and stiffened. "What kind of misunderstanding?" He couldn't hide the concern on his face. He looked down at her wrist, noticing the bracelet, as it shimmered against her skin.

"Well...he...he asked me to spend the weekend with him in Mobile," she blurted out.

"And this offended you."

"Of course it did," she said, giving him an incredulous stare.

A hint of a smile played around his lips. Turning his head to the side, he placed the washcloth on the bed. "So...did you tell Lane what you thought about his idea?"

"Yes."

"And did you give him the same kind of treatment you gave me earlier?" he asked, searching her face and trying hard not to smile.

"No." Embarrassed, she averted her eyes from his.

"That's a pity…I think I got the treatment *he* deserves." Straightening up, he moved to the doorway.

"I think you did too! I'm sorry I lost it on you, Michael. I thought you were a night stalker."

Turning on his heels, he shot her a look. "That's the second time you've insulted me, first by calling me Goldilocks and now a night stalker! I hope my ego can recover from all of this abuse. Come on." He walked back over to the bed, took her hand, pulling her up. "Let's go into the kitchen and have a Coke and an aspirin. I'm starting to ache from Lane's beating."

Chapter 25

Telie took in the surroundings of Michael's home, marveling at the beauty of it. Everything was tastefully arranged and comfortable. The kitchen was designed as a gathering place with a stone fireplace and several comfortable chairs facing each other in front of it. The tall cabinets were a warm mahogany and stretched all the way to the top of the high ceiling with gleaming stainless steel pulls and appliances. Granite countertops wrapped around the kitchen in graceful curves. The room was inviting and elegant all at the same time.

"Your home is lovely," Telie remarked.

"Thank you. This is all Emily," he waved his hand outward. "She had a way with detail and design; everything has her stamp on it around here."

Including you, Telie thought, then chided herself for being insensitive. She saw the admiration on his face for his beloved wife. "That's why you love it here, isn't it? It brings you comfort."

"Yes, I suppose it does."

As she watched him, her heart filled with tenderness. *What is it about him that I find so endearing – is it the loss we both share, or something else?*

Looking out of the kitchen window, into the night, a fog damp and low rolled onto the grounds around the house, settling over everything.

Michael gestured with a nod toward her wrist. "The bracelet looks nice on you. I knew it would." Handing her a small bottled Coke, he placed a plate of cookies down in front of her. "Chocolate chip, right?"

"Right and thank you for the bracelet, Michael, I absolutely love it! I can't believe you thought of it." She reached for a cookie, taking a bite.

He grimaced. "What! You mean you can't believe I have a creative side or a slight imagination? Or that I could actually come up with a good idea."

"What I meant to say was, how very creative of you to come up with such a wonderful idea."

"Ah, it was nothing." His legs straddled the stool. "That's just the way I am. A man of many talents," he teased. "I hope your little confrontation with Lane hasn't given you a bad memory to attach to it." Taking a swig of his Coke, he placed the bottle down on the counter.

"No, not at all, I love it, Michael. But I especially love the thought behind it." She considered his words, then said, "I hope I haven't given you reason to think I'm dangerous or unstable or anything like that. I'm really a mild-mannered person, most of the time."

He laughed quietly. "I'm glad *you* think so. But I'll be on my guard around you from now on, I promise you that."

Yawning, she covered her mouth with the back of her hand.

"You're tired. Come on, I'll drive you home."

The drive back to Bell Forest was uneventful. The fog was thick, like driving through whipped cream. As they turned off the main road and onto the rougher dirt road that wound back around to the cottage, something appeared in front of the truck, crossing the road from the direction of the bayou.

"Did you see that?" Telie asked, alarmed. "What was it?"

"I'm not sure," Michael said, squinting. "Looked like a person, didn't it?"

"What on earth would someone be doing out here in the middle of the night?"

Michael stopped the truck and backed up. "I don't know, let's find out."

He backed up slowly and stopped at the place where they saw the apparition. Getting out, he reached behind the seat and pulled out a flashlight. "Stay in the truck, I'll have a look around."

He disappeared into the fog. Telie locked the truck doors and waited, hoping to catch a glimpse of Michael coming out of the woods. An owl sounded in the distance. "Oh perfect, what'd they say, cue the owl. Could this get any creepier?" she mumbled to herself. The light from his flashlight wobbled in the distance, getting brighter as he approached. Unlocking his door, she waited for him to report on his findings.

"Well? Did you see anything?" she asked, as the weight of his body rocked the truck. Her eyes fixed on his face.

"It must've been Theda. I followed the path all the way to her house," he said, slightly out of breath.

"Theda...who is Theda?" she asked, confused.

"She's an elderly black woman that lives alone back up in the woods. She's lived there all of my life, as far back as I can remember. She'd never hurt anyone."

Wide eyed, Telie asked, "How can you be so sure?"

"When I was a boy my mother told me that if I came across her to be very respectful, that she'd suffered a lot in this life."

"Suffered how?" Telie asked, intrigued and a little spooked at the same time.

"She didn't say, and I didn't ask. I wish I had." He put the truck in gear and eased out down the road. "I remember my mother saying that things could happen to a person that made it difficult for them to get past it. She never explained more than that and I never questioned. But, after our little talk, I looked at Theda differently."

"What do you think she was doing down at the bayou?"

"I have no idea. I remember seeing her years ago gathering flowers and placing them near the bayou. I always thought it might be some kind of a memorial or a remembrance to someone buried there. At one time there was once an old cemetery there. I don't know if she still does that or not. I should've told you about her, but honestly, I forgot. I haven't seen her for years. You shouldn't worry though, she's harmless." He smiled at Telie from across the seat.

"Perfect. I'm officially creeped out. All I need now is to hear that stupid bell!" she said, annoyed. "Michael, I hate to ask you because I know you're tired, but do you think you could stay awhile, just until after I have my bath?" She looked at him expectantly.

"If you promise next time to look before you waylay somebody in the dark," he said jokingly. "You've got a pretty good right hook." He rubbed his chin with his hand, smiled and turned back to the road.

"How's your head?" she asked.

"My head is fine; it's my shin that's killin' me. You must have your boots on. What are they – steel toed?"

"No, I don't have my boots on, just my sandals. That was my toe that kicked you and you should see my toe! I think I broke it!" she grimaced, reaching down to rub it with her fingers.

As they walked in, Michael plopped down on the couch. "Don't you miss not having a TV?"

Stepping into the kitchen, she returned a moment later with an Advil and a glass of water. "Here you go, and no, I don't miss television. I have my own entertainment and excitement around here with bells and ghosts and who knows what else down in that bayou."

"Can't argue with that," he said, tossing back the pill before taking a swig of water.

Leaning back in the tub, she tilted her head and let out a sigh. The hot water soaked into her skin, stinging where cuts tore her flesh. She didn't know how long she had stayed in that position, but her fingers and toes were starting to pucker.

A knock came at the door. "Are you all right in there?"

She bolted up quickly, splashing water out of the tub. "I'm fine. I'm getting out now."

Michael smiled at the sound of sloshing water, imagining how startled she must look at the interruption.

She got out and dried off, pulling on her sweatpants and a T-shirt. Rubbing her hair with a towel, she stepped out of the bathroom along with the steam. "Sorry…you know how it is in a bubble bath."

"No, I don't know how it is in a bubble bath," he looked at her, aggravated.

Smiling, she tossed her towel across the back of the sofa. "I think I fell asleep in there." She picked up her hairbrush from the table and sat down next to him on the sofa.

The smooth movements of her hands while brushing her hair and the slight way she titled her head caused Michael to remember Emily. Many nights he had watched her perform such womanly rituals. Snapping out of it, he asked, "You think you'll be okay here tonight, Telie? I could sleep on the couch if you're afraid."

"I'll be all right. Besides, I wouldn't want you to have to answer to Brother Simeon tomorrow if you stayed. He might not understand."

"Yeah, I don't think he'd buy the whole apparition story, do you?"

"Not likely. But I promise I'll be fine once I get to bed. I doubt I'll even move. Thanks for staying with me while I calmed down."

"Anytime." Reluctantly he moved toward the door. "I almost forgot; you had a call while you were in the tub. I didn't answer; I doubt Lane would understand my being here at this late hour. He's probably calling to say how sorry he is. Please tell him for me that he owes me one."

"I'll be sure to do that."

A mischievous smile crossed his face as he walked out, closing the door slowly behind him.

Turning her pillow over once trying to find a cool spot, her mind thought back to everything that had happened that day. She curled up under the covers, feeling warm and protected, thinking about Michael. She rubbed the silver bracelet around her wrist, wrapping her arms tightly around her pillow. *I think I'm falling in love with that man.*

Chapter 26

Telie awoke to the buzzing sound of someone slicing away with a weed eater outside her bedroom window. Pulling herself out of bed, she peered out the window. Joe was weeding around the house. *What time is it?* She wondered, glancing around at the clock. "Oh my goodness, it's 10:00!" Remembering it was Saturday she relaxed. Slipping on her jeans and a shirt, she stepped outside with her coffee. "Morning Joe, want some joe?" she asked, holding up her coffee.

"Nah, I never touch the stuff. It reminds me of cigarettes for some reason." He wiped his brow with the back of his hand. "I'll take a Coke if you've got one."

She nodded and headed back into the house to grab a Coke out of the fridge. She handed him the drink. "May I ask what you're doing here? Not that I am complaining."

Before he answered, he turned up the bottle and gulped it down smoothly. "Ah…Michael sent me down to help you out today. He said you'd had a rough night and needed your rest," he eyed her suspiciously.

"Oh...well, that was nice of him. I guess he told you about the brawl I got into last night." She peered up at him, waiting for his reaction.

Joe's eyes perked up. "No! What happened?"

She would much rather Joe to believe that she'd gotten into a fight than whatever else he was thinking. She could only imagine from the look on his face. "Yeah well," she twisted her arm around and showed him the scratches and bruises. She neglected to mention that they were all self-inflicted from pounding Michael's body. "It's a long story...but I hear the other guy doesn't feel so hot either. He grabbed me in town last night...didn't Michael tell you?"

Joe propped the weed eater up against the house, giving her his undivided attention, clearly fascinated by the tale. "No...he just said you'd had a rough night and I needed to help out down here."

"Oh...well, I've probably said too much already. Thanks for helping, Joe. Let me know if you need anything from the house." She turned and walked back up the steps, leaving Joe gawking at her retreating form.

"Poor Joe," she snickered. Something about him just made you want to tease him. "I can't wait until he asks Michael about it."

Across the yard, she saw Brother Raphael coming down the path, McKeever matching his every step. "I see you've stolen the affections of my dog once again, Brother Raphael," she shouted, over the noise of the weed eater.

"It seems like it, doesn't it? He was resting in his usual spot under the willow tree until I finished with morning prayers. You know, I think he's got some Australian Shepherd in him. You should see the way he corrals those geese down at the pond," he said, patting McKeever on the head.

"You're not suggesting my dog is some kind of a half-breed, are you?" She peered at him as he walked up the steps.

"Half, certainly not, anyone with half an eye can see that what we have here is a fine example of an undiscovered rare breed of dog." Brother Raphael pursed his lips.

Warmth spread around inside her when she laughed with Brother Raphael; she truly enjoyed his company. She'd often thought if she ever had a chance to pick out a brother, she would pick him, hands down.

"I saw your lights on late last night; did you get scared or hear bells or something?"

"I think monks have way too much time on their hands." She shot him a sideways glance. "And for your information, I'm not scared of anything, not even bells!" She wondered if the monks knew about Theda. "Tell me, have you ever seen an elderly woman down by the bayou? I'm just curious," she asked, displaying an "I'm mildly interested" look.

"You mean Theda?" he questioned, seeing her nod. "Not for a few years now. Why? Did you see her?" Brother Raphael leaned against the porch railing. He wiped the dog hair off his hands and narrowed his eyes, intent on what she was saying.

"Last night when Michael brought me home…"

"Michael?" He interrupted. "But I thought you left with Lane…Brother Simeon saw you."

"What? I guess I'm going to have to send ya'll a copy of my agenda before I leave Bell Forest from now on. I'd hate to cause confusion over there." She shook her head in disbelief and glanced over her shoulder toward the monastery. "Long story, anyway…we were coming down the road by the bayou and this ghostly figure passed in front of us…out of the fog…out of nowhere and disappears into the woods. We could tell it was a person. Michael got out and searched the woods, but all he found was the trail that led to her house. He followed it a little ways, but never saw her. He said it was probably Theda since the trail led back to her house."

"Mmm, I wonder what has her stirred up, or if she has always waited until nightfall to come out and prowl." He rubbed his chin. "Now that's interesting."

"That's interesting? That's freakin' me out! What is she doing out there? Does she wander around all over the property at night?" Plopping down on the steps beside him, she cleared her throat. "I have to know what she's doing out there. I *have* to know."

"You could always stay up to find out," he suggested, and then grinned really big.

She chewed on her bottom lip for a minute. "You're absolutely right! We'll stay up and hide near the bayou and wait for her! That's a wonderful idea, I'm glad you thought of it."

"We?" he questioned. "I don't recall mentioning 'we.' I distinctly remember saying 'you.'"

"You don't think I'm stayin' out there at night all by myself, do you? After all, it was *your* idea."

"What happened to the girl who said she wasn't afraid of anything?" He pushed off the railing with his hands; a smug look crossed his face as he headed back toward the monastery.

"See you at 10:00 tonight," she called after him.

That night they sat behind the undergrowth near the water's edge. Neither of them had seen or heard Theda coming, she just seemed to materialize in front of them.

They sat completely still. Telie's knees were pulled up with her arms wrapped tightly around them. They waited and watched in the darkness.

Theda held her hands together as if in prayer and sank down to her knees in the dirt next to the bayou. An eerie call from a night bird sounded from a nearby tree, giving the impression some ancient ritual was about to be performed. After a minute, they saw her toss a bouquet of wildflowers into the inky black water. The moon shone down on half of her face, giving it an eerie glow. Her dress moved back and forth with the breeze. She rose slowly and deliberately to her feet. Turning around, zombie-like, she walked back up the path as if in a trance. She never looked to the right or to the left as she disappeared into the woods.

"You're shaking. Are you scared?" Brother Raphael asked. He placed a hand on her arm trying to calm her.

"I'm fine. I told you, I'm not scared of anything...I just do that sometimes. So, what do you think *that* was all about?" Telie whispered. Getting up, she dusted off the back of her jeans.

"I'm not sure," he pondered. "It looks like some kind of an offering. It makes you wonder what's down there...what's she making the offering to. You're shaking again," he said, taking both hands to steady her.

Telie looked annoyed. "Why did you have to put it that way? Why couldn't you just say it looked like a memorial of some kind, that's what Michael said."

"Okay...it's a memorial of some kind," he repeated.

"Don't you think it's strange that McKeever didn't bark or growl at her? He just sat there and watched her come and go." She kept her eyes on the woods, fearing Theda might return and hear them discussing her. "Come on. You're walking me home," she stated, flatly.

"Of course I am. What kind of a gentleman would I be if I let you walk home without an escort, especially on a night like *this*?" He widened his eyes, trying to look scary. "Lead the way."

The night was soft, the kind of summer night you remember from childhood. Lightning bugs flashed all around like twinkling Christmas lights. She remembered chasing after them and the way watermelon seeds squished between her toes as she ran barefoot through the night grass. Telie sighed, thinking lastly of her magnolia tree and the many nights she would spend up in the branches of that enormous tree, staring at the summer moon.

"Nice night, isn't it?" she noted.

"I was just thinking the same thing." Brother Raphael kicked a rock out of the path and asked, "Do you ever miss home, Telie?"

"On nights like this I do. If I was eight, I'd be perched up in my tree, pretending to sail the sky."

"Your tree, you have a tree?" There was a surprised tone to his voice.

She didn't know if the words would come out. "Well," she swallowed hard, "I did have a tree. They chopped it down recently."

His face became soft. "It hurts to lose something you love, doesn't it?" he said, stopping at the back porch to the kitchen. "But you still have the memories," he added. "Sounds like you had a good childhood."

"I did…maybe that's all that's wrong with Theda. Maybe she just lost something she loved."

"Maybe so. Goodnight, Telie, and sweet dreams." Glancing back over his shoulder he couldn't resist teasing.

"Whatever you do, don't go back out tonight. You never know what may be lurking in the bayou."

As she closed her eyes that night, she could still see Theda's time-worn hands tossing flowers into the still waters of Bayou Bell.

Chapter 27

Telie was grateful the service had not yet started as she rushed down the aisle to take her seat beside June. Glancing around, she noticed Michael, sitting in the pew beside Mary Grace. Mary Grace was glaring at her smugly with her arm hooked securely through Michael's.

Turning her attention back to her lap, Telie lifted out a hymnal. Her face burned hot as she pretended to thumb through the pages. Her thoughts were on Michael. *Here I go again,* she thought. *Why do I always allow that man to distract me from worship? What is it about him that gets to me?* Out of the corner of her eye she caught a glimpse of June, her eyes sweeping over her.

"Are you all right, dear?" June whispered.

"Fine, why do you ask?"

"Your song book is upside down."

Snapping it shut, she placed it beside her. Feeling embarrassed, she grew quiet. June didn't say anything more, but by the twist of a smile that played on her lips, she knew that she understood something. Maybe something more than Telie understood herself.

Taking a deep breath, she tried hard to focus on the message.

She liked Nathan's style of preaching. It was strong and to the point. He rarely repeated words, so you listened carefully so as not to miss anything. There was something different in his voice today, something indefinable. Watching his expression go from serious concern to joyful abandonment all in a matter of seconds kept her riveted to his words. Thankfully, she needed the distraction. *Why should she care if Michael chose to sit by Mary Grace; it's a free country,* she thought inwardly.

After the service, June patted Telie's leg and walked over to speak with Mildred. She lingered in the pew, not wanting to watch Michael and Mary Grace walk out together. She waited for the church to clear out, all the while fumbling with her Bible. Glancing around, she saw the backs of a few stragglers, but for the most part, everyone had gone. She stood up and smoothed her skirt, propping her Bible on her hip as she made her way to the back of the church.

Telie paused briefly to say goodbye to June and wave at Nathan before descending the steps to the church parking lot. She rounded the corner just in time to see Michael helping Mary Grace into his truck. He glanced up at Telie, and then got into his truck, pulling away in front of her.

She wanted to disappear, vanish from sight. She didn't want to be there, at that moment, witnessing their departure. She didn't want to be seen by either of them, but she had. Passing directly in front of her, Mary Grace waved franticly, a sly smile plastered on her face.

Why should I care, she thought. *Go squeeze a few shrimp, Mary Grace, enjoy yourself.* Ashamed for allowing such harsh thoughts to creep into her mind, she admonished herself. "What's the matter with you? You haven't been out of church five minutes and you're already being witchy." She shook her head, disgusted.

Telie pulled out of the parking lot. Thoughts of going home didn't appeal to her, so she drove slowly wondering which direction to head. "Where to go." She tapped the steering wheel with her finger. "I need lunch," she told herself.

Pastor Nathan's sermon had challenged her that morning. Floating around in her mind were his words, "As a believer, you represent Christ to this lost world." Passing by Pap's Cove, she pulled off the road and slowed to a stop. Sitting for a while, she began arguing with herself and making excuses as to why she should leave. From the corner of her eye she saw the side door at Pap's swing open and Elle came out with a trashcan in her hand.

She waited in her truck, wrestling with the idea of going inside. "What else do I have to do today? Go home and feel sorry for myself." She took a deep breath and got out of the truck, crossing the road to the establishment. Entering the dining area, she looked around with new interest. The "after church crowd" was there. You could easily identify them as the ones dressed in "church clothes" with crayons and covered cups with straws scattered about. In the light of day it was hard to imagine the restaurant had a seedy side. The sun was reflecting off the cheerfully colored boats docked outside as they bobbed up and down in the harbor. The wake from a nearby boat troubled the waters, turning them a frothy green.

"Table for one?" asked the waitress. Her bright red lipstick was creeping outside the natural line of her lips.

"Yes, please." Telie answered.

She led her away from the noise of the other diners to a corner table near the bar. Handing her a menu, she asked, "What can I get you to drink, sweetie?"

"Tea please, un-sweet." *What am I doing here*, she thought. Elle brushed passed her just then on her way to the bar.

"Hey Elle, what's good today?" she asked, looking down at the menu, trying desperately to sound nonchalant.

Elle stopped, turned around and stared at Telie, not recognizing her. "Oh, I think it's the blackened Amber Jack. That seems to be the favorite today." Her voice was soft and as smooth as silk.

"Umm, that sounds good. I think that's what I'll have. Have you had lunch?"

"Me?" She sounded surprised. "Uh no, but I'm supposed to go on shift in about ten minutes."

Telie responded with a nod of understanding. "I believe we have a mutual friend...Michael," Telie said, smiling up at Elle. She knew the mention of his name would guarantee attention.

"Michael Christenberry?" A pleasant smile crossed her lips.

"Yeah, he's my boss. I came in here with him the other day. I remember you from then." She left out the part where she had been completely ignored by the girl in her total absorption of Michael.

"Oh yeah, that's right. I knew you looked familiar," she said politely with renewed interest.

Telie didn't wait for her to speak again, but said, "Sit down and talk to me until your shift starts. I hate eating alone."

"Okay sure, I'll just grab a drink. Would you like a refill?" Elle's face relaxed.

"No, I'm fine," she said, pushing out the chair next to her. It seemed she had already made a friend. Their shared interest in Michael brought them together.

They chatted all during lunch, small talk mostly and almost exclusively about Michael. Elle's ten minutes turned into thirty as she lingered at the table with Telie. The ease of conversation seemed to surprise them both.

"I was hungry," Telie said, placing her napkin beside her plate.

"Yeah, I noticed." Elle laughed, looking down at Telie's clean plate. "How do you manage to stay so small and eat so much?"

"Manual labor, it's better than aerobics," Telie said jokingly.

"Manual labor...aren't you Michael's secretary?" she questioned.

"Hardly, I'd go crazy if I had to stay behind a desk all day...every day!"

The crowd thinned out with only the occasional so-called "regulars" coming in from the docks. A few men approached the glass doors on the bay side, wearing the typical yacht wardrobe. A nice-looking man with an average build and dark curly hair stepped inside. He scanned the dining room after pushing his sunglasses to the top of his head. As his eyes adjusted to the dim light, he noticed them.

"So, what do you do for Michael?" Elle asked Telie, lighting a cigarette and pretending not to notice the new arrivals. Turning her head slightly, she blew the smoke from her cigarette over her shoulder.

"I sell plants mostly. You know – trees, shrubs and flowers. I also mow and weed gardens, clean out ponds...that kinda thing."

"You like that kinda thing?" Her eyes held a hint of surprise.

"I'd never do anything else," she said, sipping her tea. "By the way, I'm Telie McCain." Telie stuck out her hand.

"Nice to meet you, Telie," Elle said, grasping Telie's hand as she stood up. Elle leaned over the table to smash out her cigarette with her free hand. "I'm Eleanor Bragwell. But please, call me Elle."

The man with the dark hair walked slowly across the room and up to the bar. He stood with his hands on the bar, leaning into it as he looked around. His companions had taken a table near the windows facing the docks. They cast knowing glances at their friend and mumbled under their breath, laughing.

"Oh…better get to work." Elle got up and walked behind the bar. "What can I get for you?" she asked the man.

"What all do you offer?" he asked, casting a glance over at Telie.

"Well, it's Sunday so your choices are limited to soft drinks and…she's not on the menu." Elle picked up a rag and wiped it around in circles as she waited for the man to reply.

"That's too bad. Looks like I've missed out all the way around." He flashed Elle a smile and then asked for an iced tea.

This man could turn on his charm at will. She was sure it was a weapon he used whenever necessary. Elle had seen his kind before.

"Listen, I'm David Austin. All I want to know is her name and where she's from, that's all."

Elle couldn't resist the attention the man was giving her. She smiled back at him, leaned over the bar and whispered, "It's Telie and all I know about her is that she works for Michael Christenberry and she's a really nice person."

He nodded, slid his tea glass off the counter and walked toward Telie's table. "May I join you? You look terribly lonely over here now that your friend has abandoned you."

"Oh, I'm still here," Elle chimed in, walking up behind him. She had no intention of leaving Telie alone with the stranger, no matter how attractive and obviously wealthy he might be.

"Perfect, two beautiful girls to share a drink with. By the way, I'm David Austin, and you're Telie. I was waiting for an introduction, but your friend here thoughtlessly forgot to make them."

"Oh, I'm sorry. I had something else on my mind. I was just going to ask Telie if she would help us out around here with a little landscaping. You'd have a clean slate to work with, that's for sure. There's nothing out front, only sand and a few rocks. It looks like the aftermath of a nuclear explosion."

"Umm, sure, I'll ask Michael and see if he'll let me have a few plants. Do you think your boss would mind me digging around on his property?"

"Heck no, he'd be thrilled. There's no telling how much business we've lost over the years because of the way this place looks from the road. People driving by think we're some kind of a rathole."

"I'll see what I can do." She took a sip of her tea, placed the glass down gently on the table and looked at the man who so brazenly sat down next to her.

"By the way, ladies, I'd consider it a privilege if you'd join us out on the boat this afternoon," David said. He kept his attention on Telie.

"No thank you, I've got to be going. Thanks for having lunch with me, Elle." She made a mental note to talk to Michael in the morning about letting her have a few plants. "It was nice meeting you both." She grabbed her purse and headed out the door.

Chapter 28

There was no getting around it; it bothered Telie that Michael was out with Mary Grace. It had nagged her all afternoon. Mary Grace's smug face annoyed her. *Why are they together? I thought Michael said he had to be forced to go out with her.* Trying to block the thought out of her head, she grabbed a lightweight lawn chair from the back of the truck.

After changing into a comfortable pair of jeans and a T-shirt, she picked up a book from her nightstand and bounced down the steps. She lifted the lawn chair up with one hand and headed down the path toward the bay. McKeever led the way, his tail wagging as he sniffed the trail in front of them.

She chose a secluded spot, away from the appraising eye of the monastery. The fortress forever loomed in the background like a watchful brother. Taking a deep breath, she relaxed as the sound of the gently lapping waves soothed her soul.

The sunlight gleamed against the water, going dark at each passing cloud, then emerging again, brighter than before. A blue heron flew overhead, gracefully going on its way. Telie settled into the easy rhythm of the bay. The water calmed her mind, soothed her soul. She stared out to where the sun lowered into the bay. Tossing her book aside, she absorbed the serenity around her.

"Am I disturbing you?" Michael's voice came from behind, startling her back to reality.

"No, no, not at all, I'm just relaxing. Come, join me," she said, beaming. She tucked her hair behind her ears. "Are you by yourself?" she asked, looking behind him. Her heart beat wildly at the sight of him.

"Yes, thank goodness. I made my escape right after lunch. They'll just have to manage without me." He looked out over the water as if something else needed to be said. Pulling up a stray piece of driftwood, he sat down.

"They?" She looked confused.

"Yeah, Mary Grace, Nathan and Sonny. Mary Grace had a cookout for Nathan's birthday. She'd invited Sonny and me. Nathan wouldn't go unless I did and I could tell he really wanted to go. It had more to do with Sonny being there than Mary Grace. I can assure you." He ran his hand through his hair, looking out at the water again. He turned his attention to her, the deep bluish-green eyes fixed on her. "You would've been proud of Sonny. She handled herself well, considering. I think she enjoyed seeing Nathan squirm. Mary Grace was making a big show of everything as you can imagine, but the look on Nathan's face was priceless!"

"I'm glad Sonny and Nathan finally got to spend some time together. Do you think they're serious?" she asked, looking over at Michael.

"I think he's very interested in her. I've never seen him act like this before. I mean the fact that he went to Mary Grace's for a birthday party tells you he's serious." Michael picked up a stone and skipped it through the water.

Without warning, McKeever bounded toward the water, splashing as he chased after the rock, drenching Telie.

She sprang to her feet with her mouth open, her face dripping from the splash.

Michael shot up, grabbing the corner of his shirt. "Hold still," he said, laughing. He leaned over her and began carefully blotting her face.

They stood facing each other. His smile was warm and inviting as he pressed the cloth to her cheeks. She could smell the faint scent of cigar mixed with peppermint on his breath. His nearness caused a reaction in her she never expected. Her pulse raced; her heart pounded in her chest so violently she was afraid he'd hear it. As she looked down, he put one finger under her chin and raised it up slightly. Moving closer, his lips formed around hers. She responded to his kiss with caution at first, then, as his arms encircled her and he pulled her near, a passion built between them. Barriers began to crumble in that one endless moment. She felt safe, cherished, with his warm lips enveloping hers. Her head began to swim with delight. Nothing else mattered, not one other thing except for his arms securely wrapped around her.

Michael pulled away first and searched her eyes, still holding on to her.

She was out of breath, embarrassed by her response to him.

"I've wanted to do that for a long time. I hope it was all right."

She nodded, but couldn't speak. *Oh, it was better than all right, I want to say. In fact, all I want is to be lost in your arms again.*

With his arms still around her waist, he spoke low into her ear. "A while back, I came to the realization that I have feelings for you, Telie. I'm not sure what to do with them... if anything. I'm surprised by the way I feel about you and a little confused about it all. Seeing you walk by this morning as I drove off with Mary Grace made me physically ill." He sighed deeply. "I understand that you and Lane have a relationship, and I shouldn't have kissed you. I'm not sorry, but it won't happen again."

She didn't speak, but listened to him intently.

"Emily was the love of my life. I've never been with anyone else...as far back as I can remember, it's always been Emily." He stared at Telie, and then released his hold. He sat down again on the driftwood.

Telie felt her lips go dry as she stood in front of him and listened while this man who had just kissed her so passionately revealed his love for his wife. She envied the deep bond they still shared, a bond so strong that, even after death, remained.

"Today," he continued, "I felt like my heart was being ripped out of my chest when I drove away from you. All I wanted to do was grab you and take you with me without a thought to Lane, Mary Grace or anyone else for that matter."

Feeling lost in his words, her eyes widened as she blinked back tears. She stared down at her hands, without words, feeling the lump tighten in her throat.

Michael watched her, trying to read the expression on her face. "I'm sorry, I've made you uncomfortable. I didn't mean to drop all of this on you like this, but I needed to tell you what I was feeling. I am well aware of the fact that I'm also your employer. However, I want you to know that I'll never cross that line again, unless invited."

Recognizing an opening, she spoke softly, "Michael...Emily was a very blessed woman to have the love of a man like you. I'm not sure there's enough of you left for anyone else right now, and that's okay...I don't think I'm ready to trust my heart to anyone anyway." She reached down for his hand, lifted it to her lips and kissed it softly, rubbing the gold band around his finger with her thumb. "Your heart belongs to her."

He sat in stunned silence, trying to absorb her words. He knew she was right but he wanted her to be wrong. She had put her small thumb on the evidence. He was still clinging to the past love and life of his long dead wife.

That night as he sat at his kitchen table, lost in thought, his mind kept circling around the words Telie had spoken to him that afternoon. Propping his elbows on the table, he clasped his hands together and sat, staring at nothing in particular. *She's right, of course. I haven't let go of Emily. Nathan tried to tell me that very same thing.* He got up, walked around the bar and began making a fresh pot of coffee.

He looked around the kitchen. It was just the same as it had always been. As if Emily had just stepped out to run an errand, everything was exactly the same. Bending over the counter he twisted the wedding ring on his finger, thinking back to the kiss he'd shared with Telie. Feelings had been awakened in him he thought long gone and impossible to experience again without Emily. The memory of Telie's warm body clinging to his caused his heart to race. He caught the slight scent of her on his clothes. Dropping his head into his hands he grieved over his loss and over his life.

Rising up he reached over, got the coffee pot and poured a cupful. Looking down he noticed Emily's rings still in the little ceramic bowl next to the sink. She'd removed them the night before the accident before sticking her hands into the soapy water…three years ago! "She must've forgotten to put them back on that morning in her rush to her doctor's appointment," he mused. *Those rings have been there for three years! Everything has been the same here; nothing has changed in three years! I'm so stupid!* "Of course Telie would notice I haven't gotten over my wife! A blind man would notice," he said, angrily. "Is this how you want to live the rest of your life? Is this how Emily would want it?" He knew the answer to that question. The only question that remained was how to begin. He reached over, picked up the phone and began dialing Alexandria's number, Emily's sister.

After a few rings Alexandria answered, "Hello."

"Alex, this is Michael. I was wondering if you could come over. I've got some things of Emily's I want you to have."

Alex stammered, "Sure Michael. I'll be right over."

Hanging up the phone, he waited for Alex and for the hardest part of letting someone go. "Lord, please help me get through this," he prayed out loud. "Help me move forward with the life you've given me."

For the next few hours Alex and Michael sorted through Emily's belongings. Alexandria Whiteside was so much like her sister. Her gentle nature and soft voice reminded Michael of his wife. It pleased him to hear Alex say she would always cherish Emily's possessions and pass them down to her daughters whom he and Emily loved so much.

It was late into the night when they had finally finished going through all of Emily's things. They'd laughed and cried over each memory of their beloved wife and sister. Michael loaded down the back seat and trunk of Alex's car, then turned to her and handed over Emily's rings. "Give these to our girls. Emily would want them to have them. She loved her nieces so much, and I know they loved her, too."

With a tender embrace, Alex choked out a reply, "Oh Michael, thank you. I know how hard this has been for you. It's been so difficult for all of us. But I want you to know that we are so grateful to God that Emily had you for a husband. She loved you so much! I know all Emily would want is for you to find happiness again in this world."

Swallowing down the lump in his throat, he turned back to the house as her car lights ran across the yard. Relief washed over him. It was done. The thing he had dreaded for so long was finally over. He walked into his bedroom, opened the top dresser drawer and twisted off his wedding ring. He placed it in a small black box and shut the drawer.

Chapter 29

"Why can't you just be honest and tell me flat out? Why do you have to run away from me? All I'm asking is why?"

Exasperated, Telie spun around on her heels. "I told you why, Mr. Austin. I don't want to go out with you, period." Telie brushed away a stray piece of hair from her cheek.

"But why, I don't understand." David Austin persisted, following Telie's every step. "Are you serious with someone else? Is that it?"

"No, that's not it. I'm just not interested in going out with you, that's all." She loaded the last of his pecan trees, squinting against the sun. "Nothing personal, I'm just not interested."

"Do you know who I am?" he asked, piercing her with his eyes.

She didn't know and didn't care, but she decided not to answer. She wasn't certain who he was, but she'd noticed how Joe had stepped and fetched for him all afternoon like he was royalty.

He made a move and cornered her, backing her up to a post. She held her head high and met his gaze dead on.

Michael appeared out of nowhere. "Can I help you, Mr. Austin?" he asked, trying to make sense of the scene before him.

"It's okay, Michael," David said. "I'm just trying to explain to this girl who I am." He continued to glare at Telie, trapping her against the post.

"I'll introduce you. Telie, this is David Austin. David, Telie McCain." Michael stepped toward Telie; taking her arm he moved her behind him and stood facing David.

"It's not that, Michael. I know who she is; she just doesn't understand who I am and how things work around here. I simply asked her to dinner. But, she has refused my invitation," he said, amazed at the refusal. "I'm not used to being turned down so flatly but it's okay."

"It's not okay if you've upset Telie," he warned. "You have your answer, David. The lady has refused your invitation, now leave it alone. I suggest you go before I lose what little patience I have left for you."

A smile tugged at Telie's lips as she peeped out from behind Michael's shoulder. She fought the impulse to stick out her tongue; instead she raised a mocking eyebrow.

"Need I remind you, Michael, of just who you're dealing with? If it wasn't for my grandfather and all the business he throws your way, you wouldn't *have* a business!" he said, measuring his words with malice. "Remember that the next time I ask for something from around here." He released his words as he walked away.

"Are you okay? He didn't hurt you, did he?" Michael asked, wanting to take her in his arms and hold her.

"I'm fine. He's just a jerk. Who is that guy anyway?" she asked, staring after him. She watched him signal to the driver

223

of the truck hauling the load of trees before getting into his black Mercedes.

"That's David Austin. He owns the largest shipyard in Mobile; well, his family does. His mother is a Bennett. Lane is related to him somehow, a cousin, I guess. He's just a spoiled brat, always throwing his weight around. People around here cater to those people and they've come to expect it. We don't cater to them and never have. I've never once asked for their business. But he's right; we get all of it. I guess they're our largest customer."

"Oh...I hope I haven't lost our biggest customer."

Michael grimaced. "If that's what it takes to keep his business, I'll gladly lose it."

"So that guy is related to Lane? That's hard to believe."

"Why is that? Lane wanted the same thing, only he asked in a polite way. I don't see much difference," he said, annoyed.

"So you're telling me Lane is a millionaire?" She shielded her eyes with her hand as she squinted at Michael.

"I suppose so...does that make a difference to you?" he asked, aggravation seeping into his voice.

"Do you even know me?" she stated, as she turned and walked away.

He smiled and shook his head.

"What did David Austin want?" Martha asked Michael as he came into the office.

"Telie," he said, bluntly.

"I wish I'd known that, I'd have given him a piece of my mind. I can't believe the nerve of some rich folks around here. They think just because they have money you're supposed to step and fetch for them, give them whatever they want! I hope she let him have it! What did she say?"

"I didn't hear what she told him, but whatever it was, it made him furious," he added, smiling.

"Ha, serves him right. The very idea, who in the heck does he think he is?"

"A Bennett or close enough," Michael stated flatly.

Martha's eyes shot fire as she thought about the audacity of David Austin. "He best stay clear of me," she fumed, "or there will be one less Bennett around to worry us."

Things got hectic at Christenberry's. People came from everywhere to buy plants and garden supplies. The fountains were selling like hotcakes. Everyone was busy, buzzing around helping customers, loading plants and garden accessories. Even Joe turned it up a notch.

When they reached a lull in activity, Telie would catch Michael watching her. She couldn't get rid of the memory of his embrace, the smell of his skin, the feel of his rough whiskered face pressing into her face. "Oh, stop it," she reprimanded herself. She couldn't risk her heart to someone who loved another. She wouldn't! But, the more she tried to ignore him, the worse it became for her. She started watching him too: how his muscles moved beneath his shirt and the way he laughed, throwing his head back slightly. She was falling in love with Michael Christenberry. She knew it; she felt it and she dreaded it.

Michael noticed Telie, with her bottom lip bitten in concentration as she surveyed her work. Tilting his head, he read the determination on her face and grinned. She hadn't looked up yet, giving him an opportunity to study her. He watched as the wind played with her hair, lifting it up and off her shoulders and the way her skin glowed from the sun. The light sprinkle of freckles peppered across the bridge of her nose gave her a look of innocence. He leaned against a post, crossing one leg over the other, as he observed her.

Telie noticed Michael taking a break and thought it might be a good time to ask about the leftover plants and flowers back on the "soon to be mulch" pile. Coming closer to him, she asked, "Michael, you know those flowers and plants out back behind the shed – the ones headed for the mulch pile?"

"Yeah."

"Well, I was wondering if you would mind if I got them. I'm working on a little project for a friend."

"Sure, help yourself. You need some help loading them?"

"Nah, I'll get them and thanks." She rushed over to the shed and pulled out a wagon. After loading an assortment of plants into the wagon, she made her way cheerfully toward her truck.

It sure doesn't take much to please her, Michael thought, grinning. *A few half-dead plants and she gets excited.*

Just after closing Michael came up to her. "You wanna go get some ice cream? I'm hot and tired, and I could sure use a little something cold."

Her eyes lit up at the suggestion. "Yeah sure, that sounds great."

Thirty minutes later they were sitting at a little parlor table in an ice cream shop in town. Telie closed her eyes, savoring the cold creamy chocolate ice cream on her tongue. "This is so good." She saw his lips twist to cover a smile. "What?" she asked.

"Nothing," he said, grinning. "I just like watching you eat. You're amusing, the way you enjoy your food. You're like a child. I keep expecting you to start humming and swinging your feet."

"Oh, is that right? Well, I'm glad to be a source of entertainment for you."

"That you are." Taking a big bite of his ice cream he asked, "So...tell me, Telie, if you could do anything, anything at all right now, what would you do?"

She thought for a moment, looked at him and said, "Pass."

"Pass?" Curiosity got the best of him.

"Yes, I'd rather not say." Taking a lick from her ice cream cone, she looked around the shop.

"Oh...that bad, huh?" Michael tried to bait her, hoping she'd tell.

"No, that good I'm afraid."

"Oh well, now you've *got* to tell me..." He leaned in with both arms on the small table, waiting for her answer.

"I was just thinking how nice it would be to go swimming. This reminds me of when I was growing up and how after a hard day's work, my dad would drive us down to the lake and let us cool off with a swim. He'd stop and pick up a watermelon or some ice cream and drench it with ice in a cooler." Finishing her cone she said, "Isn't it funny how you remember the simple pleasures in life...they always seem to stick with you."

"You're in luck," he said, tossing the remnants of his cone in the trash. He grabbed her hand, pulling her to her feet.

"Where are we going?"

"You'll see."

They walked briskly to the truck and hopped in, making their way through town; she recognized the road as they turned onto it. Driving up the pebbled driveway, through the iron gates, she was struck by the simple elegance of his home. He helped her out of the truck. "Right this way," he said, leading her through the back kitchen door. He brushed past her toward the rear hall. She remembered his bedroom was at the other end of the hall. He called back to her. "My sister-in-law, Alex, has had a bathing suit here for the past six years. The tags are still on it. It should fit you fine. I never thought it would come in handy, but she begged me to keep it or throw it away when she was over here the other night. She'd bought it before she had the twins. It must be a painful reminder of her skinnier days."

"That sounds like a woman," she teased. "Emily has a sister?" It never occurred to her that Michael had in-laws. For that matter, it was hard to believe he had a life outside of Christenberry's.

"Yes, Alexandria, 'Alex' to me; she's a special person. You'd like her."

It was just then that she noticed a change in the house; things had been rearranged, even removed. She pretended not to notice, but it was hard not to. Her eyes went to the sink and saw that the rings were gone.

"Here you go," he said, handing the bathing suit to Telie. "Bathroom's down the hall on the right."

Closing the door to the bathroom, she slid off her clothes and stepped into the chocolate brown one-piece bathing suit, thankful for its modest and understated design. She felt self-conscious, preferring a cover-up but grabbed a bath towel from the shelf instead. Wrapping it around her waist she walked back to the kitchen. A set of French doors lay open in the gathering room off of the kitchen. She could see the fading sunlight reflecting in the water of the pool as the whirring of cicadas signaled the end of another summer day.

"Over here," Michael called to her. "Does it fit?" he asked, aware of the towel around her waist. He managed to cover his amusement at her modesty, taking note of the faint blush of her skin.

"Yes, it does." She stuck one foot in the water and let the towel drop on the tile. She then slid into the pool, swimming slowly to the other side and back again.

Telie beamed. "Aren't you coming in? I'll race you," she challenged.

Tossing his cigar into the ashtray, he strode over to the edge of the pool and dove in beside her. "So...are we betting on this race?" he asked, raking back his wet hair, smiling into her eyes.

"That depends on what you want to bet." She eyed him suspiciously.

"Winner's choice," he stated, grinning.

"Then I guess I'd better learn to keep my big mouth shut. I'm really not that great of a swimmer. I'm more of a floater actually...I can tread water, that's about it."

"I'm feeling pretty generous. I might even give you a head start," he teased.

"I'll keep that in mind," she said, floating away from him to the other side of the pool.

"So tell me, Telie, is this what you really wanted to do... swim?" he asked, swimming up to her. He took her hands in his, pulling her toward the deep end of the pool. "Hold on, this is over your head." He smiled at the panic he saw in her eyes.

When she could no longer feel the floor of the pool, she let go of his hands and clung to his shoulders. The movement of the water pressed her closer to him as she stretched her arms to avoid the encounter.

He smiled at her struggle, seeing the awkward way she arranged herself to avoid pressing into him. Having pity on her, he moved slowly back to the shallow end. Once she had her footing she let go.

"To answer your question, yes, this is exactly what I want to do." Spinning gracefully in the water, she said, "I love the way water feels on my skin, especially after a hot sticky day like today. It really refreshes you, don't you think?" She twirled in the water.

"So, your dad rewarded you after a long hot day of work with ice cream and a swim, is that right?" He pulled himself up onto the side of the pool.

"Uh huh."

"I'll bet your dad worries about you living so far away from home." He looked down at her, thinking of how he must miss her.

"I don't think so. He doesn't even know I've moved." Looking away, she moved over to the steps and sat down in the water, next to his legs.

"What?" he asked, narrowing his eyes, waiting for an explanation.

"I've lost touch with him. He started another life out in Texas…he has a new family now. I really don't think he cares too much anymore. I only hear from him occasionally."

"That's really hard for me to believe." He saw the hurt in her eyes and wished he could remove it. Hopping down into the pool, he reached for her and gathered her into his arms, holding her close.

Pushing back, she looked up at him. "I still love him, you know; it's not that. I guess I'm just finding it hard to get over the loss, to realize that he's gone from my life by his own choice. It leaves you kind of...empty."

"I know," he said, and she knew he did.

Chapter 30

The sounds of evening grew in the twilight as they sat on the patio enjoying the night. Fireflies sparked around them as an occasional croak sounded in the distance. "Are you hungry? I've got some leftover hamburgers in the fridge we could warm up. Besides, I'm really tempted to light this up," he said, rolling his cigar between his two fingers.

"Let's go before you cave." She stood, wrapping the towel tightly around her waist. "I'll not be a minute; let me change and I'll come help you."

Telie stepped into the bathroom, dried off and changed into her clothes. She hesitated, hearing a voice coming from down the hall. *Is that a woman's voice?* She finished dressing, pulling her hair up into a twist and securing it with a clasp from her purse. Emerging from the bathroom with the wet towel and bathing suit wrapped in her hands, she approached the kitchen. Peering around the corner, she saw Michael with his back to her, fixing hamburgers and Mary Grace seated at the bar, legs crossed and swinging. She was steadily chatting away.

"Hello Mary Grace," Telie spoke softly.

Startled, Mary Grace turned sharply, then glared at her. "Oh, I didn't know you had company, Michael; you should have told me."

"You didn't give me a chance," he added, smiling back at Telie.

"Michael, where is your laundry room? I need to drop this in your washer," she said, holding up the towel.

"Through that door." He gestured toward a room at the back of the kitchen.

Seeing a three-layer chocolate cake in the center of the island, Telie remarked, "That cake looks delicious. Would you care to join us for a hamburger?"

Michael glanced over his shoulder toward Telie, an annoyed look on his face.

"Thank you, I'd love to. I hope I'm not intruding. I just came by to tell Michael about Tom Bennett. I'm sure Lane has already told you about his grandfather."

"Told me what?" Telie asked, as she hopped up onto a barstool next to Mary Grace.

"Tom Bennett passed away this afternoon. They think he had a heart attack."

"Oh, I'm so sorry to hear that. Lane adored his grandfather. June spoke very highly of him also. She said he was a true southern gentleman." She took in a deep breath. "I'll bet the family is devastated."

"I'm sure Lane will want to see you, Telie. We all need comfort in times like these. It's going to be hard on him, being so close with his grandfather. He'll need you close by for support." Mary Grace blinked and stared down at the rings on her fingers, twisting them. "Did you know him, Michael?" she asked, looking up.

"Not very well, I met him for the first time the other day."

"What did you think of him?" Telie asked. "Was he as gracious as everyone says?"

"I thought he was very gracious, very hospitable. I liked him. I only wish I'd gotten to know him better. He'd asked me to drop by and visit him. I really think he meant it. He'd been a loyal customer of mine for years; it's a pity I didn't know him better. Of course he always sent one of his workers to get whatever he needed. I could never understand why someone with a shipyard business needed so many trees and flowers."

"Oh I'm sure he owned property everywhere. They say he's worth a fortune," Mary Grace chimed in.

"I don't think I'll have the same friendly relationship with some of his other relatives though." He shot a look toward Telie.

A smile of understanding played across Telie's face that didn't go unnoticed by Mary Grace.

"I wonder who'll get all of his money. His kids, I guess, and grandkids," Mary Grace blurted out rudely.

"I guess that's family business, don't you think?" Michael cut her off with his comment. "Here ya go," he said, placing the burgers on the bar. "Eat up." Michael tossed a bag of buns on the counter. He turned to get the mustard out of the fridge and placed it next to the other condiments lined up on the bar.

Telie glanced briefly at Mary Grace, noticing an odd expression on her face. It was somewhere between shock and disbelief. Telie followed her eyes to Michael's hand and saw that his ring finger was bare. A white ring around his finger, three shades lighter than the rest of his hand, jumped out at her. His wedding band was gone!

Quickly recovering, Mary Grace turned the conversation back around to Lane. "Poor Lane, he must be suffering. I can't believe he hasn't called you, Telie."

Reaching down beside the barstool, Telie retrieved her purse from the floor. Removing her cell phone she noticed several missed calls from Lane. Telie attempted to force casualness to her voice. "It looks like he has been trying to reach me."

"Oh, I'm sure." Glancing over to Michael, Mary Grace said, "Why don't you go call him. Michael and I will fix a plate for you. I'm sure he needs to talk to you right away."

Telie's chair scraped across the kitchen floor. "I'll step outside and call him."

A look of triumph crossed Mary Grace's face as she watched her leave the room, leaving her alone with Michael. "Oh really, Michael," she said. "Why do you waste your time on that hillbilly girl? She's obviously chasing you...and cheating on her boyfriend to do it!"

Dragging out a barstool, he sat opposite her. After taking a large bite of his burger, he said, chewing, "*She* was invited."

Mary Grace shrugged. "I guess you'll just have to learn the hard way. Don't say I didn't warn you."

The kitchen door opened. Glancing around the room, Telie motioned for Michael.

He was on his feet, swallowing down the last of his burger. Bending his head down to her, she whispered, "Can you take me home now? I need to change and go see Lane, he is really upset."

Nodding, he turned to Mary Grace. "We have to leave now, Mary Grace. Thanks for the cake. I'm sure it's delicious. You can stay and finish your burger, just lock the door on your way out."

Pulling up to the cottage at Bell Forest, Michael waited until Telie got out, then said, "Take your time, I'll wait on you and drive you over to see Lane."

"You don't have to, Michael. I'm sure you've got better things to do than haul me around all over creation."

"No, not really," he grinned.

When Telie got back into the truck, Michael's eyes widened. "It amazes me at how fast you can transform yourself."

She wore her hair pulled back loose at the nape of her neck, falling down her back. Her white tunic top and faded jeans completed the picture of a perfect coastal girl.

The truck roared to life as they slowly pulled away. "I take it you've forgiven Lane," Michael stated, keeping his eyes on the dirt road ahead.

"Yes, I forgave him…that same night. He asked me to and I believed him when he said he was sorry. We're still friends. And that's all we've ever been." In the silence that followed, Telie cleared her throat, causing Michael to glance at her. "I usually don't have trouble forgiving someone who asked me to."

"What if they don't ask?"

"That's where I have trouble." Her voice was like a whisper.

Michael thought about her words, full of meaning and emotion. His mood was suddenly lighter with the knowledge that her relationship with Lane was only friendship. "Your father?"

She nodded. He had more perception about him than it first seemed.

He touched her arm lightly. "It must be hard…trusting again after having the foundation of your world crumble the way it did. Being afraid that everything you once believed about your father was false. That would be difficult for anyone, Telie. I don't know how I would handle it. But I'm sure there are reasons, reasons you may never understand."

Tears gathered in her eyes, whether from the truth of his words or the understanding in his voice, she didn't know.

He reached behind her and pulled her next to him. With an arm around her, he spoke into her hair. "Change happens to all of us, Telie. Only one thing remains the same in this life and that's the love God has for us. That never changes; it's the same yesterday, today and forever."

Exhaling deeply, she leaned her head back on his arm. "I know…He's teaching me to accept that. That's hard to do. But, I do see the hand of God working in my life, guiding me."

"Yeah, He's good at that," he smiled down at her. "He's been working on me, too."

They soon arrived at the Bennett house. She slid back over to her side of the seat, opened the door and hopped out. "Thanks for everything, Michael."

"I can wait for you if you like. Take you back home."

"That's okay. I'll ask Lane to. I'm not sure how long I'll be."

With that, she closed the door. Michael watched as she walked down the sidewalk, half hidden in the overgrown boxwoods that flanked either side of the walkway. He waited until he saw Lane move from the shadowed porch to embrace her. Turning his eyes away, he reached in his shirt pocket and took out a cigar.

The evening was difficult. Tom Bennett's house was eerily quiet and still, as if the house itself was mourning the passing of its master. Late into the night, Lane drove Telie home. As she said goodbye, she promised she would be there for him to help him get through the next few days.

Sitting up with a jolt from a fitful sleep, she stared at the shadows playing across the floor. The wind outside tossed the trees wildly about as it howled around the house.

She rose, slipped on her thin white robe and went outside on the porch to wait for the approaching storm. All her life she could sense when a storm in the natural realm was brewing, but this time, she sensed a different kind of storm.

Chapter 31

Morning sunlight fell fresh on the day. No sign of last night's storm could be seen. Telie thought back to her conversation with Lane the night before. She reassured him that his pain mattered to God and that He was there with him through it all. She wasn't sure how he had received her words of comfort, or how anyone finds solace without a relationship with the Creator.

Later that day June pulled up at Bell Forest. "Thanks for letting me come with you, June. These things are always difficult," Telie said. She felt secure around June and today she needed her more than ever to provide that sense of security. She wanted to avoid David Austin at all costs, but today that wouldn't be possible.

"Don't mention it, sweetie. I'm glad for the company." June patted her arm.

Once inside the funeral home, they could see the receiving line twist and turn in and out of rooms and all along the walls of the large ornate foyer.

"He certainly was popular, wasn't he?" Telie remarked, taking in the crowd of people lining the walls. All walks of life seemed to be represented as each one entered the building.

They had filled orders all day long at Christenberry's, not something they were accustomed to doing for funerals. It seemed that even the local florists had run out of inventory. Every potted plant and flowering shrub had been sold. Telie and Martha had worked hard cleaning and polishing the leaves. They'd wrapped ribbon around the bases of the baskets, sprucing up the look of the plants.

"Telie, Miss June," Lane spoke from behind them. He walked up, hugging June first and winking at Telie over June's shoulder. Reaching for Telie's hand, he gave a gentle squeeze.

The powerful emotion in Lane's voice seemed to smooth as he smiled at them and explained how good it was to see them. Tugging Telie's hand, he said, "Come with me." Escorting them through the parlor doors, he interrupted the line and introduced them to his family.

"Telie, this is my father, Tommy Bennett, and of course, Father, you remember June."

"I'm happy to finally meet you, Telie. Lane speaks of you often. I see you're wearing that beautiful bracelet I've heard so much about." Turning to June he said, "June, it's been a long time, good to see you again. My father always loved your apple pie better than anyone's." He smiled warmly at June, then turned to the next face behind her.

The line pushed forward and carried them away with the current. June was distracted by an acquaintance, leaving Telie and Lane alone together. He was clinging to her for dear life.

She caught a glimpse of Mary Grace in the line behind her, with Michael close behind. She and Michael's eyes met briefly, then he looked away.

"Aunt Dottie, this is my friend Telie," Lane said affectionately.

"So nice to meet you, dear," she said, extending her hand gracefully.

Telie smiled back warmly as she took her hand. "I'm happy to meet you too. I'm so sorry for your loss."

Aunt Dottie squeezed her hand, pressing her lips together in an attempt to smile. The grief was evident on her face.

Dottie had a look of privilege, even in her grief. Designer clothes, exquisite jewelry, there was an understated elegance about her, as if she spent her afternoons in the country club or on the family yacht. *She's pleasant and attractive in a "well kept" kind of way,* Telie thought.

Ushering her forward, Lane said, "This is my cousin, David Austin. He's Aunt Dottie's son. David, this is Telie."

"We've met," he said, taking her hand and pressing a kiss to her fingers. He let it linger for an uneasy moment before casting his eyes up at her.

"Oh...I see." Lane looked annoyed. He turned to Telie for clarification, but she looked away. "David, you never cease to amaze me how you seem to know every pretty girl in a fifty-mile radius." Lane clenched his jaw as he brushed by him. "It's like you have some kinda built-in sonar system."

They moved along quickly, Lane still clutching her arm as they viewed the body. "I'm so sorry, Lane. I know you are really going to miss him."

"Yes, I certainly am." Turning away slowly, he led her outside to a small courtyard. Once they were seated, he inquired, "So...how do you know David?"

"From Christenberry's, he comes in there sometimes." She left it at that.

"Well, I know David...has he made a move on you yet?" He searched her face for an answer.

"You could say that," she said, smoothing her dress nervously. "But it doesn't matter; I'm not interested in him at all, Lane."

"He's a real jerk. It would be a good idea to steer clear of him." Leaning over, he placed his elbows on his knees, clamping his fists together under his chin. "He hasn't offended you, has he?"

"No...not like you did," she blurted out unexpectedly. Noticing the look of shock on his face she added, "I guess that's because I actually *like* you!" She smiled, reaching for his hand.

He ran a hand across his forehead, wiping his brow in mock response. "Whew...you had me worried there for a minute."

"Want to go back inside?" she asked, motioning to the door.

"Not really...guess I need to. Can you stay with me for awhile?" he pleaded.

He looked more adorable than ever with his unkempt hair strangely out of place with his suit and tie. "Of course, Lane. I'm here for you. I just need to make sure that June doesn't get tired."

Looking around for June, he asked, "Did you come with her, or did she come with you?"

"I came with her," she said.

"Oh good, I'll take you home. It will give me a good excuse to leave early. I hate these things." He looked nervous and agitated as he fidgeted with the collar of his shirt.

"Hmm, sounds familiar. I think you're just antisocial," she said, teasing.

"Oh, you're most definitely right about that!"

Just then, Michael and Mary Grace came through the doors to the courtyard. Telie and Lane stood up to greet them. Michael extended his hand to Lane, saying, "Lane, I'm so sorry for your loss. If I can help with anything at all, you just let me know."

"Thanks Michael, I really appreciate that. I'm glad you got to meet grandfather; he seemed to really take an interest in you."

"I am too. He was such a gentleman and he spoke very fondly of my mother."

Mary Grace slid her arm through Michael's and added, "I didn't know him personally, but I've only heard good things about him. He was certainly well thought of in the community. I mean just look around – this is the longest receiving line I've ever been in."

"Thank you. He certainly was well thought of," Lane said, softly.

Telie lifted her eyes to look at Michael. He caught her glance and smiled. "And how are you tonight, Miss Telie?" Michael asked.

"Fine, thank you."

Firmly clasped to Michael's arm, Mary Grace waved as they said goodbye. June passed them on her way to see Lane and Telie.

"I've never seen so many people turn out for a visitation. I'm glad we got here early, Telie, or we'd still be in that line," June said, letting out a deep sigh. She looked tired.

"Go on home, June; you must be exhausted. Lane will take me home later."

"Okay, dear." June patted Telie's arm, as was her custom. Lifting her hand to Lane's cheek she said, "I'll send over some more food in the morning. I can't have you starving over there."

"Thank you, Miss June." Lane smiled tenderly at her.

Telie grinned at the sight, knowing how June loved to take care of people. She could just imagine how much food she would pour through the doors of the Bennett house. She whispered in Lane's ear, "You'll be fat as butter if June has anything to do with it."

Lane laughed, caught Telie's hand and pulled her toward the door. "Come on, let's get this over with."

Chapter 32

"Get out of my way!" Tommy Bennett shouted, shoving his father's attorney, William Forsythe aside. "If I listened to you, we'd all end up broke. I'm contacting my attorney and we'll see about this!" he warned. "He made a simple mistake, that's all. He didn't know what he was doing." Tommy flipped open his cell phone and began punching numbers.

"No! Your father knew perfectly well what he was doing, and if you so much as touch me again, Mr. Bennett, I'll have you arrested for assault. Do I make myself perfectly clear?" William Forsythe fumed.

Tommy shut his phone, pausing at the door. "You'll hear from my attorney. I'll see you in court!" With that, he slammed the door, rattling the windows as he left.

Williams Forsythe exhaled slowly. Buzzing his secretary he said, "Millie, get Michael Christenberry on the phone."

Michael was in the tractor shed, greasing a chainsaw when the call came in. "Michael, you're wanted up front," came Martha's gruff voice over the outside speaker. He wiped the grease off his hands with a rag and walked toward the office.

"Who needs me?" Michael asked, as he walked through the door, looking at Martha.

"You've got a phone call. I think it's important," Martha replied, waving her pen in the direction of his office.

Shutting the door as he walked into his office, he sat down, lifted the receiver and punched the extension button. "This is Michael," he said. "May I help you?"

"Michael, this is William Forsythe. I'm an attorney for Tom Bennett and his family. I was wondering if we could get together...at your earliest convenience. I have some business to discuss with you, of a rather personal nature."

"Okay...sure, how about this afternoon? I'm available after 4:00," he said, sounding a little puzzled.

"That's perfect. Can you meet me at my office, say around...4:30?"

"I'll be there." Hanging up the phone, he sat still in his chair, lost in thought.

"Is somebody trying to sue us?" Martha asked, walking into Michael's office. Her eyes darted back and forth as she waited for an answer.

"I don't know. I've got an appointment with William Forsythe at 4:30. Don't worry I'm sure it's nothing." He picked up his cigar from the ashtray and bit down on it, staring off thoughtfully.

"Attorneys never 'good news' anybody. It probably has something to do with that bratty boy you ran off from here the other day," Martha commented, as she walked back to her desk.

Bells clanged against the door as Michael stepped into the law office on the corner of Mimosa and Main. "I'm Michael Christenberry, here to see Mr. Forsythe. I have an appointment."

Millie looked up from her typing. "He's expecting you, Mr. Christenberry. Please go right in," she said, continuing her typing.

"Michael!" William Forsythe stood up, extending his hand over his desk. "So good of you to come on such short notice; please, have a seat." He motioned to a leather wing-backed chair across from his desk.

Michael sat down, looked around and asked, "What's this all about, Mr. Forsythe?"

"Call me William. I'll get right to it. Tom Bennett hired me some time ago to manage his affairs." He cleared his throat. "In the event of his demise, I've been given special instructions on how I'm to handle his estate. That's where you come in." He eyed Michael for a moment, then took a deep breath.

"I don't follow you. How does that concern me?" Michael tilted his head slightly, waiting for an answer.

William Forsythe's voice took on a sympathetic tone. "The truth of the matter, Michael, is that Tom Bennett was your father." He let that sink in before he proceeded.

Michael widened his eyes, leaned forward and asked, "What did you say?"

"I'm sorry to have to be the one to drop all of this on you, son. I know it's a bit of a shock. Trust me, it all checks out. Tom felt that he had failed you, Michael. You were his only regret in this life. From what it looks like, he'd made an agreement with your mother that he would not interfere with your life. Apparently, she had wanted a different life for you.

247

I'm not certain why; anything I'd say would only be speculation. But the truth is, they made a bargain and he regretted it. As for your father, Mike Christenberry, he knew from the beginning. I don't have to tell you what a fine man he was. I've known Mike all my life and you were his son, and it didn't matter to him who had fathered you."

Michael sat in stunned silence, staring straight ahead as Mr. Forsythe disclosed the details of the arrangement his mother had made with Tom Bennett. "He was not to be involved in your life and no one, not even his children, was to know about you. It was her wish that you'd be spared the influences of the Bennett family and all that went along with them, including their money. I'm not sure why, Michael. I don't know any of the reasons why she felt that way. I only know that, for whatever reason, she didn't want you to be a part of them and Tom Bennett agreed with the terms."

"So...if that's what they agreed upon, why change, why drop all of this on me now? I mean...why not just leave things as they were?" He ran his hand through his hair and sighed. "I don't understand why he would want to disclose all of this to me now when they're both gone and I can't ask questions to either of them!" His voice rose in frustration.

"As you know, Michael, Mr. Bennett was quite wealthy. Like I said before, his only regret was not being there for you, not being a father to you, not getting to know you. The silver lining in all of this is that you now own one-third of one of the largest shipyards in the South. You are financially well off, and there is nothing anyone can do about it."

William relaxed back in his chair, his voice full of concern. "I understand all this may be a little overwhelming to you right now, but I'm under obligation to disclose the information and help you in any way I can. You may have an attorney that you're comfortable with, that's fine, but I'm here for you if you need me. Tom paid me well in advance for my services, but it's up to you whom you'll choose to represent you."

Something snapped in Michael. He rested his elbows on his knees with his hands folded together, leaning forward he said, "Let me see if I understand what you're saying to me. My mother made an arrangement with my...biological father, to stay out of my life. Feeling...what I assume to be guilt, he gave me an equal share of his inheritance with his children. Is that what I'm hearing from you?"

"In a nutshell."

He pondered this a minute, then asked, "Do the others know?"

"Yes." He sighed. "I'm not going to sugarcoat this, Michael. Tommy is furious and he's trying to fight it. Dottie is fine with it as long as her check keeps coming. There is nothing that can be done about the will. It was Tom Bennett's business to do with as he wished, and he specified that all the children he sired were to be given an equal share of his estate. Furthermore, if any such children were to precede him in death, their share would be given to their next of kin. The truth of the matter is that the decision has already been made. Tommy will exhaust all of his options, but he's a smart man; he knows it's a foregone conclusion."

Clearing his throat, Michael stated, "I would like to continue your services Mr.—William. I appreciate you being up front with me. I'm not sure what to do with all of this information. I'd like some time to think it over."

"Sure...I understand."

"What advice can you give me now?" Michael looked directly in the attorney's eyes.

"Don't expect help from the others. Learn what you can about the business on your own. Educate yourself; pay close attention to the details. Conduct yourself with humility and don't change your lifestyle anytime soon. Tommy will try to buy you out. Don't do it. No matter how difficult he tries to make things for you, it will be a costly mistake. Tommy keeps his people close; don't trust any of them. Remember, you are an equal partner and no decision can be made without you. Keep silent. You convey more by saying nothing than by speaking."

Michael nodded.

"I'm right here if you need me. In the meantime, while all of this works out, carry on as usual. I'll let you know how things progress with Tommy's efforts." William patted his desk.

"Just so you'll know; I don't intend to fight or use my resources to defend myself. What happens happens."

"You don't have to fight, Michael; it's all here in black and white." William smacked the papers in his hand.

Michael nodded once and stood, shaking hands with William. "Thank you, William, for being straightforward. I really appreciate that."

"I'll be in touch." William walked Michael to the door, patting his back as he left. He couldn't help but make the comparison between Michael's humble sincerity and Tommy Bennett's greedy and calculating arrogance. "Maybe Michael's mother was wiser than anyone ever realized," he murmured under his breath.

Chapter 33

Billowing clouds sat motionless, waiting for the wind to direct their course. Grayish and gathering, the clouds collected beneath the white puffs that billowed upward against the blue sky.

Telie stared up at the sky, lost in thought. Without warning, McKeever bolted up from his resting place near her feet and lunged forward.

"Hey boy," Brother Raphael said, scratching behind McKeever's shaggy ears. He took a seat next to Telie on the porch in the old willow chair.

"What brings you out on this fine day?" Telie asked. "You looking for cheap labor again? Who's coming this time, the Pope?"

"I promise if he ever does show up down here, I'll try my best to get you an audience with him. It'll take the Pope to do anything with you!"

"No, really, what's going on?"

"Oh, I don't know. I saw you over here looking so peaceful and thought I might come stir up some trouble," he said, grinning. "So, how are things going for you?"

"Why do I feel like you're trying to pick a fight?" Telie turned up her tea glass and glared at him.

Shaking his head, he replied, "I'm just asking about you; what's the big deal?" Brother Raphael dropped his head, avoiding her eyes and continued, "Have you spoken with your father since you've been here?"

"Uh…no, what am I supposed to say to him? 'Hi dad, how's the wife, the kids?' I really don't know how I can pretend everything is just great."

Brother Raphael sat still a moment, looking into Telie's eyes. He could see the feelings of abandonment written all over her face. Reaching over, he took her hand in his, explaining. "You're not the least significant person in this, you know…I'm telling you to do this for *your* healing, *your* restoration. You must forgive him, Telie…that doesn't mean you have to like it or that everything is all hearts and flowers now, but you have to forgive."

Annoyance emanated from her whole body. She shifted in her chair. "He hasn't asked for forgiveness," she stated bluntly.

"It doesn't matter. Have you ever heard of unilateral forgiveness? That's what is needed here. To put it simply, it means that you forgive even when the person who has wronged you hasn't asked you to." Tapping the dirt loose from his shoe with the palm of his hand, he turned his attention back to her.

"And *why* should I do that?" she asked, not at all convinced his advice was worth taking. Still, she kept replaying the conversation she and Michael had had a few days earlier.

"Because God commands us to – it releases us somehow and allows God's love to flow through us. If you don't, Telie, it can hurt you inside and make you bitter, hard, angry. I don't want that for you. All I'm asking is for you to consider my words and pray about it. Let God direct you, Telie." He squeezed her hand and stood up. "Remember, while we were yet sinners, Christ died for us. Well, I've accomplished all that I wanted to say, I'll go now."

"Is that why you stopped by, to lecture me?"

"You call it lecturing…I call it obeying the voice of the Lord." He grinned at her and headed back up the path toward the monastery.

"Figures, this guidance of your Lord is tough!" Telie sat quietly for the longest time, staring up at the clouds. They had shifted, becoming a gathering darkness that threatened to burst forth into thunderous display. The air hummed with the feeling of electricity as the wind picked up. The trees looked as if someone raked their hand over them. Telie glanced over her shoulder toward the monastery and, as usual, saw Brother Simeon perched in his chair like the guardian of the temple.

"Great! I don't stand a chance against the prayers of those two." She turned back to the brewing storm. "Okay Father. But I'll need your strength to navigate me to a place where I can forgive."

She shook her head, saying out loud, "How do I start?" A voice inside her simply said, "You start with love." The phone buzzed in her palm, startling her. Taking it up she noticed it was Michael. "Hey Michael," Telie said, as she answered the phone.

"Hey, do you have plans for dinner?" Michael asked, sounding more subdued than she ever remembered.

"No, not exactly. I was trying to decide between peanut butter and jelly or a bowl of ice cream, leaning strongly toward the ice cream," she joked.

"Sounds like you." Michael gave a halfhearted laugh. "Listen, Nathan just called and said he was grilling and wanted to know if we wanted to come over. Sonny is with him."

"Oh good, I'd love to go. Just give me a minute to shower. I'm a mess."

"Pick you up in thirty minutes."

Nathan's home was surprisingly comfortable. It was small, but quaint. Books lined the shelves in the den and scattered out around the furniture, resting on chairs and tables. They walked through the kitchen and out the back door to the patio.

"Hey you two, come on, pull up a couple of chairs." Nathan waved his spatula in the air.

Sonny hopped up and made her way to Telie, hugging her firmly. "How have you been? It seems like forever since we've talked. Come on over here and tell me what you've been up to," Sonny said, smiling warmly at her friend.

Telie sat down next to her, looking around the yard, hoping to catch a glimpse of Mary Amelia.

Sonny had a flyswatter in one hand and a small stuffed bunny in the other. "Mary Amelia is next door playing on the swing set with the neighbors. I've been asked to baby-sit," she said, shaking the bunny in her hand.

Telie laughed. "I can't wait to see her. Michael has told me so much about her."

Sonny looked over her shoulder toward the laughter from the yard next door. She briefly caught sight of two feet in the air before the swing swooped down again. "Oh you will. She'll jump out of that swing so fast it'll make your head spin once Nathan calls. She adores him, you know." Sonny had a look of pure adoration on her face as she looked at Nathan.

Like mother, like daughter, Telie thought, and grinned. She watched the men for a moment, noticing how they were engaged in a deep conversation of their own. They were so engrossed that Nathan forgot the burgers as the flames shot up from the grill. He grabbed a spray bottle and doused the grill, almost soaking the meat with water.

"What do you suppose they're talking about?" Sonny asked.

"I don't know, but whatever it is, it's about to cost us our dinner. It must be something pretty intense; look at the expression on Nathan's face. He's preaching. I've seen that look before," Telie said, lifting her eyebrows.

Nathan looked at Michael, pointing the spatula at him and said, "Take what's given to you, Michael. Who knows what higher purpose God has in mind. Trust Him in this; He'll direct your path." Nathan looked down as he flipped the burgers. "Sometimes though…we have to do the hard thing and go with what our heart tells us, no matter what the cost. It's not easy, but try and discern the will of God. What He would have you do. Pray about it and make the best decision you can. That takes faith. Try not to be ruled by your feelings; they'll lie to you. Let your heart be ruled by truth and love."

"I haven't told anyone about this, Nathan…the Bennetts know of course and Martha."

"You haven't told Telie?" He shot him a questioning look.

He nodded, "No."

"Why not?"

Running his hand through his hair in a nervous manner, he replied, "I don't know. I guess I'm not really sure how all of this will affect her. I mean…will she be attracted to the money, the lifestyle? Will it change her? I just don't know."

"You don't know? Look man…she's not my girlfriend but a blind man can see what kind of a person she is…not the kind that would be interested in someone for money. Think about it, Michael, if money was all she was after, why wouldn't she go after Lane? Didn't you tell me he acts like he can't function without her? He's definitely interested in her. If she was after money, she'd be out with him right now instead of you." Shaking his head, he gave Michael a disappointed look. "How is everything with you two anyway? Have you told her how you feel?"

"Sort of, I guess," he whispered. He wanted to change the subject but knew he could forget it. Once Nathan had you in his sights, you had just better lay it all out there for him.

"Sort of…what does that mean, sort of?" Nathan was not letting him off the hook.

"I told her that I have feelings for her…but I wasn't sure what I wanted to do about it, if anything."

Nathan put down the spatula, wiped his hands on a towel and looked at Michael. "Let me get this straight, you said to her, 'I kinda like you, but I'm not sure yet. I'll let you know if anything changes.' That's great, Michael…what every girl wants to hear. I can't believe you! If you're not careful, you'll run her into the arms of Lane or half a dozen other guys who would love to trade places with you." Shaking his head, he picked up the spatula, scooped up the burgers and placed them on a plate.

Michael glanced over at Telie. She and Sonny had their heads leaning toward each other talking. Sonny was gesturing with her hands as she was speaking. Telie laughed out loud, enjoying herself. "I also told her that I loved my wife."

Nathan let out a long breath. "What, pray tell, was her response to that?"

"She said she knew my heart belonged to Emily...that there wasn't any room for anyone else but that was okay; she didn't trust her heart to anyone anyway."

"Well now...don't you two make the most dysfunctional couple. I don't get you, Michael. I mean it's funny to me that you say you don't know how you feel about her when all it takes is for some guy to ask her out and you go crazy. She can sneeze and you're running to her like some kind of overprotective nurse maid."

"Is it my imagination, or do I sense a little hostility from you?" Michael eyed his friend; reaching in his front pocket he took out a cigar and stuck it in his mouth. A smile played across his lips as he waited for an answer.

Nathan gave him a sideways grin and confessed. "Is it that noticeable? I thought I was being reasonable. I guess I got carried away. I'm just worried that you'll miss a chance for happiness again, Michael. I've kinda been worrying about the same thing for myself lately."

Michael raised his eyebrows. "So are we talking about Sonny?"

"Yeah." Nathan rubbed the back of his neck, looking down at Michael. He watched Michael prop his feet up on the small table in front of him and lean back, chewing on his cigar.

"Let's hear it." A smug look replaced the defensive one.

"I love her. It's that simple." He let out a deep sigh.

"Does she know this?" Michael asked. He narrowed his eyes out of habit from the imaginary smoke from his cigar.

"Not yet. We share everything…well almost everything," he clarified, giving Michael a sheepish grin. "I can't begin to think of my life without her. The decision I make will affect so many. I've had this burden, this feeling of uncertainty, for too long now." He inhaled releasing his breath evenly. "Don't get me wrong, I'm not under the delusion that if I can convince her to marry me, that I can still pastor our church. I understand the requirements of our board and since Sonny has been married before…I know what I'll have to do."

Michael removed his feet from the table and leaned forward in his chair. "You'd leave the church?"

"No, I'd leave the pulpit. Don't think this is something I haven't wrestled with, Michael." He held him in a steady gaze. "Trust me, I've spent many nights in prayer about this. I've even sought the counsel of my pastor from back home. It's not something I take lightly. The church is vitally important to me, and I would never do anything to cause harm or confusion."

"So you think staying on as Pastor would harm the church if you were married to Sonny?"

"I do. Not because I think Sonny hasn't been forgiven for her sins the same way I'm forgiven of mine; it's not that. I believe forgiveness is available to all who seek it. But that's a requirement of this church – that a minister cannot be divorced or married to a divorced woman." He looked over at Sonny and smiled. "I know Sonny's story. I know her heart and I love her more than you can imagine. She's an incredible woman. I knew this from the first time I spoke with her. I knew she was the one."

"No wonder they get along so well," Michael said, gesturing with his head over to the girls. "They're cut from the same cloth."

"Yeah, but the question is, what are they doing slumming around with the likes of us?"

"Just so you know, Nathan, if you're looking for a job, I sure could use you. I haven't forgotten your skill with a backhoe." Michael swatted a mosquito that had landed on his arm.

"Thanks Michael. I may take you up on that. If Sonny will have me, I plan on staying at the church and serving in whatever capacity I can, just not as Pastor. I'll need to find a job," he stated. "If you promise not to boss me around all day, I'd love to work for you."

"We all get bossed around all day by Martha, no exceptions...just ask Telie."

"I'll see how all this pans out. I'm not sure how Sonny feels yet. She has a lot more to consider than I do; she has Mary Amelia."

"Speaking of Mary Amelia, how do you keep from spoiling her rotten? All she'd have to do is bat her eyes at me and I'm done." Michael smiled as he remembered her saying how 'cited she was to have a goldfish.

Mary Amelia had gotten to him, too. He felt the same way about her. It was hard for him to keep from giving into her every whim, especially when he thought about the life she'd had with her own father. It had been unstable and hostile before her father finally left them. "It's hard," Nathan replied.

"Is her ex still in the picture?" Michael asked.

Shaking his head, Nathan answered, "No, he took off about a year ago. He won't be back. He's afraid he'd have to pay child support."

"That's got to be hard on Mary Amelia." Michael winced.

"She doesn't talk about him much. Her memories are mostly painful ones. He tried his best to destroy them both...almost succeeded." A darkness covered Nathan's face, like a shadow. It caused him pain to think of the two people he loved most in this world being hurt so badly.

"Mr. Chris Berry! Mr. Chris Berry!" The excited voice of Mary Amelia brought Michael back to the present. She ran across the yard toward him.

"Hey! Slow down. You'll fall and hurt yourself!" Michael reached out and grabbed the little girl, pulling her into his lap.

"You 'member Nate; don't you, Mr. Chris Berry?" she asked, breathless. She threw both hands around his neck and locked her fingers. Michael's heart skipped a beat. He shot Nathan a glance that said, "I'm done for. This little girl owns me!"

"Of course I do. How is he anyway?"

"He's fine. He's tryin' to talk to me, but the water makes the words quiet."

"Yeah, that can make it hard to hear what he's saying. Come with me," he said, standing up. He held on to her hand. "I want you to meet someone." Walking toward Telie he said, "Telie, this is Mary Amelia; Mary Amelia, Telie."

The adoration in Michael's eyes took Telie by surprise. She'd never seen him around children. It was evident to her that he'd make a wonderful father. She thought how tragic it was for him to have been denied that privilege.

"Nice to meet you, Mary Amelia, and thank you so much for those delicious brownies you sent to me when I was sick. They helped me get better!"

"You welcome. I'm glad you feel better. Is Mr. Chris Berry your husband?"

"No, he's my friend. I hope you'll be my friend, too."
Telie smiled up at Mary Amelia, and then glanced at Michael
who was grinning at her intently.

Nathan's voice interrupted. "Who's ready to eat?"

Chapter 34

Business had picked up steadily since the funeral for Tom Bennett. They filled orders all day long for plants and flowering shrubs, something they had not previously done on such a large scale. The added business kept everyone hopping and the supply trucks coming.

Rounding the corner past the oak leaf hydrangeas, Telie grimaced as she recognized David Austin's voice calling to her. He approached her from behind. "There you are. I've been looking all over for you and here you are, hiding out in the hydrangeas." His smooth voice slithered out from between his teeth.

"What can I help you with, Mr. Austin?" Her tone was businesslike and stern.

"Hmmm, let me see. I believe you can help me by getting into my car and going off with me to some exotic place in the sun. Or maybe you would prefer another destination since you always seem to be out in the sun, somewhere cooler perhaps?"

She glowered at him, as his grin grew wider.

He leaned into her, pushing aside the branches of shrubs. "You've had Michael...Lane...now it's my turn. I promise you won't regret it." He brushed his hand down the front of her blouse, resting his hand on her hip.

Telie's chin lifted in defiance, determined not to run but to confront this guy head on.

"Get your hands off me!" She yanked his arm away, stepped back and balled her fist, planting it across his jaw. A thud followed. David's head fell back slightly, and then snapped forward.

Stunned, he grabbed her throat with both hands. Struggling to get free, she began prying his fingers loose. Suddenly his hands released her throat. Looking up, she saw fear in his eyes as he looked past her. Turning around, she saw Michael quickly approaching. She stepped out of the way. Michael pulled back and plowed his fist into David's face, knocking him backward. He landed hard into the potted plants as bits of terracotta shattered around him. He was out cold.

Michael's arms encircled Telie in a tight protective grip. "Are you all right, baby? Did he hurt you? Let me see your neck." Pulling away from her, he examined her throat, seeing the red marks left by David's fingers.

For a minute she thought it might have all been worth it just to have Michael hold her and call her baby. Snapping back to reality, she said, "I'm okay, he just crossed a line and I hit him. I guess I don't have the same kind of force behind my punch that you have, though. I just made him mad."

Joe shuffled up, hose in hand, moving like slow molasses. "What's goin' on over here?" he drawled. He looked around and saw David sprawled out on top of the potted plants, dirt and pottery scattered everywhere.

Michael took the hose out of Joe's hand and turned it on David. He gasped and spewed water, slapping his hand down his face. Michael handed the hose back to Joe.

He looked sternly at David. "You owe Telie an apology."

"You've got to be kidding!" he spewed. "Hell will freeze over before I apologize to anyone!"

"You really should reconsider, David. It would do your soul a world of good." He reached down and pulled him up sharply, a vice grip on David's soft uncalloused hand.

"Okay, okay, I'm sorry, I'm sorry," David yelled out.

"Let this be the last time I see you on my property. If you so much as think about coming anywhere near Telie again, I'll finish what I've started."

As soon as David was well away from Michael, he yelled back, "You think you've had the last word, don't you? We'll see about that. And by the way, we all know now what kind of a woman your mother was, now don't we!" He scurried into his car and sped away, slinging gravel through the air as he tore out.

Telie spoke first. "He seems like a nice enough guy; it's a pity he's so misunderstood."

"Oh I understand him," Michael said angrily between clenched teeth. "I understand him perfectly."

Glancing around, Telie picked up a rake and began cleaning up the mess from the encounter. She set the geranium pots upright and moved them around, arranging them so the broken sides were not as noticeable. Humming a cheerful melody, she worked at clearing away the debris.

He watched her, puttering around the plants. "Are you all right, Telie? Why don't you take a break? I'll clean this up."

"I'm fine. I don't need a break. I'm just going to straighten this out, then head on over to June's. She's expecting me."

"I'll call her and let her know that you'll come tomorrow." He walked in the direction of the office door, intent on calling June.

"No, Michael, I want to go. I'm fine, really. June has been waiting all week for me to help her with her garden. I can't disappoint her."

He hesitated, and then nodded. "I'll drop by and check on you later."

Telie worked in June's garden late under the afternoon sun. Cicadas grew loud in the trees as the sweltering heat rose up from the ground, making the very air feel tangible, like liquid air.

"Here you go," Michael stretched out his hand, holding the wet glass, condensation dripping down his arm. "June sent this out to you."

"Thanks." Gulping down the icy lemonade, she made a swipe with her gloved hand over her brow. "This heat is unbelievable!"

"Tired?" Michael asked. "Need a swim?"

She couldn't see his eyes behind his sunglasses, but she knew he was teasing. "Wouldn't that be nice," she said, letting her voice trail off.

"Yeah, it would." He looked away. "Unfortunately I have a dinner engagement that I'm already late for. I just stopped by to check on you." She saw his head tilt, appraising her neck. "Looks like the redness is gone, although it's hard to tell when you're pink as a grapefruit."

As he walked off she wondered where he was going, dressed as he was. He was actually wearing a tie! The white shirt he wore was so lightweight she could faintly see his tanned skin underneath. *Wow...he is so handsome*, she thought, feeling the sweat trickle down her chest. She blushed from embarrassment. *And look at me, in all my sweaty glory.*

A thought hit her, *Mary Grace*, and a feeling of pure jealousy rose from somewhere within her. She turned her attention back to the garden, yanking weeds so fast and furious she was out of breath. *I'll bet Mary Grace has never sweated a day in her life!*

She was in no mood for company. Telie walked into the Blue Plate Restaurant and ordered the special to go. While waiting for her order, a few well-dressed ladies made their entrance. She stepped aside, allowing them to pass.

"Telie, I'm so glad I've bumped into you." Mary Grace flashed a dazzling smile, running her eyes up and down Telie's dirty clothes. She scrunched her nose in distaste.

This was one of the few times Telie was actually glad to see Mary Grace. That meant she wasn't with Michael. Hardly able to contain her joy or wipe the grin from her face, she met the disgusted look of Mary Grace with a wide smile.

Waving the others away, Mary Grace turned her attention back to Telie. "I've been meaning to talk to you. You see, Michael is going through a difficult time right now." She had a look of being "in the know" as she flipped her hair back over her shoulder. "I'm not at liberty to say...you see it's a personal matter, but I wanted to make you aware so you would give him the space he needs."

Telie held up her hand, losing patience with this audacious woman. She decided it was best to stop her from saying anything more. "Can it wait, Mary Grace? I'm not in the mood to listen to you right now." Thankfully they called up her order. Brushing past her she picked up her order and left, leaving Mary Grace gaping after her.

She watched in the rearview mirror as the Alabama dust rose like smoke behind her tires. *Another hot, dry and sticky day,* Telie thought. "I don't need anyone to take me swimming if I want to go swimming," she said out loud, defiantly. "I can do whatever I want. Who's stopping me?" Arriving home, she pushed the kitchen door open, placed her dinner on the counter and changed into her bathing suit. She picked up her dinner along with a towel and headed toward the bay.

The bay was calm, warm and inviting. Easing out into the water she twisted around and floated on her back, looking up at the sky, all lavender and swirling. McKeever sat watching her from the shore. She looked up again, fascinated by the soft colors painted across the horizon. Something in her was changing. A need, a longing in her once-shielded heart began to emerge. Her thoughts danced around the notion of having a home, a family of her own.

She swam up to the shore and dried off with her towel. McKeever licked her leg once, then turned back to sit down, as if to say "good girl."

Slipping on the oversized Christenberry T-shirt, she shook her hair loose, then spread out the towel on the narrow beach, pushing away the shells with her toes. Opening her dinner container, she took out a piece of ham and threw it to McKeever. *What would it be like to sit here with my husband, enjoying this evening, talking about the day together?* She dreamed. Only one person came to mind as she contemplated sharing her life with someone, and that someone…loved someone else.

I've got to snap out of this. Busy myself with something, she thought. She remembered the discarded plants in the truck bed and got up, intent on going to Pap's Cove.

Chapter 35

After loading a few tools from the garden shed, Telie headed over to Pap's Cove. Her cell phone buzzed on the passenger seat as she pulled into the parking lot. "Hello?" she said.

"Hey beautiful, this is Lane. I'm out in the boat and thought you might enjoy a cruise. What about it? It's so much nicer at night. The stars practically fall on you. I can meet you anywhere, anywhere there's a dock that is."

"Sounds great, Lane, but I'm here at Pap's Cove helping a friend with some landscaping. In fact, I've just pulled up and haven't even started. I'll probably be working until dark."

"Oh okay, I understand. Hey listen, I might come by later and see if you're still working. Maybe we could have dinner or something." Lane's voice was lighter. Snapping his phone closed, he changed course and headed toward Pap's Cove.

"Let's see," Telie murmured under her breath. She stepped back and appraised the situation.

The front door swung open and Elle stepped out grinning, holding a shovel. "Hey!" she said, waving franticly. "The boss said I could come help you!"

"Great! I could use your help!" she yelled back.

"I'll do whatever you ask, but you'll have to show me. I don't know a thing about landscaping."

"Don't worry, I'll teach you. Now…see that area over there?" she asked, pointing to the front door.

Elle nodded.

"That's where we'll begin. It's better to have a focal point, a place that will draw the eye. The front door is the perfect spot because it will draw people toward it, see?" Telie gestured with her arms outstretched and then narrowed them toward the door.

Elle stared at the pitiful-looking entrance, all drab and dead looking. There was no grass in sight, not one living thing. Even the door itself was worn and faded out like a piece of bleached driftwood.

Not waiting, Telie unloaded the tools from her truck and began lifting out the plants, one at a time. She grouped certain ones together, rearranging them time after time until she seemed to have them the way she wanted them. "Here, go place this tree in that spot over there, next to the door. Come out about six feet from the wall."

Elle did as she was instructed. "Is this good?" she asked, waiting for Telie to give her nod of approval.

"Perfect, now let's get this fountain grass over on the other side." Picking up the large container of grass, the girls sat it down near the entryway. Telie took her foot and pushed the container around until she was satisfied with the placement. "Two more should do it."

"Does everything go in this one area?" Elle asked.

"Yeah...instead of scattering what we have all around, it's better to concentrate on one particular area...just like this. You'll see what I'm talking about. By the way, you don't know of an old bench around here, do ya?" Looking around the grounds, she noticed a few buildings. "Do those storage sheds belong to your boss?"

"Well, one of them is where I live. The other one holds old chairs, broken tables and stuff like that. We can look and see if there's a bench in there." Moving toward the shed, Elle opened the door and began digging around. "Jackpot!" she said.

Telie rushed over and helped her pull out the old bench. "This will do perfectly. Come on, I'll show you what I mean." They carried the bench awkwardly until they reached the entrance area. "Let's put it down right here, in front of the curly willow."

The bench was worn, just like the door. It had the same color tones and matched the door perfectly. "See how this bench ties everything together?" Telie tilted her head, and then grabbed another pot. "We'll plant this Jackson vine next to the door. It won't take long for it to reach the top of the door, and when it does, we'll train it to move across and then back down the other side. Now, let's get digging!"

"Hey!" called a voice from the other side of the building. "Looks good from here!" Lane threw a hand up, smiling.

"Hey Lane," Telie called. "You're just in time."

"Figures, my timing's always exceptional," he said, giving her a lopsided grin.

"Lane, this is my friend, Elle Bragwell. Elle, Lane Bennett."

As Lane looked at Elle, his breath caught in his chest. He had never seen such clear blue eyes. He extended his hand to her.

She gently took his hand and smiled softly saying, "Nice to meet you, Lane."

"Same here." Suddenly he was at a loss for words.

Telie laughed under her breath at the look on Lane's face. Turning her attention from Lane to Elle, she understood why. Elle looked especially pretty today. Gone were the too tight jeans and tacky top. She wore a nicely fitted pair of jeans and a pale blue collared shirt, slightly oversized. Her light brown hair spilled down her back in soft curls. She was beautiful.

"Here, give me that." Lane took the shovel from Elle and asked, "Where do you want the holes?"

This is going to work out good. Lane seems to be eager to impress Elle, and I'll get all my holes dug! She thought. Turning her attention to Elle, Telie said, "While Lane digs the holes, show me your house. Just the outside, I'd die if someone asked to see the inside of my house right now," she said, trying to put Elle at ease.

"There's not much to see, Telie." Elle looked embarrassed. "It's all I can afford right now, but my boss said I can live there as long as I work here."

Lane overheard the conversation, but kept digging, glancing up as they walked toward the cottage.

The gray blockhouse stood facing the bay. Two small windows flanked the single door in front. No other windows or doors existed, just those at the front of the house.

"Elle, this place has potential. Let me show you. See…right here we can hang a couple of window boxes, one on either side of the door. One small can of red paint for the front door and a few geraniums in the window boxes and, voilà, a perfect little cottage by the bay."

Elle didn't know if she should laugh or cry. It amazed her that Telie was able to transform the place so easily in her mind. She'd already turned a desolate entrance into a thing of beauty in less than two hours. "I'll buy the paint tomorrow," she said, an excitement bubbling up from inside her. "What else...I mean what else can you transform? Can you do that with people too, take something ugly and worn and turn it into a thing of beauty?" she asked, half teasing, half serious.

"No, *I* can't. But I'll introduce you to the one who gave me a do-over just a few short years ago. He's a miracle worker!"

"That's someone I need to know!" Elle said. "I could use a miracle."

Lane hollered over to them. "How many of these holes do you want me to dig?" He propped his hands on the shovel handle and waited for them to answer.

It amused Telie that Lane didn't want his work to go unnoticed for very long. "That's good, Lane," she yelled. They walked back to the entrance. "I thought you smoked. I haven't seen you light up once this evening."

"Oh, I only smoke when I'm nervous. I'm really kinda shy. Honestly, I hate the smell of cigarettes." Elle glanced at Telie, then back down to the ground.

Telie smiled as they walked up to the plants. "After we get these in the ground and water them, we'll be finished for the day." A look of satisfaction crossed her face as she took in the charm of the entrance. What was once empty and dead and is now fresh and alive. She thought about Elle's words. She needed a miracle. *Please Lord, help me say the right*

*things to her that will draw her to You. We all need You so
very desperately. We all need Your healing, restoring touch.*

Lane held Telie's hand as she steadied herself against the
movement of the waves as she stepped into the boat. "Too
bad Elle couldn't join us. I think she'd enjoy a ride. I'm
thinking of inviting her to church on Sunday, Lane. Do you
think she'll go?"

Lane shrugged. "I don't know; you can ask her and find
out." He narrowed his eyes. "Why is it you've never invited
me? Have you decided I'm a lost cause?"

His words stung her. In all the time she'd known him,
she had not once thought of inviting him to church. "Oh,
Lane, no, no one is a lost cause as long as they have breath!
Why don't you come this Sunday? I'll ask Elle and let her
know that I've asked you, too. That way she won't feel as
uncomfortable since it will be your first time as well. What
do you say?"

Rubbing his chin, he managed to give her a "maybe."

Chapter 36

The following afternoon, excitement grew as Telie drove down the rutted dirt road beside Pap's Cove. She'd waited anxiously all day to get back to Elle's so she could begin the transformation of Elle's cottage. With paint can in hand, she hopped out of the truck.

The door to Elle's cottage flew open, startling Telie. "Sorry, I didn't mean to scare you. I'm just a little excited to see you; that's all."

Putting down the paint can and brush, Telie leaned over, giving her a big hug. "Me too!"

"Did you and your boyfriend have a nice cruise yesterday? The water was a little choppy near the docks, but it looked a lot smoother out in the bay."

"Lane is not my boyfriend; he's just a friend. Is that why you wouldn't go with us yesterday, because you thought we were on a date?"

"Well, yeah. I didn't want to be the third wheel." A smile tugged at her lips, but she tried to hide it. "I'll get this lid off for you; I have a knife inside, come on in."

Looking around the tiny cottage, Telie felt a lump rise in her throat. The place was clean and neat and very sparse. One ladder-back chair sat next to the window with a small crate for a table next to it. A tiny lamp sat crookedly on top of the uneven slats. In the back corner of the room was a single bed covered with a white chenille bedspread, neatly tucked underneath. The kitchen area, on the opposite wall from the bed, had a small refrigerator and stove with a sink in the middle. Behind the kitchen, a door led to what Telie assumed was a bathroom. There was one closet, no dresser or kitchen table.

"I think this red is going to look great! I brought the window boxes with me. I caught Michael outside today and asked him to make them for us. He's been missing in action these days, and I was lucky to catch him." Telie smiled, realizing she was chattering on and on. She felt uncomfortable in the small house with the obvious need all around her. She was trying hard to seem at ease in front of Elle. If Elle noticed, she didn't let on.

"That was nice of him. I'm sure he's got a lot more important things to do than make window boxes for me," Elle stated, flatly.

"I was glad I was able to pin him down for this. You're gonna love the way they look once we get the geraniums in place." She took the knife Elle offered and walked back outside.

After the first coat of paint was on the door, Telie stood back and looked at her work. "Elle, what do you think...do we need another coat?"

"Nah...looks good to me. Should I paint the window boxes? I think I might be able to manage that." Elle picked up a corner of the box, looking it over. "Do you trust me?"

Blowing her hair up out of her eyes, Telie glanced over her shoulder at Elle. "Of course I trust you. Get busy. Oh, and Elle, would you like to go to church with me on Sunday? I've invited Lane. He got his feelings hurt when I told him I was going to ask you...he wanted to know why I hadn't asked him," she winked at Elle.

"Men." Elle shook her head. "It's been a long time since I've been to church. I know this sounds like a lame excuse, not even original, but I honestly don't have anything to wear. I'm not much of a shopper." Feeling suddenly embarrassed, her neck flushed red.

"Me either. I absolutely hate shopping. Ah, but hold on a minute." She yanked out her phone from her jeans pocket and dialed a number. "Sonny, hey this is Telie. I'm here with a friend painting, and we were just discussing our mutual aversion to shopping and our lack of decent clothing. I was wondering if you could help us."

Sonny could barely keep the excitement out of her voice, "Tell you what. After you finish painting, drop by my house. I've got a bunch of nice clothes just sitting here waiting to be donated to charity. It won't cost you a thing."

Closing the phone, Telie turned to Elle. "Good, it's all set. My friend Sonny has a consignment-clothing store behind her house. She wants us to drop by later. Don't worry about the cost; she's digging out of the charity pile. And right now I can't think of two better charity cases than us!"

The door to the consignment shop closed behind them as Telie and Elle followed Sonny into a back room. Sonny looked thrilled to be able to fix them up with clothes. She practically skipped to the back of the house, rubbing her hands together excitedly. "Look, see I told you I had everything." Picking up a box of clothes marked skirts and dresses, she pulled out several neatly folded items. "Okay...who's first?"

Telie smiled, pointing to Elle. "Don't worry; you'll get your chance to work on me. But right now, we're looking for church clothes for Elle. She's coming with me on Sunday."

"What? Oh, that's great!" Sonny's smile widened. "In that case, let's go for shoes, too. Just look at these darling sandals. I have this customer who buys all these really cute clothes. I honestly don't think she wears the same thing twice, most of these are from her."

Sonny was in her element. In less than an hour, Elle was outfitted with several adorable pieces, including shoes and accessories. Sonny chose solid colors for Elle, mostly in soft fabrics. "See how this lightweight skirt moves? You can wear all three of these tops with it and have three different outfits. Now, I personally feel that soft colors and soft fabric work best for you. A little silver on your wrist...like this." Sonny slid a few simple rings over her hand. "Perfect. Lavender blue is *your* color," she said, admiring the delicate top. "Let's bag the rest of this up for you; you're all set...now for you, Telie."

Chapter 37

A hush fell over the church as Telie entered the sanctuary, followed by Elle, then Lane taking up the rear. She smiled as she remembered the first time she'd come here and how she had felt walking down the long aisle all the way to the front. She imagined Elle and Lane felt the same way, feeling as if every eye was on them.

June looked up, surprised to see them all. She moved down to make room. Elle sat down next to Telie with Lane coming in beside her. Elle looked lovely, radiant even. Lane was adorable as usual, no matter what he was wearing, but his casual blue button-down shirt and khaki pants worked well for him, or was it his face. Something was different about his face. Whatever it was, she was glad for it.

One person could make such a difference in a life, Telie thought.

Telie remembered a quote from Mother Teresa saying, "One should do small things with great love." It's a small thing to help someone with a little planting and painting and a very small thing to invite someone to church. Maybe, just maybe, they will respond to the Lord's voice. It could change the course of their lives forever, just like it had hers.

Michael walked through the church doors, hesitating as he glanced over to where Telie and June usually sat. He didn't recognize the girl who sat next to Telie, but he instantly recognized Lane. Just as he was about to turn his head, the girl looked back over her shoulder and gave him a tiny wave. "Elle!" he spoke out loud. He walked toward them, extending his hand first to Lane, then to Elle. "Good to see you both," Michael said. He looked at Telie; the expression on his face was one of confused delight.

"We've got room, sit with us." Telie slid down the seat, making room for Michael on the end, next to Lane.

Michael took his seat, then stood a second later as Nathan walked to the pulpit and began leading them in an opening song. He handed a hymnbook to Lane, after opening it to the correct page, and motioned for him to share with Elle. Realization hit suddenly. Lane was his nephew! His nephew! He was sitting in church next to his nephew! He had never known another relation besides his mother and father. Now, here he was in church sitting next to a blood relative.

Nathan's message spoke of following Christ no matter the cost and what a believer would gain if he did. Once or twice Telie noticed Elle's eyes fixed on Nathan, as if her very life depended on his words. Telie understood that Nathan's words were God's words and that those words had life. She silently thanked God for speaking to her friends and for using her to get them there to hear His word.

After service, Lane took hold of Nathan's hand and thanked him for the message. "I'd like to talk to you sometime, Nathan, if you have the time. I've got a couple of questions…things maybe you could help me understand."

"Sure…Lane, isn't it?"

"Yes. Lane, Lane Bennett."

"Tell you what, Lane, you come by here anytime. I'm usually always around here somewhere." Nathan patted Lane on the shoulder. "I look forward to it."

Elle was outside the church standing under a shady tree talking to Sonny as Lane and Telie approached. "I was just telling Sonny how much I appreciate the makeover. I feel like a new person today." Elle beamed up at Lane.

Michael and Nathan stepped outside and saw the little group under the tree. "God works in mysterious ways, doesn't He?" Michael said, appraising his friends.

Nathan smiled, knowing the conflicting emotions Michael must be dealing with. "It will work out, Michael. God's in this; it will work out, trust Him."

Mary Grace breezed by them. "Did your friends leave you out, Michael? Looks like they're all going out. Now why would they not invite you?" She didn't even try to hide the smirk on her face.

"Give it a rest, Mary Grace; they invited me. I've just got other plans." Shaking his head, he turned to give her a look of disgust. "I really wish you'd find some other form of entertainment, Mary Grace. All this interest you have in my life is starting to wear on me."

Getting back to the cottage after having lunch with Elle and Lane at Pap's Cove, Telie looked over her kitchen garden before going into the house. It popped with color and lush green foliage. Walking between the rows, she admired the sharp bright colors of the zinnias that bordered the garden, moving their heads drowsily in the breeze. A thought came to her. Rushing inside she snatched up a pair of clippers from the kitchen drawer and ran back out to the garden. She began cutting the flowers, mixing a variety of colors. Bunching them together, she picked up a string she found near the tomato stakes and tied them together in a loose bow. *This is another small thing,* she thought. *It just might make a difference, who knows.*

Just before sunset, Telie strolled silently down the path toward the bayou, flowers in hand. The well-worn path told her of the many visits Theda had made to the bayou. She bent, placing the bouquet down gently with a note that simply read, "To Theda."

The following day a mist covered the early morning ground damp with dew. Telie started down the path, anxious to see if the flowers had been taken. Her eyes scanned the nearby woods and the place where she'd laid the flowers. No flowers. A slow smile spread across her face.

A young mother with a baby on her hip stood listening to Telie. She moved from side to side, rocking the baby gently as she listened to her give instructions on how to care for her newly purchased plants.

"Loosen the roots first with your fingers like this," she said, demonstrating, "especially if they're in a tight mass like this one. And water every day until the roots become established."

"For how long?" the young mother asked, bouncing the baby up and down on her hip as she tried to listen over the whimpering child.

"A few weeks should be fine." Telie smiled at the baby, bent down and picked a long-stemmed daisy and gave it to the child. *It worked,* Telie thought, *it was just the kind of distraction that poor mother needs to buy her some time so she can finish her shopping.*

"Thanks," the young mother said. "She was working up to a full-blown wail!"

"Telie!" Martha shouted, "Come here!"

Smirking, she said, "Excuse me...I'm being paged. Call me if you need help with that."

Waving in the air, Martha called to her, "Go tell Mr. Evans that his order is ready."

Scanning the crowd outside, she saw several men hanging out around a truck up front. "Okay, which one is Mr. Evans?"

"He's the bald guy over by the white truck. The one that looks like he's got a package of weenies strapped to the back of his head."

"Oh, *that* guy." She loved the way Martha described people. She could only hope and pray that no one ever asked her to point her out in a crowd. Michael once told her that Martha had insulted the president of the local bank. He was known far and wide for being a cheapskate. She'd told him to let the moth out of his wallet and buy a new plant for a change and not some pitiful half-dead stick on the discount table. That was Martha.

Telie stepped up to Mr. Evans, informing him of the order that was ready and waiting. She smiled a pleasant smile and as she turned to go, she caught a glimpse of Lane's jeep in the parking lot. "Oh, Lane's here!" she said under her breath. Looking around, not finding him anywhere, she went inside to ask Martha. "Have you seen Lane?"

"Yeah, he's in there talking to Michael," she gestured to the office door.

"Oh," she said, deflated. Walking back outside she busied herself, trying not to think about what he could possibly be talking to Michael about.

An hour or so later she saw Lane emerge from the office. He tucked a folder under his arm, put on his sunglasses and stepping onto the gravel parking lot headed for his jeep.

He reached for the handle and looked up, seeing her, "Telie!" He closed the gap between them. "Hey…I was hoping I'd get to see you while I was here. How've you been?"

"Oh fine. I thought that was your jeep, but I couldn't find you." She was waiting for an explanation, but Lane didn't offer one. He smiled down at Telie, taking her hands in his.

"You look hot, and I mean that in every sense of the word. Are you hot and tired?"

"Not too bad. I wish it would rain though and cool things off." Jutting out her bottom lip, she blew up a loose strand of hair.

Something was going on; she could feel it. She was sure Martha knew something, but she wasn't talking, that in itself was highly unusual. Michael had been distracted for weeks now. She noticed a difference in him. He seemed troubled by something; now this unexpected visit from Lane further confused her. What's going on? *It's none of my business*, she thought, trying to put it out of her mind. *If I need to know, he'll tell me.*

Lane studied her face, misreading her thoughts. "Come have dinner with me. I promise…no more propositions, just dinner." He lifted her hands to his lips and placed a soft kiss on each of them. "What do you say?"

"I say that sounds good." She smiled back at him.

"What time shall I pick you up, 5:30?"

"Perfect. That will give me a chance to get ready. How should I dress?"

"However you like, casual of course."

Excitement filled her. She loved Lane's company and the easy way time rolled by when they were together. Still, she wished someone else had asked her to dinner. *Don't think like that!* She reprimanded herself, shaking the thought from her mind.

"See you then," he said with a smile, dropping her hands gently.

Telie stood there and watched as his jeep pulled away. Hearing the door open behind her, she turned. Michael brushed past her without a word. He got into his truck and left behind Lane.

Martha came out right behind him, laughing. "You sure got him all stirred up, Telie girl. I've got to hand it to you. I never would've believed Michael Christenberry would have ever snapped out of that blue fog he's been living in for the past three years, but boy when he snapped, he snapped!"

Telie had no idea what she was talking about or what was going on. She stared at Martha's back as she went back inside. Twisting her lips, she wondered if she was the only one around that didn't know what was going on.

Lane pulled up at Bell Forest just after 5:30. He looked around marveling at the vibrant colors, the blue sparkling sea, the green lawn and pink clouds against a violet sky. It was breathtaking. Even the garden was washed with muted colors of pink and purple from the evening sky.

"I bet you wish you had your sketchpad and paints, don't you?" Telie remarked, coming up beside him in the yard. "This place is magical. I never get tired of it; it changes constantly."

"If I had my sketchpad, you wouldn't get dinner. Lucky for you that I don't," he said jokingly. "As beautiful as this place is…it doesn't hold a candle to you. You look like you belong here." Taking her hand, he lifted her arm, twirling her around, admiring the way her white dress looked fluid on her body. "You could pass for a wood nymph or water sprite, you know." His eyes moved over her admiringly.

"I just might be," she said, winking up at him. "Where are we going?"

"Oh, I thought we might go out on the boat. The water's smooth as glass. It's a perfect night for it. I thought you'd enjoy the wind in your hair. I saw how you were trying to manufacture your own breeze this afternoon by blowing on it." He lifted his hand and moved a strand of hair from her face, tucking it behind her ear.

"And dinner?" She asked, confused.

"Why? Are you starving?" He slid his arm around her waist, pulling her close as they walked down the path toward the jeep.

"Uh…yeah, follow me around for one day and you'll understand why."

"We'll have dinner on the boat. I've called ahead…they'll have it ready for us when we arrive. I've got to stop by the shipyard first; it's on the way. I need to deliver something to my dad, then we'll be on our way."

"They, who's they?" she asked, trying to piece it together. She felt like she lived in a parallel universe sometimes, especially around Lane.

"The crew." He said the words slowly as if he were talking to a child.

"Oh...well excuse *me*. I guess I was thinking we were getting on a little flat-bottom boat and needed to scrounge up something for dinner."

"Scrounge up something for dinner? Hmm...raccoons scrounge up something for dinner...people dine." His smile took the edge off of his sarcastic words. "Do I look like the kind of guy who would sail off with you in a flat-bottom boat with a bag of cheese puffs and a Spam sandwich?" He raised his eyebrows, looking down at her.

"Don't knock it till you've tried it," she replied dryly, annoyed at his superior attitude.

They pulled up to an industrial-looking gate with a guardhouse located just inside the entrance to the shipyard. Lane waved and the guard opened the gate, waving them on. They drove past towering cranes and huge warehouses; everything around them looked hard and cold. They weaved in and out of structures until they came upon an office building located near the dock.

"Come on, this won't take long." Hopping out of the jeep, he reached for her hand and led her through the front glass doors.

They walked briskly down the corridor of the office building. Telie observed the walls, made entirely of white beaded board mounted horizontally, giving the place a nautical feel. Model ships and compasses were displayed here and there. Scattered around were large captain's chairs in rich red leather. The seating arrangements took advantage of the view of the bay from massive windows across one wall. Black and white photos filled the opposite wall with scenes from the past depicting the early days of the Bennett Shipbuilding Company.

Lane opened a door leading into a conference room, pulling Telie in behind him. "Sorry to interrupt," Lane said.

They walked across the room toward the conference table as Tommy Bennett pushed back his chair and stood up.

"You're not interrupting, son; we're just getting started." Tommy Bennett smiled warmly at them. "Thanks for bringing this...and oh, everyone, this is Lane's friend, Telie McCain." He gestured with his hand to include the others sitting around the table.

Telie smiled as she nodded toward the others and froze. Sitting at the far end of the table was Michael. He stared at her without blinking...his face impossible to read. She met his gaze for an agonizing second before turning away.

"Well," Lane spoke, "we'll get out of your way." Picking up Telie's hand, he escorted her toward the door.

"Where are you kids off to?" Dottie chimed in. "The boat?"

Turning back, Lane said, "Yeah, I thought I'd treat Telie to dinner and a cruise. I think she's a little disappointed though. She was hoping for a flat-bottom fishing boat and a bologna sandwich. She's been telling me how I need to broaden my horizons and experience some of the finer things in life."

A low laughter rumbled through the room as Telie elbowed him in the ribs, her face crimson. She didn't dare look at Michael but felt his gaze on her.

Walking back down the hall she punched him in the arm. "Embarrass me next time why don't you!"

"Ah...I was just playing. Don't be mad...you're adorable when you're embarrassed...I just couldn't resist." His dazzling smile quickly melted her resolve.

A nagging question bothered her as they boarded the boat. "What was Michael doing with the Bennetts?" Going through the motions, distracted by her thoughts to the point of being led around by Lane, she didn't really notice her surroundings.

"Telie, are you not feeling well?" The concern in his voice was evident.

"No, I'm fine. Just a little bit…"

He interrupted her. "You're worried about getting sea sick, aren't you? Well, don't worry; that's why I chose to go out today…the water's like glass." He patted her hand and smiled, pleased that he'd figured out her sudden quietness. "I promise, a landlubber like you will be perfectly comfortable on the water today. Trust me."

Her mind kept circling back to Michael. She tried to understand the undercurrent that ran between them. Why did she care that he'd apparently shut her out of his life? Why did it bother her that he wouldn't confide in her the way he obviously had in others? She was just beginning to realize that there was so much she didn't know or understand about Michael Christenberry.

The evening was progressing nicely with a delicious meal and a spectacular sunset. "What's this I'm eating?" Taking another bite, Telie looked up, waiting for Lane to answer.

"That's Chicken Scaloppini. Do you like it?"

"It's not a Spam sandwich or anything, but it'll do," she said, grinning. "No, I'm kidding. It's delicious."

"Telie, can I ask you a question now that we're way out here in the middle of the sea and you can't run away from me?" Placing the fork down on the table, he looked up, waiting for her answer.

"I can still jump ship you know…but go ahead, I'll risk it." Taking another bite of her chicken, she waited on Lane to speak.

"Why do you have to be so...moral? I mean...don't you ever feel like you're missing out on something...that maybe you could be enjoying yourself more, enjoying life more, experiencing more?" He let his words hang in the air as he watched her reaction to his question.

"It may be hard for you to understand, Lane, and even harder to explain, but I'll try. You see, when I became a Christian a few years ago, I decided to live my life His way, God's way, and not my way anymore, fulfilling my own desires. Sometimes that's *very* hard to do, but I've found that His way is always best. Don't misunderstand; God is not trying to keep me from pleasure, Lane. He invented it after all. He just knows that the kind of pleasure you're talking about is best between a husband and wife." She waited a moment before adding, "I simply want what's best, Lane, not sexual recreation without a committed, loving relationship. That's too shallow of an existence for me. Does that make sense to you? I'm just holding out for the best."

"When you put it that way, it makes sex outside of marriage sound cheap! What are you trying to do, Telie, take all the fun out of it for me?" He laughed and stood up. "Well, I asked for it, didn't I?"

"That you did." Cutting a piece of broccoli with her fork, she fought to keep from smiling.

"And you gave me both barrels, God *and* relationships. The two things in life I'm not that comfortable with."

Telie hoped that Lane would consider her words.

Lane seemed lost in thought, as if he were weighing something...turning it over in his mind. Once or twice he would start to say something, then stop. Whatever was bothering him, he kept to himself.

"What do you think of Elle?" Telie asked, breaking the silence.

Lane met her gaze and shrugged. "Beauty inspires."

"That's not what I'm asking."

"What *are* you asking? Am I interested in her?" Suddenly, he was fighting a smile. "I really hope you're jealous."

"You know I'm not jealous, I'm just curious." She placed her napkin down beside her plate and pushed back from the table slightly.

"That's what I was afraid of." Placing his drink down on the table, he said, "I think she's very charming. Of course we're polar opposites. I was born into privilege, and she, into less than desirable circumstances from what I gather. But it's strange, Telie." He furrowed his brow. "When I'm around her, I feel strong, capable. I don't feel that way often. I guess I've lived a pretty self-centered life. My family's money has allowed me to enjoy the finer things in life. But, truth be known, none of it really satisfies. I enjoy painting and making a living by my art, but even that sometimes leaves me empty."

"Life can be more, Lane. Beauty draws us to the one who created it – God. Only He satisfies."

Chapter 38

"Where's Telie?" Michael demanded as he stepped past Martha. He flung his sunglasses across the room; they landed against the wall with a thud.

"Out back...why?" She peered at him over the top of her glasses.

Ignoring her question, Michael stormed out the back door, his eyes searching the grounds until he spotted her.

Telie saw Michael's fast approach and wondered what was wrong. From the look on his face she determined something bad had happened. She braced herself, waiting for him to speak the dreadful news.

Stopping directly in front of her, he spoke in clearly measured words. "I guess Lane told you about me." His face was flushed with anger, his teeth clenched. Glaring at her, he asked, "Well, what did he say? What did he tell you when you were out with him on your little sunset cruise yesterday?"

She looked up at him innocently. "I don't know what you're talking about. Lane hasn't told me anything about you. Why would he?" The wind whipped her hair around her face; narrowing her eyes she searched his face, trying to make sense of his sudden anger.

"Oh come off it, Telie. You can't tell me he said nothing to you about me. That's all those Bennetts are talking about!"

"Sorry to disappoint you." She turned her back to him, walking away, not knowing how to respond to his accusations. All she wanted to do was get away from him before she said something she'd regret or worse…cry. She felt a lump rise in her throat in reaction to his harsh words. He'd never spoken to her that way before.

"Wait just a minute, I'm not through with you," he said harshly. "Don't ever walk away from me while I'm speaking to you!"

Turning around to face him she could hardly believe he was the same person she'd known for the past few months. Where had Michael gone? Who was this person?

Anger mixed with resentment filled her. She spit the words out carefully and precisely. "Who do you think you are speaking to me that way? I'll go whenever and wherever I please!"

"I'm your boss, that's who I am!" His eyes turned a dark seething green.

"Not anymore you're not!" She slammed down the spade in her hand and jerked off her gloves, flinging them away. She turned away from him, steadily walking toward the office.

Stunned, he could only stare after her in disbelief. He felt as if he were watching the whole thing play out in slow motion before his eyes. He watched her enter the office, and in a flash, the door flung open and she was outside again. She climbed into her truck, and drove off.

"Nice work!" Martha said, approaching him from the office door.

He just stood there, dumbfounded.

"You've just successfully run off the best employee we've ever had. What the heck is wrong with you, Michael? I mean...have you forgotten how to let someone know you love them? Just a little hint, for future reference, that ain't how."

He blinked, and turned to Martha. "I don't know, Martha; I honestly don't know what is happening to me."

"That's your problem, boy. You're allowing things to happen to you that should never be happening in the first place. You go home and think about what I just said. If you're smart, you'll go after her. Don't let someone else's life ruin yours. There's more to life than money, Michael, way more."

Telie turned down the dirt road leading to Bell Forest, dust rising from behind her speeding truck. She was still shaking from the confrontation. "I've got to get out of here," she murmured under her breath. She had learned to stifle her emotions for so long it surprised her when tears sprang up from her eyes, stinging and hot. Everything around her was out of focus, blurry.

Once inside the cottage, she tried not to think past packing her belongings. She hurried around the cottage, methodically gathering her things and placing them by the door. She made her bed and cleaned the sink in the bathroom. Wiping down the kitchen counter, she placed everything back the way she'd found it when she first arrived. Reaching up, she removed the painting Lane had given her from the mantle and placed it near the kitchen door with the rest of her belongings.

McKeever looked confused, pacing back and forth with his tongue hanging out. Propping open the door, she began loading her things into the back of the truck. After the truck was loaded, she walked around, straightening and sweeping until the place was clean and orderly. Turning around in a hurry, she plowed right into Theda.

"Where you goin', child?" Theda asked. Her glassy brown eyes darted around the room.

Telie was startled, speechless. Finding her voice, she replied, "I don't know, just away from here!"

"You mad at somebody? Runnin' away? Come on to my house, child; you can stay with me until you figure out what you gonna do." She headed toward the back door as she spoke. "You better hurry up…there's only one way outa here and them monks have sure enough called Michael by now. You go on and drive around to that dirt road," she said, pointing down the road toward a stand of trees. "The road to my house is just on the other side of those trees; don't miss it, looks like a rabbit trail. I'll meet you at the house."

She knew Theda was right. Brother Simeon never missed a thing. Although she didn't know how Theda knew that or how she knew Michael might be headed that way. She could only pray that the monks were at evening prayer and hadn't seen her. The thought of facing Michael again made her physically sick. Hurrying now, she loaded the rest of her things into the truck, including McKeever. She took one last look around the place she had come to love. Letting the screen door slam behind her, she cranked her truck and pulled away.

Telie watched as Theda ambled up the path. She got out of her truck and waited for her beside the steps leading up to a slightly tilted front porch.

Theda's house was old. The wooden siding had once been white; now, a dull faded gray covered the planks. Two worn-out rockers with the cane bottoms torn and fraying sat facing each other. A single pot of geraniums was perched beside the front door. The yard was neat and well kept, mostly a sand-dirt mix with a single patch of grass directly in front of the steps.

McKeever ran up to greet Theda excitedly, pushing his noise under her hand. She patted his head and kept on walking. "Goodness gracious, girl, go on inside out of this heat," she said with a wave of her hand.

Telie shook her head. "I'll wait for you."

"Okay then…I'm comin', I'm comin'. Old ladies can't be rushed."

Taking hold of the rail, she climbed the three steps, resting after each one. Shuffling over to the front door, she bent down and stuck a finger into the soil of the potted geranium. "Needs water," she stated before opening the door. "Come on, come on. Now, you want some tea?" she asked, pausing in the doorway.

"That sounds good." Telie patiently inched inside behind Theda, glancing around the room.

The small, sparsely furnished living room was bright and clean. Three orange vinyl cushioned chairs with metal studs were placed around a small Formica table in the dining room. A loveseat with sagging "watermill" cushions and a simple pine coffee table were all that filled the living room. A worn-out Bible and a blue canning jar with a few drooping stems of Queen Anne's lace graced the table.

Theda extended her hand, holding a glass of iced tea out to her before sitting down. "Now, tell me, girl…your name is Telie?"

"Yes, Telie McCain. How did you know?"

Theda laughed, holding her chest with one hand. "Just 'cause I'm quiet, don't mean I can't hear! I heard that monk hollering at you one day...clear over here." Shaking her head, she looked at Telie. "Things were peaceful around here till you showed up. You just like Joy Christenberry, all full of life. Bell Forest is just on the other side of those trees." She gestured with her hand, looked up and smiled. "I been seeing you...you and Mr. Monk...hidin' in the bushes, watching me." She broke out in a high-pitched squeal. "I tried to look scary...give ya'll something to gawk at." Dabbing her eyes with her apron, she tried to compose herself. "How'd I do?"

"Oh, you scared me all right...," shaking her head, amused at the little old woman. Her buttery gold skin and shining eyes made her seem soft, like a well-loved doll. *I can't believe I was ever frightened of her. She must have been a beauty in her day.* "Who is Joy Christenberry?" Telie raised her eyebrows, waiting for an explanation.

"Michael's mama. She lived down here for a while. Yes, Lord, she loved it down here." Theda seemed lost in thought for a moment, then continued, "Now, why are you runnin' away, child? Has somebody been mean to you? Not Michael, he would never be mean to nobody. He's good, like his daddy."

Something about Theda made you want to tell her your business. Something in the way she looked at you, like a grandmother. "I just don't understand what's going on, Theda. Michael has changed. He yelled at me at work today for no reason. He wanted to know what Lane Bennett had said about him. Lane is..."

Theda interrupted. "I know Lane...and the rest of them Bennetts," she said firmly. "Go on with your story."

"I told him that Lane hadn't told me anything about him. What's there to tell? He didn't believe me; he thought I was lying." Tears gathered in her eyes, frustrating her as she wiped them away with her fingers.

"Oh child, don't be upset with him. He's just scared." She reached over and patted Telie's leg.

"Scared, I've never known Michael Christenberry to be scared of anything!" She looked skeptical of the comment. "What would he be scared of, Theda...tell me."

"Well, it's not mine to tell. But if you ask God, I'm sure He'll give you the answer you need. He always does." Taking a sip of tea, she cleared her throat. "I can tell you this; Michael is confused right now...he needs you now more than ever. If his mother was alive, I know what she would tell him. She would say to stay away from them Bennetts. I do know that much is true."

Trying to make sense out of it, she asked, "So how do you know all of this, Theda? How did you know I was leaving Bell Forest? How do you know what's going on with Michael and the Bennetts?"

"Oh my, so many questions, well let me see...I knew you was leavin' when I saw your truck backed up to the door and all this stuff flying out all over everywhere. And I know what's goin' on with Michael because my sister, Mae, works for Dottie Bennett and that's all they talkin' about. Any more questions, Miss Priss?"

Telie shook her head, and then paused. "Yeah, why do you visit the bayou in the middle of the night?" There, she had finally asked it. No more stepping around it, she wanted to know what was going on with this lady before she divulged any more details of her life.

A hoot came from Theda's lips. "I'm not crazy, child...I know that's what everybody thinks, and I let them think that just so folks will leave me alone. To answer your question, I go down to the bayou to visit the grave of my baby...my sweet Lilly. The waters overtook her grave awhile back when the bayou started creeping up this way. "

"Oh...I'm sorry, Theda, I didn't know." She mentally chided herself for being so direct. "So you lost your baby?"

"Yes, girl, I did." After a lingering moment, she continued. "The old cemetery for black folks was down near the bayou. There are only a few graves left; most of the others have been relocated. The bayou waters covered over the few that are left. I just don't have it in me to move her. I kinda like it that she's nearby so I can walk over to her. I go at night in the summertime because of the heat, and I don't get out much in the winter. I might keel over down there if I ain't too careful."

Telie spoke softly, "Has your little girl been gone a long time?"

"Hmm? Oh yes, girl, a mighty long time. But she's in my heart," she said, tapping her chest. "I'll be seein' her in heaven. One day soon I'd imagine. One day soon."

Theda convinced Telie to stay awhile at her place while she decided her future. The two of them quickly settled into a lazy rhythm, each one needing the other. Telie was finding it difficult to think too far ahead. Theda encouraged her not to rush God, but to wait patiently for His guidance. "He always takes care of His children," she repeated often.

"Theda, you want me to replace the light bulbs for you in the bedroom? One is already out, and I bet it won't be long until the other one goes too."

"Heavens yes, child, and there's one in the oven that's shot. See if you can reach in there and get it out; careful now, that one's tricky."

Telie grabbed the ladder from the shed and carried it inside. She changed the light bulbs, looked down and said,

"While I've got this ladder out, why don't I run to the hardware store and pick up a couple of smoke detectors? I've noticed you could use a few around here. I wouldn't want you to get caught in this house by a fire." She climbed down the ladder and retrieved her purse from the bedroom. "I'll be right back."

"You know what's best." Theda responded. She waved her hand as she walked back to the kitchen. "Don't put them things anywhere near my kitchen. I'd be settin' them off all the time," she said, laughing.

"You need anything else while I'm out?"

"Pick me up some grits from the store. I want some grits to go along with that ham you cooked."

Climbing into her truck, she headed down the road toward the hardware store. She pulled up to the curb, finding a parking space on the side of the building under the shade of a tree.

Once inside the store, a friendly voice called from behind the counter, "Can I help you?"

"Yes. I'm looking for smoke detectors."

The man behind the counter pointed to the back row. "Last aisle, lower shelf, on the right."

"Thanks." Looking around, she found several different types of detectors. She picked up each one to read the details. "This one has a built-in rate-of-rise heat detector," she said, under her breath. "What the heck is a rate-of-rise heat detector?"

A clang sounded as the front door opened. Her breath caught in her chest as Michael entered the store. Dropping down slightly to hide behind the shelves, she peered at him between the fire extinguishers. He was barely recognizable. His face was unshaven and scruffy; his light brown hair longer than she'd ever remembered it, hanging over the collar of his shirt. He looked tired and worn out.

"Hey Michael, how's the project going?" The man behind the counter asked, smiling.

"Going well, I'm almost finished. Just need another can of varnish to finish up." He looked around the store quickly as if he sensed someone's presence.

She ducked, almost dropping the smoke detector that she gripped in her hand. She held it to her chest. Her heart pounded frantically in her chest. She was afraid he had seen her.

The clerk walked past Telie, eyeing her suspiciously, then picked up a can of varnish and headed back to the counter. "Here you go. What else can I do for you, Michael?"

"That should do it, Pete. Thanks," he said, laying his money on the counter. He looked around one last time before heading out the door.

Waiting until she was sure he had gone, she walked up to the counter. Aware of the strange look the clerk was giving her, she felt as if she needed to explain, but decided not to. He rang up her purchases; she paid and got out of there.

"How old are you?" Theda asked abruptly while Telie was installing her smoke detectors. She craned her neck up to look at Telie.

"Twenty-six," Telie said, as she snapped in the batteries. "Why?"

"My Lilly would have been thirty-one this year. She's Michael's half-sister, you know. Yes, thirty-one. She didn't even live one full day. Poor baby, I miss her so much." Her voice melted away smooth.

Listening, Telie nodded, afraid if she spoke Theda would stop talking. The shock of her admission was not evident on Telie's face. She managed to continue working on the smoke detectors. She smiled slightly and held her mouth shut so it wouldn't drop open.

"That's how come me and Miss Joy was so close. We shared the same grief."

Not able to handle it any longer, Telie asked, "So you and Miss Joy were friends?"

"Why heavens yes, child! We had ourselves a regular soap opera around here for a while. She was a fine lady that Joy…a beautiful, fine lady. I miss her so much."

Looking away, Telie struggled with how to phrase the question in her mind. "So, Mr. Christenberry fathered your child?"

"Oh for heaven's sake, no, child, Mr. Christenberry would never do such a thing. He was a fine Christian man. He would never do nothin' like that. He loved Miss Joy more than anything in this world. No…Tom Bennett forced his self on me. I was their cook…worked for him twenty years cookin' and helping him raise his children after his wife passed…until that day. I'll tell you something else. Them Bennetts don't know what it means to do without! They've never been denied. Miss Joy, she knew that too…how spoiled they was. I don't blame her for not wantin' her son raised up in that mess. Mr. Bennett came to me after she done rejected him. He was drunk as Cooter Brown!"

Theda's words landed on Telie with a jolt. "So, is that what's wrong with Michael? He found out about his father?"

"Land sakes, child, I didn't say nothing about Michael! How did you go and figure that out? You kids today...just too smart for your own good!"

Relief flooded her. *He must be so hurt and confused!*

That certainly explains his behavior for the past few weeks and why he has been with the Bennetts. That even explains his rough appearance, she thought. *He's depressed!*

"What you thinkin' about, Miss Priss – goin' to find him? I tell you this...you better wait till he finds you. A man don't want sympathy from a woman."

She was right. That's probably the reason he hadn't told her in the first place. After seeing him at the hardware store, his face haunted her. He was suffering; that was plainly evident. "Theda...pray for him."

"Oh of course, child, you know I will."

Chapter 39

The last few weeks had been a struggle for Michael. After Telie disappeared, he went on an all-out search for her. June was the first person he'd stopped by to see, hoping to find her. He told her to call him if she heard anything from her. It was June who suggested that she might have decided to go back home to Coldwater.

Home, Michael thought. *This is her home. This is where she belongs.*

He slammed his truck door and strode across the yard in front of Mila's home, silently thanking God for small towns. Getting directions had been easy in this close-knit community; everyone knows everybody and all too happy to tell you what they know.

Mila was hurrying out the front door, keys in hand when she looked up and saw a man in her yard, walking toward her. Startled, her purse dropped out of her hand, landing with a thud on the porch floor.

Michael scooped it up, handing it back to her. Lifting his eyes, he met her gaze and found himself staring into the exact same eyes as Telie. He was struck speechless.

"Thank you," Mila said. "May I help you?" She saw the shock on the man's face and briefly wondered if the handsome man had gotten the wrong address.

Seeing her confusion, he smiled reassuringly and said, "I hope so. I'm looking for Telie McCain."

"Oh." Relief flooded her face. "I'm sorry, my daughter is not here. She moved away to Moss Bay months ago."

He pursed his lips. "Hmm…" After a moment, he asked, "Mrs.?"

"Mila, please call me Mila."

Telie was right: her mother is beautiful, he thought. "Mila, I…well, I'm Michael Christenberry." His name seemed to register on her face. He held up his hand, signaling that he needed to explain. His voice broke. "We had an argument. It was completely my fault, all of it. I haven't been able to find her since." Raking his hand through his hair, he looked troubled and tired.

Having pity on him, Mila asked, "Would you like to come inside?"

"Oh no, I don't want to bother you. You look like you're about to go somewhere."

Shaking her head, she said, "Please, come in. I was just going to the post office; that can wait."

Walking in behind her, Mila called over her shoulder, "I'll fix us some tea. Want ice with yours or just cold and straight?"

"Ice…thanks," Michael replied.

Looking around, he saw a group of silver-framed pictures on the mantle. Moving in for a closer look, he picked up a picture of Telie, laughing with her back against a magnolia tree. She must have been about seventeen or eighteen. His smile was both happy and sad as he studied the picture.

Stepping back into the room, Mila handed Michael the iced tea. "She's lovely, isn't she?" Mila observed the tender way he handled the frame, watching as he placed it carefully back on the mantle.

"Very." The ice clanged in his glass. Sipping his drink he looked around, not sure where to begin.

"Sit down, Michael," she said, pointing to a comfortable-looking armchair. "You seem terribly upset," Mila noted, taking a seat across from him on the couch. "Would it help you to know that I talked to her this morning?"

Surprise lit his face. "This morning, did she tell you where she was?" Leaning forward, hope filled his voice.

"No, no she didn't. I just assumed she was calling from work. She hasn't told me about the argument." She hesitated a moment, then asked, "If you don't mind my asking, Michael, why do you care so much about finding my daughter?"

His hand froze in midair, holding the tea glass. He placed it on the coffee table, then said, "Because I love your daughter."

A smile spread across Mila's face. "Does she know how you feel?"

"No...that's why I need to find her."

When Michael left that afternoon, Mila prayed a simple prayer. "Oh God, please help this man find my daughter."

Michael woke up to rain spattering on his bedroom window and slid deeper under the soft quilt, not wanting to face another day. Reluctantly he rolled out of bed and hopped into the shower. After dressing he took his coffee and walked down the steps and out into the garden. "Another fork," Michael noted to himself, stepping over the rows in the garden. The rain had hammered the plants. He gently lifted the tomato vines, placing them back securely in the cages. Fingering the prongs of the silver fork, he pulled it out of the mud, wiped it off and stuck it in his pocket.

Placing the fork on the table, he thought how Telie would enjoy the wind chimes he'd made out of the silverware. The soft tinkling signaled when the wind was up or a storm was approaching. "She'd like that," he said under his breath.

The only place he hadn't checked for Telie was Pap's Cove. *Hopefully Elle might know something*, he thought. Elle and Telie had gotten close. Pushing aside his apprehension, he drove out to the cove. "Telie," he whispered. With stabbing loneliness, he realized he'd traveled this way before, with the same heavy heart, down the same one-lane road. He'd not let himself sink into despair this time. This time he'd called on God for strength and guidance. Stepping out of his truck, his boots hit the gravel. He felt weighted down, heavy. From the corner of his eye, he spied Lane's jeep. Elle and Lane were leaning against it, talking.

"Michael!" Elle shouted. "Over here." She waved to him as Lane turned around.

Michael looked distraught. A half-hearted smile tugged at his lips. "Hey…ya'll are out early this morning. Goin' fishin'?" He saw a tackle box and a picnic basket beside Elle's feet.

"Yeah…we thought we'd try out Telie's idea of a good time. Elle fixed bologna sandwiches, and I brought the cheese puffs!" Lane said, the laugh not quite reaching his eyes. "So...what brings you out, Michael – want to come along?"

"Oh, no thanks, I was just wondering if either of you have heard from her."

Shaking her head, Elle looked down, not wanting to see the disappointment in Michael's eyes.

"Sorry Michael, we haven't. We were just talking about that. I've called repeatedly...no answer. Elle asks everyone that comes in if they've seen her. It's like she's vanished. I want to plaster her face on every milk carton in town," Lane said. He swallowed hard. "The truth is, Michael, it's not like her to do this to us. I know you said that you two had an argument, but why would she not talk to us?"

"I don't understand it either, Lane." Michael looked around, noticing for the first time all of the changes. "New ownership?"

"Nah...Telie did all of this, except for the window boxes on my place. I believe you helped with that." Elle smiled. "I think about her every time I come outside."

Michael nodded. "Yeah, I see her everywhere these days too. You know what's even more pathetic? I thought I smelled her the other day. I was at the hardware store, and I could have sworn I smelled her perfume."

"Lemons," Lane whispered.

Elle got choked up and started to cry. Lane gathered her into his arms, looking over the top of her head at Michael, he said, "Man, we're praying for her...you too. If we hear from her, you'll be the first to know, I promise."

Hesitating at the truck before he got in, Michael looked over at the curly willow tree he had slated for the trash pile. It was growing tall and lush and full of life. Haunted, that's how he felt, haunted by her memory. He saw her in every aspect of his life: at work, moving among the flowers; at church, sitting on the front row with her hair twisted and loose, and at home at Bell Forest.

He remembered when he'd discovered she'd gone, and the powerful emptiness that came over him. He was not quite prepared for the emotions that assaulted him as soon as the screen door slammed behind him at Bell Forest. He crossed the hardwood floors and looked around at the barren, empty room. It was as if her leaving took all the life out of the place.

In the bedroom he sensed her presence the strongest. Walking over to the bed, he trailed his hand along his grandmother's quilt. Lifting her pillow from the bed, he caught the faint hint of her fragrance. Choking back the emotion, he stepped out onto the porch. He saw the rocking chair, now vacant. He recalled the times they'd watch storms roll in together, seeing her eyes light up with excitement as the lightning flashed across the sky. He'd made the decision to move into the cottage that very night. He felt closer to her when he was there. He knew she loved it there. In the back of his mind, he hoped she'd come back to Bell Forest.

Chapter 40

Michael had grown attached to Bell Forest and seldom left it. After work he usually headed straight home and busied himself outside until dark. He grabbed the shovel and set out across the yard. He forced the shovel into the dirt and lifted out a soggy mass of mud; he tossed it to the side. Sizing up the hole, he picked up the small magnolia tree and planted it into the soft ground. Patting around the little tree firmly with his foot, he said, "There, that should do it." He reached in his front pocket and took out a cigar, chewing on it while he appraised his work.

It was late in the evening. Michael finished supper and stepped outside with his coffee to watch the sun sink slowly into the bay. Hearing something approach, he turned toward the commotion coming up beside the house.

Suddenly, McKeever came into view, bounding up the steps. He lunged toward Michael, wagging his tail excitedly. Michael jumped to his feet, brushing past the overeager dog, he ran down the stairs, frantically searching the area for any sign of his owner.

McKeever ran to his side, panting happily. "Where did you come from, boy?" He reached down and patted McKeever's head. "She wouldn't leave you behind."

A distant sound caused McKeever's ears to perk up, and then he bolted across the road and disappeared into the woods.

Michael ran after him, slowing down as he approached Theda's home. Out of breath, he stopped in the clearing. His eyes scanned the small house until they rested on a figure sitting on the steps. "Telie," he whispered. His heart beat wildly at the sight of her. Gathering his composure, he calmly walked toward her, stopping a few feet away.

"What are you doing here, Michael?" Telie felt a rush of heat climb up her neck and onto her face. Seeing relief play across his face, she softened her words. "Are you okay?"

"I need to talk to you, Telie. I *have* to talk to you, now, if that's all right." He stiffened as Theda came through the screened door, slamming it behind her as she stepped onto the porch. "Hello Miss Theda," Michael said softly, never taking his eyes off Telie.

"Hello Michael. It's a fine evening, don't you think?" A wry grin played around the corners of her mouth.

"Yes, Ma'am," he agreed.

"I'm goin' to the bayou, Telie. I won't be back for awhile." With that she slid past him, McKeever close on her heels.

"Telie," his voice broke the awkward silence, "there's something I need to say to you. Will you come with me to the cottage?" He held his hand out to her.

Looking up into his face, she couldn't resist the pleading in his eyes. Placing her hand in his, he gently raised her to her feet. "You think you can control your temper? My guard dog just left." She looked at him suspiciously, and then smiled.

"I'll be on my guard, I can assure you," he said, in a tone that let her know he was dead serious.

He held her hand down the path, pushing back limbs in front of her so she could pass. Once they climbed the porch steps, he pulled her near him so he faced her directly.

"There is no excuse for my behavior, Telie. I'm so sorry that I've hurt you. Can you ever forgive me?"

"I forgive you, Michael," she sighed. "Everyone loses it from time to time. Things can happen to us, make us lose our way for a little while."

Searching her eyes for reassurance, he asked, "Can you, Telie? Can you ever trust me to never hurt you like that again?"

"Michael…I'm not sure what's happened to you, but I do know that you've never treated me like that before. I'll try and understand what's going on with you if you'll just give me a chance."

Taking a deep breath he blew it out slowly. "I'll try to explain. Come on, let's sit down."

"Would you like something to drink?" he offered. "I don't have much, but I do have coffee."

Shaking her head, she headed for the willow chair and sat down. He moved to the rocker beside her and began. "I recently found out that Tom Bennett is my biological father." He waited for her to say something; when she didn't, he continued. "He included me in his will, making me an equal partner with his other children, Tommy and Dottie. His business, Bennett Shipbuilding is…well…massive to say the least."

Telie didn't say a word, but let him continue.

"For some reason my mother didn't want me to be involved with them. I'm beginning to see the wisdom in that decision." He forced a laugh. "She asked Tom not to be a part of my life." He shrugged. "Guilt, regret or something else caused him to change his mind and, subsequently, include me in his will."

"So, that's what you were doing with the Bennetts the day I saw you in the conference room," she stated, aware that his pensive mood was taking the form of sorrow rather than of pain.

"Yeah, I've been spending a lot of time with them lately. I've endured constant ridicule, snide comments about my mother and obnoxious arrogance to the point of becoming embittered. You can't imagine the stress of it all." Turning to look at her he said, "When I saw you with Lane that day…I lost it. You looked so sweet, so adorable; I couldn't stand the thought of you being near him…being near any of the Bennetts. I hardly slept that night. I couldn't wait to get to you the next morning. I started out just wanting to explain everything to you, then, I guess some of the poison that had seeped into me just came out. Lane, I know now, is not like the rest of them. He's the only decent one among them. I'm sorry if I lumped him in with all the rest."

"It's okay, Michael. I understand," she said. Reaching over, she put her hand on top of his, trying to reassure him.

Taking her hand, he wrapped it up tightly in his own. "There is no excuse for my behavior." He twisted his lips to one side and continued. "After losing you, everything came into sharp focus for me. I called Mr. Forsythe, my attorney, and then I called Tommy Bennett and Dottie Austin and set up a meeting. I wanted out…to be set free from them before I became one of them." He broke off and glanced at her, waiting for her reaction.

She smiled sweetly and squeezed his hand.

"I sold my share of the business to them." A mischievous look came into his eyes. "I'd be lying if I said I didn't enjoy making them buy me out." Laughing, he said, "I can't wait to tell Nathan we can finally pave the church parking lot."

Smiling at his words, happy to see the joy return to his face, Telie chimed in. "Oh…that'll thrill him. He'll probably call another workday just to celebrate."

"I was willing to do anything to secure my release from them. I felt like I was paying my own ransom. I know that financially it was a mistake, but it came down to this: did I want to spend the rest of my life fighting with these people over money I didn't earn?" He shook his head. "I knew what I wanted. I want you, Telie. I only want you and the life we can build together. Thanks to Tom Bennett, we can pay off the business and our homes and continue working without the financial stress."

Telie's mind was reeling. *Our? Did he say our?* She tried to grasp everything he'd just told her. Blinking, she asked, "You want me…why?"

"That's what your mother asked me."

"My mother, you've talked to my mother?" Her mouth dropped open, waiting for his answer.

He nodded once. "When I couldn't find you here, I headed up north to your hometown, thinking you might have gone back there." He stopped short of calling it her home.

"So you met my mother?" Her tone was incredulous. She leaned forward, waiting for an explanation.

"Yes, and you're right…she does look like the Sun-Maiden." The tension left his face as he continued, smiling. "She was a wealth of information, too. I found out all kinds of things about you." Clearly his sense of humor had returned full force.

Her mouth flew open. "Oh you did not!"

Lifting his hands in a gesture of futility, he said, "Don't blame me. Your mother was more than willing to spill it. All your little quirks, your hardheaded stubbornness...that kind of thing, she just went on and on," he teased. "I had to stop her from telling me anything more."

Telie rolled her eyes mockingly.

"There is something else to this story." He looked off in the distance, then fixed his eyes on Telie again. "Tom Bennett had another child, a little girl named Lilly. She lived only a day, and her mother is Theda."

Telie nodded. "Theda told me about her. She's the reason she visits the bayou late at night...Lilly's buried down there."

"For now maybe, but not for long."

"What do you mean?" Telie furrowed her brow, as she questioned Michael.

A slow smile spread across Michael's face. "I met Theda's sister, Mae, at Dottie's house during one of our many board meetings. I'd stepped outside to get some air and regain my composure when Mae approached me and offered a drink. We began talking. I asked about her family and she told me about her daughter who was an attorney in Mobile and how proud she was of her. Then she surprised me by telling me about her sister, Theda, and what had happened to her all those years ago."

"When Tom Bennett forced himself on her?"

"Yeah...you know about that?" He looked surprised.

Smiling crookedly, she replied, "Once again...Theda."

"He'd been drunk, he said, but the damage was done and Theda carried his child. Confronted with the news of the baby, he quickly contacted his attorney to 'right' the matter...offering her a settlement for her silence. She refused, asking only for proof that he was the father with the agreement that she would not press charges. He agreed and the rest, as they say, is history. I told Mae what that meant and asked for her daughter's number in Mobile. I contacted her that night and set up a meeting with Mr. Forsythe. Theda finds out tomorrow that she is now a very wealthy woman. Mae and her daughter plan to come down tomorrow to help her sort through her options."

"That's what you call poetic justice!" Telie said, her eyes dancing with delight.

Laughing, he rose to his feet and reached for her hands, pulling her up. His arms encircled her as he leaned into her. "You haven't told me to get lost yet, so I'm assuming you have forgiven me."

Telie nodded, then smiled nervously, not quite sure what to make of it all.

"May I kiss you? I told you once that I wouldn't kiss you again, unless invited, but it doesn't look like I'm going to get an invitation."

Telie grinned. "Sure, why not."

Bending his head down, his lips met hers in a tender kiss. Warmth spread over her as her hands held on tightly to his strong arms; she reached up to encircle his neck in a possessive grasp.

Pulling back, he said, "Stay right here. Close your eyes and no peeking."

She did as she was told, smiling at the game he was playing. After hearing the sound of something heavy being placed down on the porch, he announced, "Open your eyes."

In front of her sat a beautiful wooden rocker. It was made out of a pale, light brown wood with a slightly greenish cast. The lines were smooth and curved softly. She stood there, speechless. She had never seen anything like it. "It's so beautiful!" she said, running her hand over the smooth finish. "Did you make this, Michael?"

"I did...I made it for you." He was thrilled to see the pleasure in her eyes. The way she ran her hand over it admiringly.

"What kind of wood is this? I've never seen anything like it." She looked over the piece, running her hands all over it, unable to identify the wood. "I'm speechless." Her eyes told him everything he needed to know.

"Oh you've seen *this* wood before. As a matter of fact, you know it quite well."

"What do you mean? I don't understand." Waiting for him to explain, she held her breath.

"I made this for you out of the wood from *your* magnolia tree."

Chills ran up her arms. Taking in a sharp breath, she looked back at the rocker. "Michael!" Tears sprang from her eyes. Gasping, she tried to choke back a flood of tears. A sensation of warmth spread over her entire being like honey. She felt as if every part of her was covered in love and acceptance; her heart came back to life.

"There's just one more thing," he broke off, sounding like he was talking to himself now. "Sit down. I want you to sit in your magnolia chair for this...bear with me."

Taking a seat in her chair, her hands lovingly rubbed the smooth arms. She watched him nervously rub his hands together.

Reaching in his front pocket, where he normally kept his cigars, he pulled out a small blue velvet box. Opening the lid, he lifted out an oval-shaped diamond ring surrounded by platinum. Bending near her ear, he whispered, "You told me once that you didn't think you could trust your heart to anyone. But I'm asking, if you will entrust it to me, I promise to love and cherish you all the days God grants us on this earth. With all that is within me, will you be my wife?"

Shaking her head frantically, unable to speak, she finally choked out, "Yes!" Tears ran down her cheeks, as she looked up at him, smiling. "As long as we both shall live." She stood, wrapping her arms securely around him, as she pressed her cheek into his chest. "I love you, Michael, and I'll love you for eternity."

He slipped the ring on her finger and held her face in his hands. "I love you, Telie. Never leave my side."

CPSIA information can be obtained at www.ICGtesting.com
Printed in the USA
LVOW09s0350030215

425383LV00007B/95/P